MURDER IN
LA GALERIA D'ARTE

MURDER IN LA GALERIA D'ARTE

A
MARCO IN SPAIN
MYSTERY

PAULA B. MAYS

First published by Level Best Books 2026

Copyright © 2026 by Paula B. Mays

This novel is entirely a work of fiction. The names, characters, and incidents portrayed in it are the work of the author's imagination. Any resemblance to actual persons, living or dead, events, or localities is entirely coincidental.

Paula B. Mays asserts the moral right to be identified as the author of this work.

Author Photo Credit: Heather Simpson

First edition

ISBN: 979-8-89820-059-6

Cover art by Front cover art by Level Best Designs and Paula B. Mays. Back cover Art by Suzanne L. Wilson

This book was professionally typeset on Reedsy. Find out more at reedsy.com

To my alma mater, Saint Timothy's school, and Randy Stevens, Headmaster, for offering a world-class education and developing, fearless women in an atmosphere of joy and respect, where hard work and kindness are valued.
Thanks for keeping the Big Blue story alive and well.

Praise for Murder in La Galeria d'Arte

"Readers will be hooked from start to finish. In this masterful second installment of the *Marco in Spain* trilogy, Paula Mays delivers a richly layered mystery…steeped in art, history, and the seductive charm of southern Spain. At a glittering gallery opening, while the town's elite are still swirling their wine glasses, the museum director is strangled to death in the sculpture garden outside his office. The story unravels around a long-lost 15th-century masterpiece, stolen in the shadows of war and resurrected on the night it was meant to be unveiled. *Murder in La Galeria D'Arte* is an unforgettable blend of art-world intrigue and old-world mystery."—**Karen Gray Houston**, award-winning journalist; Emmy Nominee, author of *Daughter of the Boycott,* a 2020 *O Magazine* recommendation

The Gates of Justice

The lowly Pilgrim, lay
prostrate. The
burdens of the past,
strapped to his back.
Weigh him down.
Lethargy,
slows him from reaching
his dream across the cordillera.
He links arms with a flock of,
trekkers,
Who left all they ever known,
With only faith as sustenance.
Guiding them,
to a centuries old archway.
Leya, beckons weary travellers.
"Step thru the gate," she says,
here you'll find me.

Prologue

"The ruling Moors of this region lived here until January 2, 1492, when Boabdil heaved his last sigh and gave the keys to the city to Ferdinand and Isabella."
—*Spain the Root and the Flower*, John A. Crow

Addison Mason paced back and forth, glancing at his Cartier watch. His hand twitched. One hour until the unveiling. The atmosphere in the exhibit hall felt electric. *Glamour on display*, Addison thought as he looked around at the array of people. Men wearing tuxes or black suits, except a few who expressed their independence in wild outfits and colorful dyed hair, the kind of dress often expected from celebrities at the Grammys; plenty of local celebrities were in attendance for this night's soiree. Dresses also came in a variety of styles, from traditional black cocktail dresses to long gowns with sequins. Addison had chosen a mixture of styles in his own dress, typical of him and his artistic brain. He wore a black tux with a bright purple tie with a picture of Salvador Dali on it, and a cummerbund. A matching purple handkerchief poked from his top breast pocket. He'd put a touch of mascara on his long lashes, a trick he'd learned from his hairstylist. His curly dark hair fell to his face, covering his porcelain skin. He felt his outfit reflected both his avant-garde nature and his eclectic sense of style.

Addison smiled. Everything was going as planned. Albéniz's "Asturias" played in the background. The flamenco dancer he'd hired looked great. Addison scurried around performing a final check. He strode over to the object in the corner of the room resting on an easel and smiled at the star of the show. His heart fluttered from nerves and his stomach hurt, as it often did when he felt worried or stressed. He'd been diagnosed with IBS. He'd been able to manage it, except in times like now. Addison took a few deep breaths and rubbed his stomach.

As time for the unveiling grew closer, Addison felt intoxicated with glee. He'd given up everything for this museum. He'd forsaken a social life, threatened his marriage. The painting about to be unveiled, the jewel that allowed him to stage the museum's opening with great fanfare, had been worth it. The painting itself had been lost to the world for over eighty years since the Spanish Civil War. *The Gates of Justice,* as it was titled, depicted a fifteenth-century gate in Arabesque design. The work represented the welcoming of people of all faiths on pilgrimage to the capital of Vivirrambla. The gate consisted of three arches in a symmetrical design. A Pilgrim is seen posted at the gate, sitting in profound thought. The painting, a masterpiece of Islamic art in the period before *la Reconquista*, The Reconquest, would finally be seen by the public again. Its resurrection created a buzz in the art world. Talk of the discovery hit the press as far as the US and Australia. For lovers of ancient Islamic art, the reclamation of the *Gates of Justice* equaled the finding of a lost Caravaggio in Italy. Addison's museum had achieved recognition before it even opened.

The Museo d'arte of Vivirrambla, a small gallery in the center of town, in a restored townhouse, had white painted walls that contrasted with the dark wooden beams that ran along the length of the high ceilings. Spanish tiles led visitors from one exhibit room to another. A sculpture garden, designed by landscape architect Christine Church, located off the patio of Addison's office, was completed only a week ago. The garden contained one large piece of modern art and a few modern bronze statues.

Addison grabbed a glass of champagne from one of the waiters and spoke to his assistant, Amy. "Can you keep everyone happy for a few minutes? I'm going to check a few things. I'll be back in a bit."

Amy nodded. "Of course," she said.

"I'm a little nervous. I have a funny feeling in my stomach," Addison said, squinching his face.

"Don't worry, Addison, everything's perfect. It's going to be a big hit," Amy said.

Addison thanked Amy and walked in the direction of his office. He wanted to check the paperwork again. The painting's legacy had already been tainted as it'd been stolen; Addison hoped his lawyers had put it all in order. He flipped through the papers. Everything seemed to be okay. He could relax and enjoy the rest of the evening. He looked out at the garden at stars above. Then, he turned his head. In the darkness of the night, under the light of a lamp, he saw a shadow of a person that wasn't himself. A tall looming figure behind him.

"What are you doing here? You should be out front with the rest of the guests. I'm about to do the unveiling," Addison said.

Addison felt a sense of doom, like being trapped in an underwater sea vessel with no escape, as the unwelcomed visitor grabbed Addison and forced him out the patio door and into the sculpture garden. Addison looked up at the sky. One big star, likely a planet gleamed brilliant light. It was the last thing Addison would see on earth as he struggled to remove the object from around his neck.

* * *

Amy Bloom wore a short black cocktail dress that came just above her knees; it had a collar that glittered. Her black heels were over five inches high with pointed toes, making her five-foot-two frame appear taller. She frowned and looked at her watch. "Hmmm," she said. "What's taking Addison so long? He said he'd only be gone for a moment."

An hour had gone by, and Addison hadn't returned to the exhibit hall. It was past the time they'd set to unveil the painting. Amy walked over to one of the museum board members, Nicholas Thompson, a British lawyer, and whispered in his ear. "Addison hasn't returned yet. He said he'd be back in a minute."

Nicholas winked at her. "Don't worry, he'll be back soon."

"I hope so. He worked so hard to make this evening a success. He didn't want anything to go wrong," Amy said.

"It'll be perfect," Nicholas said, smiling.

The guest continued to socialize with one another for another hour as they waited for the evening's highlight. A tall, slim Swedish man, wearing blue and white striped pants and a blue seersucker jacket, sidled over to Amy and slapped a wet kiss on her cheek." Nice opening, when can we expect Addison?" he asked.

The man, Sven Bjorgen, owned a museum in Puerto Bella that featured experimental modern art. Amy knew him only by reputation. His art museum, which featured mostly unknown artists and dark works, had been declared strange by most art critics.

Amy smiled a half smile. "Sven, thanks so much for coming. Addison should be here in a few minutes. I know he's anxious for everyone to see the painting."

"Well, I can't wait to see it," Sven said.

Nicholas Thompson put his arms around Amy's waist. "I'm sure Addison's on his way. He's probably just hung up on a call."

Amy shrugged her shoulders. "Okay, I hope you're right."

"Sure, he'll be here in a minute. There's no point getting agitated," Thompson said.

* * *

Amy couldn't concentrate on what the guests were saying to her. She rubbed her hands together, as was her habit when she worried. She turned to Nicholas. "I'm going to see if I can find him."

Amy moved to the center of the room. She clapped her hands to get everyone's attention. "Thank you all again for coming. I hope you're having a wonderful evening. Addison should be here shortly. In the meantime, enjoy the food and the rest of the museum."

"Addison could be lost forever. We all know how he gets wrapped up in his work and loses concentration," Sven Bjorgen said. Everyone laughed.

Amy ignored the comment and headed out of the exhibit hall to Addison's office. The door was open. *Hmm strange,* she thought. Addison was nowhere to be found. Normally, he was meticulous about locking the door when he wasn't in the office. Amy shut the door and started to search the museum's other rooms, including the basement, where paintings and other items were stored. She unlocked the door to a small room that held antique silver. She sighed. No Addison.

"I wonder where he could be?" she pondered aloud.

She went back to his office, hoping that maybe he'd returned. This time, she noticed that the patio doors that connected to the sculpture garden were ajar. Maybe he stepped out to get some fresh air. She walked out onto the garden in her five-inch heels and tapped across the stone tile. "Addison?" she cried out. "Are you out here?"

Something drew her attention over to a large sculpture to the right of the door. She gasped. Her mouth open, she stood, paralyzed, staring at the figure on the ground next to the Christine Church cubic structure. Addison, his head tilted to one side, his body contorted, blood seeping from every pore, lay unmoving at the head of the sculpture.

Amy could hear her own heart pounding in her chest. "Oh, my God! Addison!" she screamed.

Forgetting she had on her most expensive, Amy kneeled over the body and lifted Addison's limp wrist to check his pulse. Nothing! She put her ear next to his chest. Nothing. Not a single sound. She tried CPR. No response. She looked down at the blood around her and the blood on her hands and on her black dress. Amy sat on the ground amidst the stones, crossed her legs, and screamed.

Chapter One

Marco pledged to enjoy himself for the worthy cause as they dressed for the evening. Belen insisted he dress like a VIP, whatever that meant. He'd opted for black slim-fit trousers, a collarless white button shirt, and a two-button black blazer. His pointed-toe black shoes were buffed and polished. His thick dark hair had been cut and shaped in the back, and he was clean-shaven. As a final touch, Marco splashed on Hugo Boss cologne, which Belen had bought him for his birthday.

It always took Belen ages to get dressed. Marco wandered into the kitchen to grab a beer but thought the better of it and poured himself a glass of Lanjarón water while he waited for her.

Belen appeared a half-hour later. "I'm ready," she said, putting on her white shawl.

She'd twisted her hair up in a chignon. Sparkling diamond stud earrings shone on her ears. She wore high-heeled Mary Janes to boost her petite frame. Marco thought she looked breathtaking in a tea-length blue dress with a large black bow on the back. She smelled of the feminine version of the same scent as he.

"You look wonderful, sweetie" Marco said.

Belen smiled. "You don't look so bad either. I just hope I get everything right; these are new guitarists I'm working with," she said.

Marco kissed her on the cheek. "You'll do great as usual, honey."

Belen grabbed her garment bag, and Marco picked up the keys off the side table next to the front door. The duo headed out for the short walk to the center of town.

Fuchsia Bougainvillea espaliered the walls of the white-washed stucco houses of Vivirrambla. Las narangas, orange trees lined the streets, emitting a citrus scent throughout the plaza. Marco and Belen inhaled the fresh air as they strolled through the Casco Antiqua. Marco held Belen's hand as they ambled along. He didn't relish going to what he called "fluffy" parties. Those that served tiny finger foods that never filled him up, pretentious wines, and beautiful people out glamorizing one another, competing to be noticed. Marco felt awkward making small talk with fancy guests, something Belen was natural at. He'd accompanied Belen to several recent events given in honor of the late singer, Kijamba, who'd been tragically murdered, a case Marco helped to solve. Since the posthumous release of Kijamba's last video, which featured Belen as one of the principal dancers, they'd been invited to all kinds of important city events. They'd made it to the A list, a list Marco never strived to attain.

They walked up to the brick structure and opened the large wooden doors to the museum. The room, with its high ceilings, was already crowded with extravagant guests buzzing around and pontificating about the Arabesque art pieces in the room. Marco wanted to turn around and go home and watch futbol.

Chapter Two

The town's most important people, including the mayor, milled around the exhibit hall. A sturdy-looking wooden easel, illuminated by recess lighting, supported a large rectangular-shaped object covered by a heavy black drape. Various onlookers meandered over to examine it. Marco joined those speculating as to what they would see at the unveiling, while Belen went to change into her flamenco costume.

The curious object was a painting by the fifteenth-century artist, Sumaya Runya, entitled. *The Gates of Justice.* The work of mixed pigment oil and tempera had just been cleaned and restored. The painting would be seen for the first time since it'd been lost during the period of La guerra civil, the Spanish Civil War. Marco had read about the painting's reemergence in *El País* the Spanish newspaper. He'd been excited to see the famous painting by a Moroccan artist. He'd seen plenty of art in places like El Prado and Bilbao that featured works of European artists such as Picasso, Francisco Goya, and Diego Velázquez, but he'd seen few celebrated pieces by artist of Moroccan descent. Marco's grandmother, Jaddah, who lived in Tangier, cried when Marco Face Timed her to tell her about the painting. She'd told him stories about the lost Runya painting, when Marco, as a youth, had gone to stay with her during the summers, where he spent lazy hot days kicking futbols with his cousin, Karim. Runya's painting was considered a lost treasure. Moroccan people would be thrilled to learn the painting had been recovered and restored.

A slender man in his thirties with dark, curly, mop-like hair and deep-set brown eyes entered the exhibit room. Addison Mason, the museum's director and founder, wearing purple and black, welcomed the guests. His dark brown eyes flitted with glee.

"I'm so excited this evening is finally here," he said, in the accent of an Eton school graduate.

All of the fancy dressed guests clapped and nodded in approval.

"I just want to thank you all for coming. This is truly a special evening, and many of you made it all possible. The pièce de resistance will be unveiled to you shortly. In the meantime, enjoy the entertainment and refreshments."

Addison put the microphone back on the stand and floated through the exhibit hall, smiling and shaking hands, promising guests that they wouldn't be disappointed.

Marco grabbed a tapa from the silver tray that passed in front of him. He looked for Belen, whom he spotted chatting to a tall man with blond hair, wearing a colorful outfit. Marco took a bite of the garlic shrimp, followed by a swig of beer. He meandered around the room fascinated by the art on display. Much of it appeared to be Arabesque. Pieces of pottery, decorative mosaics, and ancient tile pieces in glass cases. Marco learned that the museum contained some works touted to be over five hundred years old. He wandered from exhibit to exhibit admiring the ancient works.

Marco realized he'd been walking around for a while. He glanced at his watch. It'd been almost an hour since Addison Mason announced that the painting would soon be revealed. Marco furrowed his brows. There'd been no sign of him since. A few minutes later, a young British woman with dark blue eyes walked over to the veiled easel, holding a microphone. Everyone turned to listen to her when she tapped on it, and the noise of feedback filled the room.

"Hi, I want to welcome you all again on this special evening. I'm Amy Bloom, Addison's assistant. I hope you all are enjoying the evening and this beautiful new museum." Several people nodded their heads. "In addition to all the delicious food we've provided, we've asked one of our celebrated local dancers to perform this evening." Amy acknowledged Belen, who'd entered the temporary stage that had been erected for her appearance. A singer and a guitarist who accompanied her to the center of the room took a bow."

"Afterward, Addison will reveal this beautiful work." Please enjoy and visit the exhibits, and let me know if you have any questions," Amy said.

Once Amy finished, the lights dimmed. Belen, who'd changed into a long, form-fitting dress of white satin with ruffles which flared out at the bottom and trailed behind her like the train of a wedding dress, shone under the spotlight. She seemed coy, holding a decorative white fan in front of her mouth. A large white flower was pinned to the side of her dark hair. The guitar player sat on a stool next to Belen. The other musician sat beside him. They wore shirts with ruffled tops that matched the bottom of Belen's dress. Belen began to twirl, while the singer crooned, and the guitarist strummed. Like a Sema dancer, her body moved in rhythm, telling a story of love and longing with each movement. She finished to enthusiastic applause. Marco felt his chest swell.

The lights returned, and the guests went back to mingling, eating, and drinking. Belen joined Marco in the exhibit hall after she'd changed back into her cocktail dress.

Marco kissed her on the cheek. "You were wonderful, Bel," he said.

Several guests came over to them to congratulate her on her beautiful and inspiring dance.

Marco looked at his watch again. Another hour had passed. Addison hadn't returned. *Hmmm, I wonder if anything's gone wrong,* he thought. As a former police officer, now police consultant, Marco had been trained to be suspicious when things didn't go as planned. He began to get a sinking feeling.

Belen whispered in his ear. "You think anything's wrong. Addison hasn't reappeared. According to the schedule they gave me, he should have done the unveiling some time ago."

"I wondered the same thing. We haven't seen him since he spoke," Marco said.

* * *

Amy Bloom rushed into the exhibit hall, a look of horror on her face as if she'd been confronted by an apparition. She panted out of breath. "Is anyone out here a doctor?"

"Why? Has something happened?" Marco asked.

Amy looked over at Marco. "Are you a doctor?"

"No," Marco said.

"We need a doctor, right away!" Amy said.

A woman wearing a long azure blue gown piped up. "I'm a doctor."

Amy gestured with her hand. "Please come with me."

The woman scurried to join Amy as they left the room. The guests looked around quizzically at one another .

"What's going on?" someone asked.

People began to chatter amongst themselves, buzzing about what to do next. The doctor who'd been called to assist returned to the exhibit hall after a time to retrieve her gold evening bag that was being held by a man, Marco assumed was her partner. She said a few words to him and told him she needed to hurry. Word traveled through the exhibit hall like a bullet train.

Marco rushed to follow the doctor through Addison's office and out onto the sculpture garden. There, he saw Addison Mason's twisted body next to a statue, covered in blood. The rest of the guests followed, rushing to the garden to see what had happened.

Amy Bloom stood next to the lifeless body, her face ashen.

"Has anyone called an ambulance and the police?" Marco asked.

The doctor who'd accompanied her hung her head, symbolizing the futility of doing any more examination.

Chapter Three

Emergency and police arrived within a minutes. A few reporters from the local newspapers were already in the museum for the unveiling, but when word got around about the dead body, swarms of national news outlets, including *El País*, tabloids, and various paparazzi, invaded the exhibit hall like storm troopers.

When Detective Flores arrived, media swarmed him. He declined to comment to anyone who asked or stuck a microphone in his face. Flores, always the straight cop and by the book, wore jeans and a bright green vest over his striped jersey shirt. The badge hanging from his uniform identified him as Malaga police. His large ears jutted out from his short-cut brown hair. He pulled an Altoid out of his coat pocket and stuck it in his mouth. He always chewed on Altoids when he was at a murder scene. It calmed his nerves to chew on something.

Flores spotted Marco in the room. He went over to him, opening the small box in his hand and holding it out to Marco. "Mint?"

"No thanks," Marco said.

What are you doing here? I didn't think hanging out at fancy cocktail parties was your thing," Flores said.

"Definitely not. Belen performed for the museum opening."

Marco and Detective Alberto Flores worked together on several high-profile cases in the past. They had a very high success rate for solving difficult murder cases, despite their different styles of operation. Their strengths complemented one another. Marco had good instincts, and Flores was an expert on procedure. Opposites in temperament, they'd developed a level of respect for one another.

"Did you see what happened here?" Flores asked.

Marco shook his head, no. "Belen and I were with the rest of the guests in the exhibit hall. We were all waiting for the unveiling of a painting."

"What unveiling? Can you give me some background?" Flores asked.

Marco still dressed in his evening attire said, "This was the museum's opening night. See over there?" he said, pointing to the still covered easel. "A famous lost painting was going to be unveiled. We were all waiting for the ceremony. The deceased, Addison Mason, owned the museum."

"I see the mayor and all the town hotshots are here," Flores said.

"Yeah, the opening's a big deal. The painting to be unveiled was regarded as a masterpiece. It'd been lost for some time. I don't know the whole story. Earlier in the evening, Addison announced that the unveiling would take place soon. Then he left and never returned. Amy Bloom, the woman over there," Marco said, pointing to a distraught-looking woman. "She's Addison's assistant. She first told us Addison had been delayed. The next thing you know, she comes running back in, asking if anyone in the room's a doctor."

"Did they find a doctor?" Flores asked.

Marco nodded. "She's over there," he said, pointing to the woman in the long blue dress still standing near the body, talking to the emergency services and police.

"I see my officers are getting information from her. So, this Addison guy never came back to the exhibit hall, but then he somehow ended up dead in the sculpture garden," Flores said.

Marco shook his head. "Yep, that's what happened. Addison's wife's over there," he said, directing Flores's attention to a woman in a lilac dress.

"Okay, I'll send someone over to talk to her," Flores said.

Flores examined the area around the deceased. "I don't see any weapons; no tool marks anywhere. Not a lot of blood from the looks of it." Flores bent down to look at the body. "Looks like he's been strangled."

He summoned the police photographer over. "Take some close-ups of his neck and upper area, would you?"

The photographer lifted his camera and zoomed the lens in on the neck area of the deceased and snapped pictures."

Marco pointed to a spot on Addison's shirt. "What's that spot. I don't remember any spots on his clothing when he came to talk to us."

"Hmm, looks like orange paint," Flores said.

"I wonder where he would've encountered paint. He seemed fastidious from his dress. Maybe he got it when he went to his office. Loose paint on the walls, perhaps," Marco said.

"I'll send it to the lab. It is a museum. Paint could have been anywhere. I see Javier's arrived," Flores said.

The coroner, Javier Bortello, in his early fifties and balding at the top of his head, was bent over the dead body. He took out a pair of black-framed glasses and peered at the corpse.

"I think he's been strangled," Flores said.

Bortello looked at the body and the head and neck area. "I'd agree, strangulation. I don't see any pattern evidence except large ligature marks on the neck. No evidence of a struggle. The perp had to be male, pretty tall, I'd guess, seeing the position of the body. Looks like he was left-handed from the positioning of the marks and the dominant marking being on the left side."

"Thanks, we'll look for DNA and dust for prints on him. Can you tell us anything else?" Flores asked.

Bortello shook his head. "I don't see anything else right now. I'll have to get him on the table. We'll take him to the shop once I'm done."

Marco thought it interesting that Bortello referred to the morgue as "the shop."

"Thanks, Javier. Marco, let's go to the exhibit hall and let Javier finish up," Flores said.

"Okay, I need to tell Belen to go home. She's pretty upset, and I don't want her to have to hang around here any longer than she needs to," Marco said.

"I'll get one of my officers to take her home," Flores said.

Chapter Four

Marco found Belen in the exhibit hall consoling an elegantly dressed older woman who stood weeping.

"Marco, what's happened?" Belen asked.

"Seems as if someone has strangled Addison Mason," Marco said.

The woman let out a loud gasp.

"What? How could that have happened? We've all been here in the museum all night. How could someone strangle him without anyone noticing?" Belen asked.

Marco shrugged his shoulders. "His assistant found him lying next to a statue in the sculpture garden."

The older woman heaved as if she couldn't breathe. Belen patted her gently on the back.

"Marco, this is Carmela Sanchez," Belen said.

"Mucho gusto," Marco said.

Carmela wore a Chanel tweed suit with intertwined pink and blue colors and gold buttons bearing the Chanel double "C" symbol. She had on several solid gold bangles and pearls around her neck. Her dark hair was in a bun. She seemed to be one of those women who carried themselves with effortless grace. Her olive skin had few lines, and her eyes had a few creases.

Sniff, Sniff. "I can't believe it, Addison, dead. It can't be true. He seemed happy and excited just a little while ago. He'd been waiting for this day for some time. He said we'd all be awed by what we saw when he revealed the painting. Then we never saw him again. He's too young to have a heart attack or anything like that," Carmela said.

Carmela's large diamond ring flashed light as she moved her hand. She told them she was a member of the board of directors who ran the museum. She said she'd invested heavily in it. She'd been excited to see the painting, which she'd helped to secure.

The police will do all they can to find out what happened," Marco said. He told Belen an officer was waiting to escort her home. Belen let go of the crying woman.

"Take care, Señora Sanchez. I'm sure the police will figure out who did this," Belen said.

A uniformed officer approached, and Belen followed him out.

Once Belen had gone, Marco rejoined Detective Flores.

"The guests all seem pretty shook up, but maybe we can talk to a few of them this evening, and my officers can interview the rest. Let's see what else we can find out from the woman Belen had been talking to," Flores said.

Carmela stood in the same spot, weeping. The two of them walked over to her.

"I'm sorry to have to disturb you again, Señora. Did you see anything unusual happen this evening?" Flores asked.

Carmela shook her head. "No, everything looked wonderful, just as planned. I stopped by the museum several weeks ago when the exhibit hall was still under construction. I couldn't believe Addison had gotten it all finished and looking like this in time for the opening."

"Did you know Señor Addison well?" Flores asked.

"Si, Addison, and I were close. He considered me like a mother to him," Carmela said.

Carmela pointed to one of the paintings on the wall, an Arabesque drawing. "Isn't this fantastic in the lighting? Addison asked my opinion when he decided to focus on ancient North African and Islamic art. He expressed concern that it might not attract visitors accustomed to attending museums dedicated to European artists. I told him it was a wonderful idea and that his museum would be different."

Marco agreed. He'd never seen such a museum in Spain, which featured the art of his ancestors. He wished his grandmother were with him.

"Do you know if Addison received any complaints or threats?" Flores asked.

Carmela shrugged her shoulders. "Do you mean about the art? Just a few vague complaints here and there. Addison worried about it a lot. He wanted the museum to be a success. He poured so much of himself into it. I felt good seeing him so happy when he came into the hall this evening, so full of life. How can he now be gone?"

"Did you see him again after he came into the hall that first time?" Marco asked.

Carmela dabbed her eyes with a tissue from her beaded purse. "I never saw him again. I don't understand how this could have happened."

"We'll do everything we can to find out, Señora," Flores said.

"Thank you," she said, still wiping her eyes.

Flores could see Carmela becoming weary. He'd get no further information from her now. He asked her to write down all her information, including her address and phone number. Then he sent her home.

"We'll need to speak to you again, Señora, since you are a friend of the victim," Flores said.

She nodded a weak nod.

Marco turned to Flores once Carmela left them. "She looks familiar, but I can't remember where I've met her."

Flores and Marco decided to split up for the rest of the evening and talk to the few remaining people in the hall. Most of the guests had already gone, and only a few media remained scrounging for crumbs of information and pictures.

A while later, Flores caught up with Marco again. "Let's call it a night. I didn't get much of a chance to talk to Señor Mason's assistant, Amy Bloom. We'll need to meet with her soon," he said.

Javier Bortello walked in the room like a lost puppy, looking around the exhibit hall. He spotted Flores and went over to him. "The victim's started to stiffen up. Nothing more I can do for now. You can take him away."

As a final act for the night, Flores directed that the now fully stiffened Addison Mason be removed from his newly opened museum in a body bag.

Chapter Five

Marco wiggled and kicked his legs, trying to find his way from under the large fluffy white comforter. He felt restless and stared at the ceiling, unable to sleep. He'd seen a lot of bodies, but this latest one disturbed him. He'd seen Addison Mason only a short time before he lay dead in his museum's garden. Life is short; like most clichés, the saying had been based on truth. He thought about his own life and his future as he tossed and turned. He needed to decide what he wanted to do and whether he wanted to get married and make that final commitment. He'd always believed he had plenty of time. Addison's death gave him a jolt of reality. He sighed and turned over.

He noticed a restless Belen tossing and turning as well. She had a right to be upset. It was the second time she'd been dancing at a function where a man died. It had taken her some time to get over the death of the pop star, Kijamba, who'd been murdered while she performed in his video. Marco wondered how he could comfort her. He leaned over and whispered in her ear. "Are you alright, sweetheart?"

"No, not really." She felt cold and shaky. He pulled her to his arms and hugged her tight.

"I know this is hard. None of it's your fault. I love you, and I'll always be here to protect you," he said.

"Logically, I know it's not my fault, but I'm still starting to wonder if I'm bad luck."

"Of course not. You could never be bad luck, Belen, you're warm, caring, and loving. Nothing you do would ever bring anyone bad luck."

She cried in his arms, tears dropping on his bare chest, until eventually she fell asleep and rolled over. He must have drifted off, too, since when he looked next at the clock, it said five o'clock in the morning. He got up and wandered off to the kitchen for a glass of water and climbed back into bed. He awoke again when the alarm sounded at seven. He decided he needed a swim to ease the tension in his body before he went to meet Flores to interview witnesses.

He tiptoed into the bathroom, so as not to wake Belen, changed into his swimwear, and grabbed a towel from the linen closet and headed to the beach. In the early morning light, the waves floated like the smooth rhythm of a Marvin Gaye song over the turquoise waters of the Mediterranean. Marco dove in; the sea felt like a balm to his soul. He let the water wash over him as he moved his arms and feet, doing a few laps. Then he emerged from the water and slipped on his flip-flops.

He shook his thick, dark hair to air dry it. The bright sun glistened on his deep brown-toned olive skin. His muscular arms rippled like David posing for Michael Angelo. After drying himself, he walked back to the apartment. Belen had awakened by then. She sat at the kitchen table drinking coffee. She wore gray sweats and a ponytail.

"Good morning," she said as Marco entered the kitchen. "Did you have a good swim?"

Marco, wearing a robe over his swimsuit, walked over and kissed her. "I did. It was just what I needed. I hope you're feeling better this morning, my love."

She nodded. "I'm still in shock, but I'll stay in today until it's time to go to work."

Marco kissed her again and grabbed a bottle of Lanjarón water from the refrigerator. "Call me if you need anything."

"I will. Have a wonderful day. I love you," Belen said.

"I love you too," Marco said, walking out of the kitchen, blowing her a kiss.

After he'd showered and dressed in khaki pants and a light blue shirt, Marco said goodbye to Belen, grabbed his watch and keys off the front table, and left the apartment. He walked to work most days, except in the summer when it got too hot. In the crisp, cool air of the spring, he enjoyed strolling through the Old Town, past patrons sipping cafés con leches at the outdoor restaurants. Devout old couples sat on the stone benches waiting for the start of morning mass at Iglesia Nuestra Señora de la Encarnaćion.

Marco stopped at Alvarez's café across from his office, his regular stop for morning coffee, where over the years, he and the middle-aged, balding Alvarez had become friends. Marco pushed open the door and hopped on his regular bar stool in front of the large glass-covered counter that displayed fresh tapas and pastries made daily.

Alvarez, sporting a cleaning rag over his shoulder, greeted him.

"Marco, como estas? I heard about the museum thing. The owner killed on the day of the opening. What a mess. What kind of world do we live in? Will you be investigating the murder?" Alvarez asked.

"Yep, I'm getting started on it this morning. You know I can't start anything without your café con leche, though, right?" Marco said.

"*Si, si, por supesto*, Señor. Coming right up. You do look a bit tired," Alvarez said.

"Yeah, I didn't get much sleep last night."

"Hopefully, this will perk you up."

Alvarez walked behind the counter to the machine where he created coffee like a magician conjuring up a magic trick. He put the grounds into the espresso maker, and milk in a small silver carafe. He flipped on the machine, which whirled, making a grinding noise. When it finished, Alvarez removed the carafe and poured coffee into a cup, followed by steamed milk. His hands moved with precision, like a skilled surgeon, as he finished the coffee with a swirl of foam. The aroma of freshly made coffee wafted through the restaurant.

Marco picked up a copy of *Vivirrambla Today* at the end of the counter, while he waited for his drink. The front page had an article entitled *"Murder in the Museum."* Pictures of Flores and other police officers examining the scene featured on the front page. The article said the police had no leads and would be opening an immediate investigation into the heinous crime. Alvarez handed him his coffee, and Marco read the rest of the article as he drank it. When he took his final sip, he closed the paper and returned it to the counter. He hopped off the barstool and paid for his coffee. "*Gracias, Alvarez para el cafe.* I've got to get to work," he said, putting the money on the counter.

Alvarez, who'd been serving other patrons, walked down to Marco's end of the counter, and swept up the money. "*Buen dia, Marco. Muchas suerte* with the investigation. This sounds like a hard one."

"*Buenos días, jefe.*"

"Gracias, Alvarez."

Marco walked across the street to his office. His assistant, Eva, greeted him when he arrived.

"Buenos días, jefe," she said. She had a habit of calling him "boss" in Spanish. "Detective Flores said he'll be here to pick you up in an hour. I'm shocked at what happened at that new museum last night. Someone murdered the owner right before his grand opening. I can't believe you and Belen were there."

"I know. Belen was still pretty shaken up when I left her this morning. Since Kijamba died, she thinks these deaths are her fault. She was dancing while Addison Mason was murdered."

Eva's eyes widened. "Oh, my God! Of course, it isn't Belen's fault. She must feel tortured. I read that a bunch of dignitaries were there."

"Yeah, the mayor and everyone important. The opening had been touted as a major town event," Marco said.

"I've seen the advertisements. That's crazy. Can I get you anything before you go?"

"No thanks, I had coffee at Alvarez's. I'll be in my office until Detective Flores arrives."

"Okay, *jefe*, let me know if you need anything. Tell Belen to call me if she needs me."

Marco's assistant, Eva, had been with him from the start. She'd answered his ad in the newspaper when he opened his own private investigation firm after being fired from the Vivirrambla police force. On the day of her interview, a perky young English woman, with long blond hair and blue eyes, who spoke perfect Spanish, sashayed in. She said she'd been living in Vivirrambla for several years with her Spanish husband and one child. She was looking for a job where she could use her skills as a college graduate. She and Marco had gotten along well from the beginning, and she'd been helpful to him in researching cases as well as doing his administrative work. Sometimes, he felt she knew him too well.

Just as Marco sat down at his desk, Eva appeared.

"Detective Flores is here."

Flores followed on her heels, sweating and out of breath, as if he'd just run the Vivirrambla marathon. He wore an ill-fitting suit jacket and navy pants. Marco always felt the urge to tell him to start exercising and get into shape as he was getting older. It wasn't that he appeared to be overweight; he just looked flabby like he led a sedentary life and didn't get enough sun or exercise, despite living in a town with three hundred forty-six days a year of sunshine.

"Hola, Marco, are you ready?" he asked, panting.

"Let's first take a visit to Addison Mason's wife."

Marco rose from his chair. "Yep, ready to go. Where does Señora Mason live?"

"Benahavis. I'll drive," Flores said.

"That's good. We'd have to go back to my house to get my car." Marco said, certain Flores wouldn't want to walk the half mile to his house in the beating sun.

"We're leaving now. I don't know when we'll be back," Marco yelled to Eva.

"Okay, *jefe*."

The odd duo hopped into Flores's light blue Citroën, parked on the street, and Flores drove them to Ben Havis to speak to the grieving widow.

Chapter Six

They neared the address Flores put into the locator in a nice area of town, not the uber-wealthy part called the Golden Mile, the Beverly Hills of Spain, but still a nice area surrounded by greening olive trees and large homes. Benahavis, a town of whitewashed houses, situated on the southern slopes of the Sierra Blanca Mountains, sat at the edge of the Mediterranean Sea. Like many other towns in the Andalućian Provence, it attracted European golfers and expatriates seeking sunshine and a slow pace of life. Marco golfed on the rich green courses of Benahavis once in a while. He wasn't an avid golfer, but he enjoyed an occasional nine holes with his best friend, Oscar, and some of their mutual friends.

Flores pulled into the expansive driveway of the house, a large structure in classic villa design surrounded by windows. Flores and Marco walked up to the front door and knocked on an ornate brass knocker. A petite woman with neck-length dyed blond hair and sharp eyes the color of a swimming pool answered the door. Small lines around her eyes exhibited signs of aging, though she didn't appear to be very old. She wore tan slacks and a white blouse.

"Malaga police," Flores said, holding up his badge.

The woman narrowed her eyes to look at it. Then she opened the door. Flores extended his hand to her. "I'm Detective Alberto Flores, the lead detective on this case."

Marco also extended his hand and introduced himself.

"Please, come in, Officers. I'm Estelle Mason," she said.

Flores and Marco entered the house and followed Estelle through the front entrance hallway, walking over rustic colored Spanish tile flooring. They turned the corner into a drawing room covered with beige carpeting. The room had a powerful floral scent from the condolence flowers on every table. A large peach colored sofa sat in the center of the room. Chairs upholstered in silk anchored the sofa. Several pieces of artwork in modern and antique frames hung on the walls. Contemporary abstracts added color to the room. Estelle sat on the sofa and invited Marco and Flores to sit in one of the chairs.

Flores took a small black notebook from his shirt jacket. Some of his fellow officers had begun to bring laptop computers with them on interviews, as Marco did, but Flores preferred the feel of the pen. He liked writing everything down on his notepad. He'd also feared his data would get lost or there'd be a computer malfunction.

"Señora Addison," Flores said. "We're so sorry to disturb you. I know this is a difficult time for your family. We're looking into who murdered your husband. We want to find out who did it as soon as possible."

"Gracias," Estelle said. "I'm still in shock. I've had to take tranquilizers every day since it happened. I can't believe he's gone. Addison was so excited about his new gallery and the opening. Unveiling the lost painting thrilled him, the highlight of his career." She turned to look at Marco. "You were there, I think. You saw how excited Addison seemed, didn't you?"

"Si, Señora, I was at the opening with my girlfriend. Your husband seemed very excited," Marco said.

"Oh yes, the pretty young woman who did the beautiful flamenco dance was your girlfriend, right? I saw you two together," Estelle said.

Marco nodded. "Yes, Belen."

Estelle smiled weakly.

Flores shifted his hips on the sofa. "Hmmp, Señora, tell me a little about your husband. Do you know anyone who might have wanted to harm him? Did he have any enemies?"

Estelle shook her head. "No, of course not. My husband was well-liked here and back home in England. He got along well with everyone."

"Where in England are you and your husband from?" Flores asked.

"We're both from Surrey. We met at university, and we've been together ever since."

"When did you move to Vivirrambla?" Flores asked.

"We loved the weather and the relaxed atmosphere when we came here for vacation. Like a lot of expats, we decided to move here permanently. Addison had been a curator for years at some smaller museums in the UK. When he got the chance to move to Spain and open a museum, we couldn't pass it up."

"How long ago was that?" Flores asked.

"About five years ago. We met a woman called Carmela Sanchez on one of our visits, when we went to her restaurant in town. We loved it. So, whenever we were in Spain, we'd go back there. Carmela and Addison started talking when my husband commented on the artwork on the walls. We were there for hours that night. Addison told her that he worked in museums, but that he'd always wanted to own his own museum and feature the kind of art he loved. Camela said that it was a coincidence. She'd spoken to the mayor just a few days earlier about opening a museum in town and adding to the cultural life of Vivirrambla. It seemed like fate. The two formed a relationship, and she helped him get the funds to open the gallery," Estelle said.

Flores looked at Marco. "Carmela's the woman we met that night isn't she?"

"Yes, she's the woman Belen was talking to," Marco said.

"Did Carmela help to secure investors?" Flores asked.

Estelle nodded her head. "Yes, she knew a lot of people in Spain."

"I'll need their names and addresses if you have them," Flores said. "The night of the opening, did your husband seem upset about anything. Did he act unusual at all?"

Estelle raised her eyebrows. "No, Addison seemed in good spirits. I had to calm him down a bit as he'd been hyper all day. Addison tended to get over-excited. He took IBS medication. If he got too nervous or excited, his stomach would flare up. I tried to keep him calm."

"Did either of you receive any kind of threats, strange phone calls, or anything like that?"

Estelle paused for a moment. She sniffed and pulled a Kleenex from her pocket. "Not that I can think of, I don't know any reason why anyone would kill my husband, especially on his big night."

"Addison spoke to us right before Belen danced. He said he'd be back for the unveiling in a few minutes," Marco said. Did you see him after that?"

Estelle shook her head. "He came over, kissed me on the cheek, and thanked me for supporting him. He said we'd celebrate when we got home. He said he needed to go to his office for a minute, but that he'd be back in no time." Estelle lowered her head. "Then I never saw him again."

"Carmela Sanchez seemed terribly upset about Señor Addison's death," Marco said.

"Yes, she and Addison had become good friends. Besides being on the Board of Directors, she's a huge donor to the museum. I think she may have helped to get the Runya painting," Estelle said.

"The Runya painting?" Flores asked.

Estelle looked over at Flores. "Yes, the fifteenth-century painting by Sumya Runya that was to be revealed that night."

"So, you think, Señora Sanchez had something to do with getting that painting?" Flores asked.

Estelle shook her head. "Yes. She's very wealthy and she has a lot of connections."

"I see," Flores said.

"Señora Sanchez. I thought she looked familiar. Her family owns Sanchez's restaurant, right? My family used to go there when I was a child," Marco said.

"Yes, Carmela's now the owner. She's the one who made the museum possible, as I explained."

"I see, that makes sense. Her family's been in Vivirrambla for generations. They've always been art enthusiasts," Marco said.

Estelle nodded her head in agreement.

"Tell me more about this Runya painting," Flores said.

"I don't know as much as my husband. I know that a well-known painting by Sumya Runya, a fifteenth-century painter from Morocco, had been lost for years. Legend had it that it was stolen right before the Spanish Civil War." Estelle started to tear. "Do you think you'll be able to find out who killed my husband? I don't know what I'm going to do without him."

"We're going to do our best, Señora. Do you have any children?" Flores asked.

Estelle nodded. Yes, Addison and I had two children. They're grown and live in the States. They were devastated to hear their father'd been killed. They're both flying in tomorrow."

"Did you and your husband get along well?" Flores asked.

Estelle shifted in her seat. "I'm not going to lie. We had disagreements like every other couple. Thirty years of marriage, that's bound to happen. We argued about him never being home anymore. I know the museum took a lot of his time, but he'd started spending nights there as well as days."

"What did you think about Amy Bloom, his assistant?" Marco asked.

Estelle crossed her leg. "Sweet girl. I know Addison depended on her. Why do you ask?"

Marco and Flores exchanged glances.

"Just routine questions. We need to ask about everything," Flores said.

"Did you have a disagreement the night of the museum opening?" Flores asked.

Estelle dabbed her cheeks. "No. I felt like something was bothering him, but we'd decided to table the discussion until after the opening." Estelle shook her head. "Addison kept a lot inside."

"I assume your husband left his estate to you. Did that include the museum?" Flores asked.

"He left the house and everything to me. As far as the museum is concerned, that's not how it works. Once Addison died, it's up to the Board of Directors."

"Did your husband have any life insurance?" Flores asked.

Estelle folded her hands. "I believe he had a policy."

"Do you know how much it was worth?" Flores asked.

Estelle thought for a moment. "I believe a couple million Euros. It's been a while since I've looked at it. I can get the paperwork for you."

"No bother, I can look up the information. Just tell me the name of the insurer," Flores said.

Estelle got up from her seat, went to a wooden desk, and retrieved a card with the name of the insurance company.

"You're going to be a wealthy woman, Señora," Flores said.

Her eyes narrowed. "That's not important to me. I'd give any money to have my husband back."

"What about the museum paintings, including the Runya? What happens to them?" Marco asked.

Estelle looked over at him. "Yes. As far as I know, the Runya belongs to the museum. It's up to them what they do with the paintings."

"Do you have any idea how much that painting's worth?" Marco asked.

Estelle shook her head no. "I don't have any idea. I didn't get involved with the museum's business too much."

Flores closed his little black notebook and put the pen in his suit pocket. "Alright, gracias, Señora Mason. That's all we need for now. I'm sure we've taken up too much of your time. We may have additional questions for you in the future."

Flores and Marco rose from their seats.

Estelle got up from the sofa, still holding a Kleenex like a child holding onto a toy for security. "Thank you, Detectives. Please do what you can to find out who killed Addison. You will let me know if you find out anything, won't you?"

Flores took a card from his jacket. He felt a hole in the lining. He'd have to replace it soon. "Of course, Señora. Here's my card. Call me at any time if you need anything."

"Two million Euros. That's quite a motive, huh?" Flores said as they ambled back to his car.

Chapter Seven

Back to the Citroën, Marco hopped in the front seat as he and Flores headed to their next stop. It was going to be a long day. After a fifteen-minute drive, they knocked on Addison Mason's assistant, Amy Bloom's door. She answered, wearing shorts and a tan shirt. Her eyes puffed out underneath. She invited Flores and Marco in and gestured for them to sit on one of the modern-looking chairs in her simply designed second-floor apartment overlooking the sea. She sat across from them on the rectangular gray sofa of cotton fabric.

She'd decorated the walls in colorful museum prints bearing the art of well-known painters, such as Degas and Monet. Light streamed through her windows highlighting the colors in the paintings. The room seemed bright and airy. The air smelled of potpourri, or one of those scents women liked.

"Thanks for agreeing to see us so early," Flores said.

Amy looked down. "No problem. This whole thing seems so surreal."

"I know it's a hard time for you. We won't take up much of your time," Flores said.

On a table next to the sofa, an electric kettle perked. A tea pot covered with a decorative yellow knitted cozy fit snugly around the kettle. Amy opened the lid of the pot to see if the tea had brewed. She'd placed three cups on a silver tray on the coffee table in front of the sofa. "Would you like some tea? Take as much time as you need, if it will help us find out what happened to Addison," she said.

"Thank you," Flores said.

Marco nodded in the affirmative. Amy lifted the pot, poured two cups of tea, and handed them to Marco and Flores. Then she poured herself a cup. "Would you like milk and sugar?" she asked.

Marco and Flores nodded yes. Amy put the requested amount into their cups using a spoon of solid silver and silver tongs for the lumps of sugar. She placed decorative silver spoons with designs next to their cups for stirring. Marco noticed that the spoons had a flower design on the handle. They looked expensive and seemed formal in such casual surroundings.

Flores took a sip of tea. Then he turned to Amy. "I understand the type of art featured at the museum was somewhat controversial. Had Addison or you received any recent threats?" he asked.

Amy shook her head. "No, not really any direct threats. A couple of people left nasty messages on the office machine about how a museum in Spain should feature Spanish and not Islamic art, but that was to be expected. Nothing that alarmed us."

"Why do you say it was to be expected?" Marco asked.

Amy looked over at Marco. "We'd heard grumblings about the museum from the outset. A few people disagreed with the concept, but the mayor and most of Vivirrambla expressed their excitement about it. They thought it would be a wonderful thing to have diversity in the town. They guessed it would bring in more tourists, especially wealthy Arabs who liked to golf in Spain. The mayor hoped the museum would make rich visitors spend more money and buy more property in Vivirrambla."

"That sounds like the mayor," Flores said.

All three of them laughed.

"Did you know of anyone in particular who objected to the museum?" Flores asked.

Amy raised her eyebrows. "The loudest objection came from the owner of a gallery in Puerto Bella. He attempted to organize a protest, but only a few people showed up to picket in front of the museum. Addison said the owner, Sven Bjorgen, was just afraid of competition, as his own museum wasn't doing well. It verged on closure.

"Would you say this Sven Bjorgen seemed angry enough to harm Addison?" Flores asked.

Amy shook her head. "Oh no. I doubt that. Kind of a weird guy, but I didn't get the impression he'd harm anyone. Sven was only a blip. I doubt anyone even took him seriously."

"I see. Can you think of anyone else who may have wanted to harm Addison, maybe someone else who opposed the museum?" Flores asked.

Amy took a sip of tea. The cup made a tinging sound when she put it back on the saucer. "No, not really."

"How long have you worked at the museum?" Flores asked.

"I've been working there for a year. I came over from England about a year and a half ago. I worked in an Antiques shop, which featured a lot of art, before I came here, but the owner was retiring. So, it was good timing when I found out about this job from my friend, Nicholas Thompson. Nick's on the Board of Directors. I'm sure you'll meet him," Amy said. "I've always been interested in art. This seemed like the perfect opportunity to get my foot in the door and maybe become a curator someday."

"As Señor Addison's assistant, what exactly did you do?" Flores asked.

Amy chuckled. "Assistant slash gopher you mean. I did everything. I helped decide which paintings would be hung where; I managed Addison's calendar, set up meetings with the board of directors, fielded calls from donors, helped raise money, got coffee—Addison drank at least four cups a day,—kept his scheduler, and anything else Addison needed."

"You must have seen everything that went on in the museum then," Flores said.

Amy nodded. "I did. It was the most exciting job I'd ever had."

"The opening was a huge event for the museum, especially with the painting unveiling. You must have worked even harder than usual," Marco said.

Amy nodded. "Yes. I worked all the time. That painting was Addison's prize acquisition. Everything centered around that painting. Addison had also been planning a 3D immersive exhibit featuring the life and works of the artist Sumaya Runya once we were up and running."

"That interesting. How did Addison acquire the Runya painting? You must have helped," Marco said.

Amy picked up her highly polished silver spoon, which glistened in the sunlight, and stirred a second cup of tea. "I'm not one-hundred percent sure about the acquisition side. I believe our board member, Carmela Sanchez, had something to do with it. I'm not officially on the Board. I just take notes. You'll need to speak to the Board members."

"Is there anything else you can tell us that might help us discover what happened to Señor Mason?" Flores asked.

Amy peered into her teacup as if she could find the answers to Addison's murder in the bottom, like a genie in a bottle. She shook her head no. "Addison was a wonderful person. He gave me my chance in the art world. He was the smartest, kindest man I've ever known."

Marco and Flores looked at one another. "Sorry, I have to ask, were you and Addison merely colleagues?" Flores asked.

Amy turned to look at him through moist eyes. Her cheeks flushed. "We were close if that's what you mean. We worked together all the time. We saw each other every day. You can't help but be close to someone you're with like that."

"I see. How close were you?" Flores asked.

"He was like a brother to me."

"Were you having an affair with him?" Flores asked.

Amy twirled a piece of her hair. "I wouldn't call it an affair. Sometimes we'd end up working late, too late to go home. So, we'd sleep together. I think we both appreciated the coziness."

Flores arched his eyebrow. "You slept together in the museum?"

"Yes, there's a pull-down bed in his office near the bookcases. He had it installed when we were working fifteen-hour days trying to get the museum up and running."

"Did Addison's wife know you slept together?" Flores asked.

Amy shrugged her shoulders. "I doubt it. We were very discreet. We mostly just snuggled at night. His wife's always been super nice to me whenever she came into the museum. I doubt she suspected anything."

"How often did you all 'snuggle' together?" Flores asked.

"Just a few times. It wasn't a full-blown affair, more like we needed each other at that moment," she said.

"Did anyone else know about your affair?" Flores asked.

Amy shot him a sharp look. "It wasn't an affair. I may have told my friend Nicholas Thompson, but that's it."

"Why tell Nicholas Thompson?" Flores asked.

Amy flicked her hair back. "He's one of my best friends. I tell him everything."

"You said Thompson's on the Board, right? Can you give me a list of the board members and their contact information?" Flores asked.

Amy got up, picked up their teacups, and put them on the silver tray. Then she opened the drawer of an antique wooden desk of cherry wood on the other side of the room. She extracted a folder from it and removed documents. "Here you are, I keep copies in these folders, so I don't have to go online to look up their numbers and emails each time I want to contact them."

Flores took the documents from her. "That's smart. Thanks."

"Have you heard what's going to happen to the museum?" Marco asked.

Amy shook her head no. "From what I've heard from Nick, they want to keep the museum going. The collection is ready, and everything's in place. They'll have to search for a new director."

Flores closed his black notebook and stuck it in his breast pocket. Marco followed suit and shut down his laptop. They rose from their chairs.

"I think that's all we need for now. Thank you for taking time to talk to us, Señorita. We'll let you know if we need anything else. You aren't planning on leaving Spain, are you?" Flores asked.

"No, I'll be here. I hope to still have a job at the museum. Will you let me know if you find out anything?"

Flores handed a card to Amy. "We'll keep you updated. If you need anything, or if you remember anything else, you can call me or the station anytime."

"Thank you. This whole thing is just so unbelievable," Amy said.

* * *

"I'll drop you off at your office," Flores said to Marco when they got back to his car.

"Thanks. Amy certainly seemed fond of this Nicholas Thompson. Her face lit up every time she talked about him," Marco said.

I noticed that too, Flores said.

Chapter Eight

"[T]he glorious movement, which is what he called his revolt."
Spain the Root and the Flower, John A. Crowe

In Spain, as in any other country, great wealth can bring a life of comfort and ease, but wealth doesn't make one immune from life's controversies or pains. Flores and Marco had an appointment to speak to one of the town's wealthiest residents. Carmela Sanchez lived a life of luxury in the hills of Vivirrambla. Her father, owner of Sanchez's restaurant, had been a regular buyer of Marco's father's daily sea catch. Marco's father, *un pescador,* a fisherman, supplied freshly caught fish daily to all of the finest restaurants in Vivirrambla. Sanchez's being one of his main customers.

Memories of Carmela Sanchez and her family flooded back to Marco's mind. He hadn't seen Señora Sanchez since he was a teen. Her once tight smooth olive-skinned face now bore the fine lines of aging. Small bags rested under her eyes. Her neck had lost elasticity and had formed creases. Yet, her beauty had not faded but had transformed into a sophistication.

Sanchez's restaurant opened a few years before Franco ruled Spain. It stayed open when other restaurants closed during the Franco years. Some had speculated, but there'd never been proof, that Señor Sanchez supported Franco, who in turn made sure his restaurant prospered even in some of Spain's leanest years. Vivirramblians frequented Sanchez's for special occasions like birthdays, anniversaries, and weddings. Marco had gone there on many birthdays and for his graduation. Since his father supplied the fish, they enjoyed a heavy discount. Otherwise, they couldn't have afforded the high-end restaurant, something his father explained to him years later.

Sanchez's brought back good memories. At one point, Marco knew the entire Sanchez family. He'd go with his father back to the kitchen to deliver the fish. Marco'd see the whole family working together, cooking, and preparing the meals. Señor Pedro Sanchez, an olive-skinned, pudgy man with white hair and a moustache, the family patriarch, ruled the restaurant like the leader of a small authoritarian nation, Franco in the kitchen. Everyone quaked in his presence. Marco thought him scary as well. He did everything to avoid running into the old man. Señor Sanchez had one daughter, Carmela, and a son, Diego. He seemed to dote on the teen Carmela. He softened when he spoke to her, and kindness replaced the normal scowl on his face. On the other hand, he bristled at even the sight of his son, Diego, who likewise tried to avoid him.

One day, word came that Señor Sanchez had died of a heart attack. Marco wasn't surprised as the old man ran around huffing and out of breath with his large belly bouncing up and down. Carmela, now an adult, took over the restaurant. In time, as he got older and less agile, Marco's father had begun to cut back and stopped delivering fresh fish to all but a few restaurants. Carmela secured another fish supplier. It had been years ago now, and Marco had long forgotten his memories of Sanchez's. He did recall reading an article in *Vivirrambla Today* magazine some time ago about Sanchez's and how the new owner, Carmela, daughter of the formidable Pedro, intended to modernize the restaurant with a paint job and more modern paintings. Marco remembered the restaurant having traditional paintings of figures from Sicily, including a large portrait of an elderly Italian woman. Carmela, the story said, had inherited her love of art from her father, which had led her to become a patron of the arts.

Marco recollected a more recent article that reported on a local restaurateur who wished to remain anonymous. The owner had given a substantial donation to the new museum to secure the lost painting that had been the subject of the unveiling the night Addison Mason was killed. The donor was quoted as saying:

"An important painting has been found. I'm so glad I've been a part of this endeavor and a part of the opening of the wonderful Museo de Galeria d'Arte, here in Vivirrambla. Our unique new museum will attract visitors from around the world."

Marco now knew the anonymous donor to be Carmela Sanchez. It seemed like fate that after all that time, he'd be meeting her again as a police consultant investigating a murder.

Flores and Marco made their way to see Carmela. This time, Marco drove, which meant he didn't have to ride in Flores's uncomfortable Citroën with his knees squashed against the dashboard.

"You handle most of the interview this time, since you know her," Flores said.

Carmela Sanchez lived in the town of Ojen, just above Vivirrambla, *un pueblo*, wedged in the mountains, brimming with sprawling, white-washed houses. Marco pulled into the expansive driveway of the modern-looking villa in the hills on the edge of the Sierra Blanca. Large windows that reflected green light from the trees surrounded the exterior of the home. Large palm and orange trees graced the perimeter. The orange trees emitted the fresh smell of oranges that soared through the air. Flores sped in front of him as they approached the door. He did that at times when he wanted to seem important and assert his authority. A middle-aged woman with her hair in a bun granted them entry after they rang the musical doorbell.

The woman led them down a long corridor of mosaic floors and Spanish tiles into a drawing room with a wide, huge stone fireplace and a view of the Sierra mountains. The room had traditional furniture. A light green Louis XIV sofa and two cream-colored antique chairs covered with fine silk took up one side of the room. Copies of *"Traditional Home"* magazine sat atop a wooden coffee table in front of the sofa. Curio cabinets held pictures in frames and knick-knacks. An eclectic group of paintings on the walls hinted at the owner's love of art.

Carmela entered the room wearing a black knit skirt, white button-down top, and black sweater. Her hair behind her ears allowed large, thick gold hoop earrings to be visible. She looked as if she was on her way to an important business lunch.

"Gentlemen, please sit down," Carmela said, gesturing with her hand.

Marco and Flores obeyed like children listening to their grandparents. Each took a seat on one of the silk chairs. Flores took a black notebook from his jacket. Marco opened his iPad.

"Señora Sanchez, I'm sure you know why we're here. You remember Detective Flores?" Marco asked.

She turned to Flores and nodded, "Yes, of course. Thank you for coming to see me, Detective. Marco, how's your father? I haven't seen him in quite some time. I remember he always brought the freshest fish to the restaurant. You'd come with him and visit us in the kitchen."

Marco smiled. "He's fine. He's retired. He misses the food at your restaurant. His diet is more restricted these days."

"Of course. I miss the old days sometimes, when Vivirrambla was a small fishing village. Everything's changed now. It's all commercial; we get our fish from a mega company now. I'm lucky, though. The restaurant is still doing well."

"Yes, you've been fortunate to have remained in business all this time," Marco said.

"Enough about my business. I know you came to talk about Addison. It's quite shocking what happened. I'm having a tough time dealing with it. We'd become dear friends. You know I've been one of the museum's biggest patrons. I couldn't imagine someone trying to kill such a nice young man," Carmela said.

"Si, Señora, we're all shocked," Marco said.

"It all happened so fast. One minute, we're waiting for Addison to unveil the painting. The next minute, we're all running out to the courtyard, just to find him like that." She looked down, shaking her head.

"How was Señor Addison when you last saw him alive? Did he seem worried or troubled?" Flores asked.

Carmela shook her head. "No, not at all. He made the rounds, greeting and welcoming everyone. He seemed in such a good mood. He kissed my cheek and thanked me again for my patronage. He said he'd soon unveil *our* painting; he called it."

"How did you become involved in the museum?" Marco asked.

"I've loved art since I was a child. My father also loved art. We had a lot of paintings in the restaurant."

"I remember," said Marco.

"I used to spend hours staring at them. I told Papa I wanted to go to art school, but he said women didn't do that." Carmela paused and looked over to Marco and Flores. "There'd be no future in it, he said. It was a different time. He insisted I marry someone of his choosing and continue running the restaurant. My father knew a lot of very important people in town. He was determined to find me a suitable husband." Carmela shrugged her shoulders. "I had no choice. I got married to a man of Papa's choosing, whom I didn't love. Papa left the restaurant to me when he died. I finally felt free to pursue my interests in the arts and to support artists. I put all my attention on my children and the restaurant. I met Addison and his wife when they came into the restaurant. We started talking, and he told me he was a curator in London and that he'd dreamed of his own gallery. He said he and his wife had thought of moving to Spain some time ago."

"So, you decided to help him?" Marco asked.

Carmela turned her head, revealing a small, upturned nose. "Yes, we developed a business plan. Addison told me that he had a particular interest in ancient African and Islamic art. An interest he developed in university, and when visiting Morocco. That intrigued me. It all came together in about a year. We found the space. Addison contacted artists he knew, and I helped him to get investors. It took another year to construct the museum. Then we got lucky and acquired the Runya painting. Kismet. It seemed the perfect time to open the museum and display the painting.

"How did you acquire the painting?" Marco asked.

"Ah, yes, quite by accident, really. Addison told me that a friend of his, an art historian, found out that the painting was being sold at a private auction. We agreed we wanted it. The Runya had been lost for over eighty years. It was a great find for the museum." Carmela said.

"How much did you pay for the painting?" Flores asked.

Carmella pursed her lips. "We paid one point five million, plus the auction fees. Someone tried to run up the bid, but the auction house excluded their bid as being illegal."

"Did you find out where the painting had been all these years?" Marco asked.

Carmela shook her head, No. "We never found out. The seller wanted to remain anonymous, which is why he wanted it sold at a private sale through the auction house. Addison had the painting authenticated. We were all nervous to find out the result, but it came back as the real work of the artist, Sumaya Runya, from the fifteenth century. You can't imagine how excited we were. Addison had it cleaned and repaired by a specialist. None of us on the Board had seen the painting after it'd been restored." She turned to Marco. "We were going to be as surprised as you at the unveiling."

"Did you ever find out who wanted to run up the bid?" Marco asked.

"We never found out. The auction house just told us that they'd discovered a fake account. They said these things happen sometimes. All they could tell us was that the bidder tried to wire money from a UK account. The auction house didn't try pursuing any additional charges, as the false bidder was removed from the bidding process."

"How did someone else find out about the painting if the auction was private?" Marco asked.

"The auction house listed us as preferred customers. That didn't preclude others from finding out. They could have found out in any art trade periodical," Carmela said.

"Do you know of anyone who may have been angry at Señor Addison?" Flores asked.

She sat back in her chair; her legs crossed at the ankles. "No, not that I know about. We had a few disagreements on the Board, but nothing anyone would kill over."

"What kind of disagreements?" Flores asked.

"Some of the board members wanted the museum to feature strictly Islamic art or art from that period, and maybe add African art. Others thought the museum should be focused on European art and add other exhibits from time to time. Many of us felt there are enough museums with European art. That by branching out, we could show unrepresented works of beauty that the public may never have seen. Addison had even spoken to American artist James Marshall about exhibiting at the African American museum in America. Addison and I took a trip, a year ago, to America to visit this fantastic museum."

"Would you say any of the board members were bitter about the art choices?" Flores asked.

"I wouldn't say bitter. We had a few heated discussions at the meetings. I remember the English lawyer, Nicholas Thompson, being the most upset over the issue. I doubt he'd kill Addison over it, though. They'd been friends for many years, since school."

"Do you know of anyone else who may have been upset with Addison?" Flores asked.

Carmela thought for a moment. "No, I heard him arguing on the phone with someone a few days before he died. I'd come to the museum to check on a few things before the opening. He hung up when he saw me. He said one of the suppliers had been giving him grief, and it was no big deal."

"You don't know who he was talking to?" Flores asked.

"No, I took Addison's word for it, and we went on to talk about the opening and other business," Carmela said.

"Was there anyone else you would consider to be particularly angry about the museum's art or anything else having to do with the museum?" Flores asked.

"No, not that I can think of," Carmela said?

"Is there anything else you want to tell us about the museum, or about Addison?" Flores asked.

Carmella shook her head No.

"*Vale, gracias*, Señor Sanchez. You have been most helpful," Flores said.

"I want you to find whoever killed Addison," she said.

Marco and Flores thanked Carmela. Flores invited her to contact him if she thought of anything else.

"You think someone killed him over the painting?" she asked.

"We have to look at all possibilities, Señora. Call me if you need me," Flores said, handing her his card.

Chapter Nine

Marco decided to go over the notes he'd made from witness interviews they had had so far, to see if he could find any clues. His computer pinged as he worked. "Have you heard from Bortello?" Flores asked.

"Not yet," Marco said, responding to the text message.

"Can you go and see what you can find out about the autopsy? The Chief's on my back and wants answers," Flores said.

Marco agreed to visit the coroner's office. He closed the Excel sheet he'd made and shut down his computer. "I'll go see him right now."

Javier Bortello, the prickly head coroner for Vivirrambla for the past twenty years, was known for his thoroughness in examining bodies. He'd been instrumental in helping to solve difficult cases. His office, if you could call it that, a dark room that contained dead bodies, was located in the basement of the Vivirrambla hospital. Marco walked over to the medical center and took the elevator to the basement. He pushed the steel doors of the morgue and wrinkled his nose. The pungent smell of chemicals assaulted him as soon as he entered.

Marco chalked up Bortello's snarkiness to his job of looking at the dead all day. Javier sat at a wooden table on the side of the room, peering through a microscope, examining something. Marco didn't want to know what he was looking at.

"Hola," Marco, said as he approached Javier.

Javier grunted.

Javier had reached late middle age. The only hair he had remaining on his scalp formed in a grey semicircle around his head. His chin was covered with a gray goatee. He wore a white lab coat over his slim physique. Small rectangular black reading glasses sat perched on the end of his nose. He sat on a black stool in front of a desk with a computer.

He removed his spectacles and placed them on the table beside him and looked up at Marco. "I suppose you're here about the Mason case."

"That's right. Flores wants to know if you have any information. High Priority. He's getting a lot of pressure," Marco said.

Bortello grunted. "They're all high priority," he said. "As you know, since you were there, the victim must have been killed less than an hour before we got there. No rigor had set in. I can tell you for sure that he was strangled. I know we initially said the killer used his bare hands, but it looks like they used a rope or something solid from the marks on his neck. Let me show you."

Marco followed Bortello over to one of the silver steel drawers where they kept bodies for examination that once moved and breathed. He pulled out the silver tray labeled Addison Mason. Marco noticed how tall Addison seemed in that position, over six foot. Javier pointed to Addison's neck and the marks that looked like large scratches. He turned the dead man's body so that his face seemed to stare at them. Marco felt a shiver in his spine.

"There are marks on both sides of his neck. Someone really did a job on him," Javier said.

"How could anyone do that much damage in such a short time? We were all in the museum, and no one heard or saw anything," Marco said.

"You'd be surprised. Strangulation only takes a few seconds. My guess is someone approached Addison from behind and forced him into the garden. The police found drag marks on the ground and on his shoes. Once in the garden, they used a rope or similar object to cause asphyxia." Javier pointed to another area of the body. "Look here, the killer cut his jugular veins, causing a collapse of the trachea. There are scratches on his right arm indicating he may have tried to fight off his attacker, a futile endeavor as the assassin struck with precision. Petechiae's visible, and on the brain on autopsy."

"What does the presence of petechiae tell you about the murder?" Marco asked, having no idea what petechiae meant.

"Petechiae are red, brown, or purple dots that appear when blood capillaries burst under the skin. I noticed it on the inside of the eyelids and around his ears. They let us know that at least ten seconds of uninterrupted venous compression occurred. See here how the ligature's been positioned," Bortello said, pointing to a spot on the neck of the corpse.

"So, in essence, someone forced Addison out onto the garden. Then, standing behind him, pulled some kind of rope tight around his neck to strangle him," Marco said.

Bortello shook his head. "Exactly. I also found skull fractures. The brutal attack didn't last long, but it did a lot of damage. That's why we saw little blood in the area. You found that paint on his shirt, I recall."

"Yeah, Flores sent it to the lab. Did you find any more paint evidence?" Marco asked.

Bortello shook his head, no. Then he closed the drawer with the silver tray containing Addison Mason. "That's all I can tell you. The rest is up to you and Flores to find the killer."

"Okay, thanks, Javier. You've been thorough as usual," Marco said.

"The victim was tall. So, the perpetrator had to be able to reach Addison even if he was sitting down. I'll leave that for you to figure out. I think you figured out he was left-handed. I agree."

"*Gracias, Javier*. I'll relay all of this to Flores."

Marco took the elevator back to the lobby. He took a deep breath and stepped outside. He drank in the fresh air, erasing the horrid smells of the morgue. When he returned to his office, he phoned Flores to update him.

"Javier's confident that Addison was strangled. He says he may have tried to fight off his assailant. Javier thinks the killer must have been tall and left-handed, due to the positioning of the body, but he can't tell us much else, except that it happened fast. He showed me the ligature marks and bruises on Addison's neck that verify his findings. Bortello's going to finalize his autopsy report and send it over," Marco said.

"Okay, we'll work with what we have. We're going to have a challenging time solving this one," Flores said.

Chapter Ten

The media continually speculated as to who killed Addison. It'd become a popular whodunit, with many guessing the killer over social media. Internet sleuths tried to solve the crime. Some had more faith in the internet sleuths than the Malaga police force to solve such a complicated case. After one particularly scathing article appeared in the local paper, the Chief called Flores to his office.

"I'm being pulverized in the press," the Chief said. "I didn't know everyone cared so much about museums."

Flores assured the Chief that they were making progress in finding Addison Mason's killer. "We've got some good leads to go on," he said.

He updated the Chief that they'd interviewed several witnesses and taken statements from everyone who was at the museum that night. Once they found a motive, they'd narrow in on the suspects.

"Have you arrested anyone yet?" the Chief asked.

Flores shook his head, no.

The Chief said it wasn't enough. He needed immediate answers, something concrete to tell nosy reporters hounding him. The mayor had also been calling him daily. "Make no mistake. Your job's on the line." The Chief told him when they met early in the morning.

People are intimidated by anyone in a position of power who seemingly have control over their lives. Flores was no exception. He cowered when he had to face the Chief. His head pounded after his morning meeting. They'd have to speed up the investigation, which meant he'd have to pull officers from other cases. He took an *aspirina* and rubbed his temples. Then he sat down to review the notes he'd made from interviews and what he'd learned so far. Everyone said Addison seemed excited that night. He didn't look worried about anything. He didn't have any enemies. The only clue they had so far—a few outsiders had disagreed with the exhibits, a weak motive for murder in his estimation. He picked up his cell and called Marco.

"It's time we speak to the board members. Maybe we can get some answers from them," Flores said.

"I agree. Maybe they know something no one else has told us," Marco said.

"The lawyer, Nicholas Thompson, is the board chair, according to my notes," Flores said.

"Yes, that's the information I have."

"Can you get a hold of him and arrange a meeting for us?" Flores asked.

Chapter Eleven

arco set a date for their meeting with Nicholas Thompson, Esquire, and the members of the museum board. Prior to the interview, Flores and Marco got together to review the information Amy Bloom had given them about each member.

"Quite an eclectic group," Flores said.

- **Carmela Sanchez** - Wealthy restaurateur, instrumental in getting the painting and opening the new museum.
- **Nicholas Thomas, Board Chair**- UK lawyer, had been a friend of Addison's since childhood. The two had gone to a posh public school in Britain. Nicholas divided his time between Gibraltar, Spain, and the UK. His family still lived in the UK.
- **Luis Castillo**, General Counsel to the Board from Vivirrambla. - Castillo, in his mid-forties, was a well-known entertainment law lawyer. He represented many of the town's celebrities and was a friend of Carmela's.
- **Farah Zine** of Tangier, Morocco - early thirties, a top model who appeared in several magazines. Farah served as the poster face for the museum. She'd been in numerous advertisements and in several editions of *Vivirrambla Today* discussing the new gallery. Farah's husband was a computer technology and 3D specialist.
- **Oliver Hall** of the UK, Board Secretary, and treasurer - Oliver, an antiques dealer and art historian, lived in Spain. He also had a house with his partner in London. Addison had been friends with Hall since

University, where they both majored in art history.

Marco arrived at the museum early on the appointed day. Flores arrived a few minutes later. The front of the museum remained roped off with a "No Entry" sign. Flores showed his police badge to the guard, who let them inside. The unveiled painting remained perched on the easel where it'd been when it was about to be revealed. Marco and Flores walked up a set of winding stairs to the boardroom at the top of the three-story building. Flores panted out of breath when they reached the top. There were no exhibits on that floor, only the boardroom and another unused suite of offices. Inside the boardroom, a long dark cherrywood table dominated the space. A life-sized portrait of Addison Mason hung centered above the table. Addison, his lips turned up in a smile, looked forever young. Like Dorian Gray, Addison would never grow old. His youth remained eternally in the portrait. He wore a gray suit and blue silk tie—his dark hair combed back. He sat on a leather chair with his legs crossed, amid an impressionist pale blue background. His eyes stared straight ahead at the viewer as if watching the board's every move.

The board members filed in and gathered around the table. They went to a particular seat, as if they were school children with assigned seating. Marco and Flores sat in the two remaining leather chairs. The members chatted amongst themselves until Nicholas Thompson, Chair, called them to order and explained the purpose of the meeting.

Marco noticed that Thompson wore expensive clothing. His dark gray suit and a silver tie were set off by sterling silver cufflinks. He stood and spoke from his position at the head of the table. "We all know why we're here," he said. "The police need our help in finding out who killed our beloved Addison."

"I don't know how much we can help. We were all in the gallery waiting for the unveiling of the painting when he was killed," Oliver said.

Everyone nodded in agreement.

"You may have some useful information to aid us in our investigation. Something you may not have thought important at the time," Flores said.

This led to more chatter among the board members until Thompson again called for order.

"Let's just hear what the detectives have to say," Thompson said.

"Well, I don't know how much help we can be," Oliver Hall said.

Member Farah Zine spoke. Farah was, by all accounts, beautiful. She had an oval face and slim body. Her raven hair flowed down her back like the waves of the sea. Her dark skin, the color of milled honey, was smooth and clear. Her long eyelashes fluttered when she spoke. "Let's just listen, like Nicholas said."

Flores pulled out his notebook and a pen from his jacket. Then he addressed the board. "Thanks for taking the time to meet. I'm sure you're all busy, but we'd be grateful for any information you can give us since you all knew Addison better than anyone else."

"Yes, of course, we're happy to help if we can," Thompson said. "I'm sorry this happened to Amy; she must have been so frightened to find Addison in that state," he said.

Marco's eyes narrowed. He wondered why he singled out Addison's assistant, Amy.

"We were all very upset, still are," said the proper speaking, Oliver Hall.

"Did Addison have any enemies that you know of? Has the board had any issues with him?" Flores asked.

Nicholas Thompson fidgeted in his chair. "None that I know about. We had our minor disagreements, but we all respected Addison and his dedication to this wonderful museum."

"What were your disagreements about?" Flores asked.

"Mostly exhibits, where this or that painting should hang, which paintings we should acquire, which paintings would cost the museum too much, that type of thing. Nothing you'd murder anyone over," Thompson said.

Oliver spoke. "We all loved Addison and wanted him to succeed and the museum to do well. We expected it to be a major tourist draw for Vivirrambla, especially with the Runya painting on display."

"I understand some outsiders complained about the museum and that some of you board members disagreed with the focus being on Islamic and African art," Marco said.

"At first, but I think we all got on board later. Addison assured us he knew what he was doing," Thompson said.

Everyone shook their head in agreement, except Farah Zine, who started to speak but then hesitated.

"Were you going to say something, Señora Zine?" Marco asked.

Farah shrugged. "Nothing important. Just that Addison did receive a couple of nasty emails, but nothing we considered to be a real threat."

"Did you save those emails?" Flores asked.

"Amy should have them. They were pretty general. From what I remember, they said something about not ruining Vivirrambla's history. Of course, they didn't seem to understand that Vivirrambla's history included four hundred years of Muslim rule. Few are aware of our history," Farah said.

Marco nodded in agreement. "Were there any direct threats in the emails?"

Farah shook her head. "No, not threatening, just nasty and ignorant as to Vivirrambla's and Spain's history.

"How were the museum's finances?" Flores asked.

"Thanks to a lot of generous donors, especially people like Carmela," Carmela blushed. "We're in the black and doing well. Addison raised a substantial sum to keep the museum going for at least a couple of years. We projected that with visitors, the museum should thrive for the foreseeable future," Oliver Hall said.

"We'd never have been financially sound if Addison had listened to Nicholas, who didn't want to feature the Runya at the opening," Luis Castillo said.

Nicholas shot him a sharp look. "That's not true, Luis. I just thought it shouldn't be the main feature of the opening. I thought it should be mentioned but not be a focal point for the whole evening."

"Well, you were wrong. The painting, and its being lost, drew in a lot of important people and a lot of potential investments, just like Addison said it would," Luis said.

"It all worked out in the end. The museum's in good shape," Carmela said, sounding like a mother appeasing her two sons.

"When will we be able to reopen?" Thompson asked.

"I can't say right now. It's still early in the investigation," Flores said.

After a few more questions, Flores handed out cards to each of the board members and encouraged them to contact either Marco or himself if they remembered anything, even if it didn't seem important. He and Marco thanked them again for their time and left. They heard chatter behind the closed door once they exited.

"I sensed a bit of tension in there," Flores said.

"Yes, I did too. They tried to act like everything's fine, but I have my doubts," Marco said.

"Maybe one of these board members got upset enough to kill Addison," Flores said.

Chapter Twelve

"Prosopagnosia is face blindness. It is a condition where you see a face, but you don't recognise it. We are consciously and actively invisibilising certain stories, certain identities, and certain social movements."
—*Behzad Khosravi Noori*, discussing his art exhibition,
The Life of an Itinerant Through a Pinhole

Marco stumbled upon an article that had made it all the way to the national paper, *The Guardian*. Local museum owner, Sven Bjorgen, a Swedish expatriate, wrote a scathing editorial about the new Galeria de' Arte museum scheduled to open in Vivirrambla. The article quoted Bjorgen as saying the museum symbolized the dangers of "cancel culture," which he said was spreading throughout the world. He claimed that Addison Mason had merely capitalized on what Americans called "wokeness," an attempt to control the narrative of what's acceptable. A museum featuring Islamic and African art, he claimed, "is a classic example of this phenomenon." Sven stated that his museum featured European art, the kind of art Vivirrambla needed.

The critique sounded like disguised racism. Those with this belief argued that their sacred past culture has been suppressed in favor of new inclusiveness, not understanding that there's enough room for everyone. Marco recognized this subtle form of hate. He'd faced it often enough. Being of half Moroccan origin, he'd been subjected to comments about his appearance, being called *un gitano*, Gypsy, implying that he engaged in thievery. Others looked down on his Moroccan heritage. Spain, they saw as a sophisticated European nation, and therefore, somehow superior to neighboring Morocco, an African country. Those with Sven's worldview wanted to ignore the true history of Spain, as Farah Zine noted, in favor of their own narrative of the past.

Marco also sensed a rivalry in Bjorgen's biting words and perhaps professional jealousy. *I need to know more about this Sven.* He thought. He pulled up a search for Sven Bjorgen on his search engine. Wikipedia listed Sven as a Swedish artist who'd been educated at the Konstfack school of art in Sweden. He'd moved to Spain after school, and a few years later opened Bjorgen's Modern Art Museum in Puerto Bella. Sven was married and had one child.

Marco decided to visit Sven Bjorgen's museum. Belen didn't have to go to work until late. She loved going to museums and knew a lot about art. He called her to see if she had plans for the afternoon. He invited her to go to the museum and have lunch on the water in Puerto Bella, ten minutes away. Belen said she'd love to go. Marco said he'd pick her up in an hour.

Marco read a few more articles, then headed to his car to pick up Belen. Belen slipped in the seat beside him. She wore a flowered sundress and large, round earrings. She looked bright, like a morning star. Marco took the coastal highway to Puerto Bella, the town famed for its wealthy ex-pat residents and rich tourists. He parked in the overpriced garage, and they walked to the entrance of the town. They joined the British, Swedish, and Germans, with pasty white skin, strolling along the paseo. They trudged only a few feet from yachts bobbing up and down on the turquoise water. They sauntered past patrons eating in outdoor restaurants or sipping drinks at the Ellington bar. They found the address Marco had notated. **The Museo of Modern Art of Puerto Bella** was located next to the Versace store, inside a large white edifice with grey windows, which also contained offices. Marco and Belen walked into a the stark-looking entrance. The small museum was empty, except for an attractive black couple who spoke with an American accent. Various pieces of dark art hung on white walls. The American couple looked puzzled as they moved from picture to picture.

"This looks more like a warehouse than a museum," Belen whispered.

"It looks like a basement where an artist would store their rejected pieces. All the pictures are so dark," Marco said.

A tall man with white-blond shoulder-length hair approached them, brandishing a broad smile. He wore blue checkered pants and a pink oxford shirt. He spoke with a Swedish-sounding accent. "Good afternoon, I'm Sven, welcome to my museum."

"Pleased to meet you," Marco said.

Sven paused and put his thumb and finger on his chin and studied Marco. "Oh yes, I remember seeing you at Addison's opening. Have you been here before?"

"This is our first visit," Marco said.

The man looked at Belen and smiled. Marco noticed a glint in his eyes.

"How long has your museum been here? We live in Vivirrambla, but I don't remember seeing it before," Marco said.

"Yeah," Sven laughed aloud. "We're tucked away next to the fancy stores. We're a hidden gem," he said, chuckling at his own joke. He turned again to smile at Belen. The corners of his mouth turned up, forming a leer.

Marco glared at him. "Yes, a hidden gem."

Sven turned to Marco. "You from Morocco, or are you what they say here, 'Un Gitano'?"

Belen squeezed Marco's hand as if to say, please restrain what you say.

"No," Marco said. "I was born in Vivirrambla."

"Ahhh. If I remember, you were working with the police, weren't you? Tragic about Addison, huh? I wonder what will become of the museum now?" Sven asked.

"I don't have any idea about who will take over the museum, or even if it will stay open," Marco said.

"Ah, yes, maybe closing it would be the best thing to do for everyone. I told that detective who questioned us that night to let me know if I can help the police in any way," Sven said.

"I'm sure he appreciated that," Marco said.

Sven grinned a wide grin. "I'm always happy to help law enforcement,"

"I'll keep that in mind," Flores said.

Sven turned as if to leave. "Well, don't let me hold you up," he said, making a sweeping semicircle gesture with his hand. "Please, look around. Take your time. Our museum is different from the traditional gallery. My art collection is innovative. I feature unknown European artists and bring them to life. Take a look at the gift shop while you're here."

Marco and Belen looked at one another.

Belen asked where to find the facilities. Sven pointed her down a hallway. Then, he sauntered off to another area of the museum. The American couple passed by, frowning, trying to study each of the paintings.

Marco walked around the strange museum. Surreal paintings hung amidst stark lighting and weirdly colored walls. The room he stood in was painted a deep purple, almost gothic. Other paintings depicted dark scenes and figures in various positions. Something in the atmosphere felt cold and uninviting. It wasn't minimalism for which the Swedes were known, but something else. Something sinister.

Belen caught up with him in one of the rooms. "I've seen Picasso's Guernica. It's dark, but it was meant to represent the hardness and destruction of the Spanish Civil War. These paintings just look like a collection of bleak pictures by disturbed artists. The only thing I liked was the small figurine of a horse that I saw displayed in the gift shop, a beautiful orange hand-carved figure with a floral design. I think it was called a Dala horse the label said. Pricey though, two hundred dollars, but it's by far the nicest thing in here," Belen said.

Marco stifled a laugh. "I don't know much about art, but I have to agree with your assessment."

Marco and Belen continued through the various exhibit rooms, hoping to see at least some pastel color in any of the pieces, but it was the same in every room they went into: dark, disturbing paintings and prints. Even the descriptions at the bottom of the paintings didn't help to explain their meaning. Marco knew of modern art and the idea that a painting could be up to interpretation. Try as he might, though, he found no deeper meaning in anything he saw.

"I've had enough of this depressing place," Belen finally said. "Let's go and get something to eat, honey."

Marco put up no argument. They found Sven, who hovered over the African American couple, waiting for them to give a reaction to one of the paintings.

"Sven, thank you for letting us look around your museum," Marco said.

"Si, gracias. I saw a charming wooden figurine of a horse in your shop," Belen said.

Sven grinned. "Oh yes, excellent taste. It's the Dala horse, a symbol of my home country, Sweden. I sell a lot of them to tourists."

"Really lovely," Belen said.

They bid Sven good day and walked over to Pizzeria Picasso for lunch, appropriate for the day's visit.

"I need a beer after that," Marco said.

"I need several glasses of wine to get those images out of my mind. The pizza's better art than anything in that place. Why did we visit there again?"

"It's part of my investigation." He showed Belen the article he'd read in *The Guardian*. "Sorry, I didn't realize it'd be such a horrible exhibit."

Belen perused the article as they waited for their meal. "So, he's against Addison's beautiful and interesting museum, but we're supposed to enjoy that travesty he calls an art gallery."

Marco agreed. They finished lunch and decided to take a stroll on the water before going home. They held hands, their fingers intertwined as they walked on the water's edge. Marco spotted Farah Zine walking with an older man; they both licked ice cream cones, catching the ice cream dripping down the sides with their tongues.

The couple stopped in front of them. "Marco," Farah said. "So nice to see you here."

Belen narrowed her eyes and twisted her nose.

"Farah, good to see you," Marco said, kissing her on both cheeks.

Marco introduced her to Belen.

Farah smiled a broad smile, displaying pearl white teeth. "Mucho gusto. This is my husband, Bernard."

Belen and Bernard both nodded. "Un pleasure," they said.

"We've been over to Sven Bjorgen's museum," Marco said.

Farah scowled, still holding her dripping ice cream. "That museum stinks. Excuse me for being so blunt. I can't believe he wrote such horrible things about Addison when his own place is trash. Bernard knows Sven. He says Sven is considered second rate in the art world."

"Really?" Marco asked. "Is your husband an artist?"

Farah glanced over at her husband. "Not really an artist per se. Bernard owns Faruq Industries. It supplies 3D equipment and helps customers develop three-dimensional immersive art exhibits. Bernard's worked at galleries all around the world, including El Prado, the Louvre, the Philadelphia Art Museum, and the American Smithsonian museums. Sven Bjorgen asked Bernard to install some fancy 3D imaging to perk things up in his museum and attract more visitors. Bernard refused the job. He wanted no parts of that disaster."

"Addison Mason had been working with us to install a 3D exhibit in the museum. Sven heard about it and wanted me to do the same for him," Bernard said.

"What kind of 3D exhibit?" Marco asked.

"Addison designed a three-dimensional prototype which displayed fifteenth-century Islamic pilgrims. He said it was Runya brought to life. The idea was that visitors would be immersed in an ancient world. He'd hired me to develop it and set it up. I told him I'd help him get a patent for the design, which is something else my company does. Addison had planned to open the interactive exhibit as soon as everything had been completed. It's so sad he died before we could finish it," Bernard said.

"That's really a shame. I would have loved to see such an exhibit," Marco said.

"That sounds really amazing," Belen said. "I'm sorry to cut this short, but honey, I've got to get ready to go to work."

Marco looked at his phone. "Oh, yes, you're right. We'd better get going. Farah it was nice to see you again, and to meet you, Bernard."

They exchanged goodbyes, and each went on their way.

"She certainly is a beautiful woman," Belen said, as they retrieved the car from the garage.

Marco looked straight ahead at the road. "Yeah, Farah's a model. Her husband seems nice."

He dropped Belen off at home and gave her a quick kiss.

"I'll see you after the show sometime," she said, getting out of the car.

When he reached the office, Marco went straight back to researching information on the Board members. After a few hours, his eyes grew weary from looking at the computer screen. He shut everything down and decided to go home. Eva had gone some time ago. Belen wouldn't be home yet. So, he decided he'd stop and get something to eat from the super mercardo.

As he approached his car, he felt as if someone was watching him, though he didn't see anyone. He turned around to look. He beeped the car door open with the electronic key and started to get into the car. Before he could move, something hit him from behind. The blue of the Mediterranean turned to stars that floated around his head. He felt dizzy and light-headed, but he remained conscious. He looked around; the culprit had gone. He sat on the ground for a time with his head between his knees. He felt able to move after what felt like hours, but his watch showed only a few minutes. He put his hand on his head and checked himself to see if he was bleeding. He seemed to be okay, except for still feeling dizzy. He walked around again and checked the street in front of and behind him. Nothing. No one in sight. The assailant had vanished. Marco, a former trained police officer, didn't see it coming. Someone wanted to send him a message.

Chapter Thirteen

Marco called Flores to let him know what happened. He still felt woozy. Flores advised him to go to the hospital. Marco assured him that he didn't need a doctor. The assailant hadn't struck him that hard. Neither of them had any clue who could have tried to harm him or why. There was nothing they could do but be on the lookout. Marco decided not to say anything to Belen as he didn't want to worry her. He made himself something to eat, took a couple of aspirina, and went straight to bed. He didn't even hear Belen when she got home later.

Marco slept hard. When he woke up he had a dull headache. So, he took a couple more aspirina. He looked over at the bed to see Belen still sleeping. He tiptoed around, trying not to make noise to wake her as he showered and dressed.

He didn't stop for his usual coffee at Alvarez's but went straight to work and on to his computer.

As he was deep into his search, Flores pinged him. "How's your head?"

Marco rubbed his temples. "It's not too bad. I'm lucky it wasn't worse."

"You're lucky you weren't killed. Let me know if you need protection. We're stretched to the limit, but I'll see what I can do to have someone sent around if you need it."

"Thanks, but I'm ok. I can handle it," Marco said.

Marco sensed the hesitation in his voice. "Okay. Listen, I need to talk to you about something else. My officers have been watching the museum since the murder. Last night, one of them saw something strange," Flores said.

"Really? What was it?" Marco asked, saving his Google search."

"Officer Adelo saw Amy Bloom leaving the museum in the middle of the night, carrying a large, heavy bag. It attracted his attention because she looked surreptitious, like she was trying to hide it. My officer thought they saw something bulging out of the sides of the bag. Amy looked around and surveyed the area before putting the satchel in her trunk. Officer Adelo had no reason to stop her. He had to let Bloom go. I want to find out what she had in the bag. I need you to watch her and see what you can find out."

"Sure, do you want me to tail her at home or the museum?" Marco asked.

"We're still watching the museum. I need you to watch her house," Flores said.

"I'll get right on it," Marco said.

"Take care of your head," Flores said.

Marco saved all the searches he'd done on an Excel sheet. He'd have to finish later. He thought about waiting until morning to start the surveillance, but by then she might have destroyed whatever she'd been hiding. He called Belen to tell her he'd be home late. She wasn't upset as she said she'd received a call to replace one of the dancers at a performance. She expected to be very late as well. Marco was glad of that. At times, she didn't seem to understand that the nature of his work meant he could be called out at any time.

As he wasn't prepared for a stakeout, he had no food for dinner. He walked over to Alvarez's to order a bocadillo and coffee, something he could eat easily while sitting in the car.

The café was empty as it was late in the afternoon. Alvarez sat on one of the stools at the end of the bar, watching an Oviedo futbol match on the large screen television. It felt strange to see him without the ubiquitous cleaning cloth slung over his shoulder.

"Kind of late for lunch for you, isn't it?" Alvarez asked.

"Yeah, I've got to do something this evening. I don't have time to go home and get dinner."

"Oh, is it one of your exciting sleuthing adventures?" Alvarez asked, smiling.

Marco laughed. Alvarez loved to hear about his work as a private investigator. He told Marco once that he'd always wanted to do something exciting, but fate had intervened. He'd taken over his father's café when he got married and had a family.

"I'll have to live vicariously through you," Alvarez had joked.

Marco waited while Alvarez prepared his bocadillo and coffee. He thought how it would be nice to sit in front of the TV and watch a futbol match with a couple of beers. He hadn't seen his friend Oscar in some time. They needed to catch up with their favorite sport. He made a mental note to give him a call.

Alvarez returned with two bocadillos and a large thermos of coffee. "I thought you might need a little extra fuel," he said.

Marco thanked him and left. Alvarez had become a good friend, and Marco felt grateful for him. Armed with dinner, he got in his car and pulled up Amy's address on his locator and headed to her apartment. She lived less than ten minutes away in Estepona in a large white building near the beach. Marco had to search to find a parking spot where he could see her apartment, but where he couldn't be seen. He found a place a few yards away. He pulled out his camera. He could see Amy's comings and goings in her second-floor apartment.

Tedious work, surveillance duty, but it gave Marco time to catch up on his reading. He pulled out a copy of *Vivirrambla Today* he'd found at home. He turned the pages to the large write-up about Addison's Museum. The informative article was an education on Islamic art. Attending school in Spain, he'd learned more about Goya, Velazquez, and Picasso, whose home he'd visited in Malaga, than he did about Islamic art heritage. The most visible part of his heritage were the famous Cathedrals and churches, such as La Mezquita in Cordoba, and those in Sevilla, and elsewhere in Spain where a Catholic church had been erected atop an ancient Mosque. The lace tiling and other elements, characteristic of Arabesque art, were still evident in these churches. Marco felt emotionally torn. He loved his Spanish heritage passed down from his father, but he also loved his mother's Islamic heritage and the lineage of his grandmother and cousins and family in Tangier. He wished he knew more of that history.

Once he finished the article, Marco took out Alvarez's bocadillo of *jamon y queso* and began to eat. Nothing seemed to be happening in Amy's apartment. He poured himself a cup of coffee and watched people saunter along the paseo and go in and out of her building. Just as he finished his sandwich, he observed a dark blue Mercedes pull into the parking lot. Museum board member Nicholas Thompson emerged from the car. Marco sat up straight and pulled out his long lens camera. Thompson, dressed in a pink short-sleeved Oxford shirt and navy pants, strolled into Amy's building. Marco had a view of them once Thompson entered the apartment. Amy handed him a duffel bag, which seemed to be the same as the one Flores described. Thompson moved closer to Amy and looked inside the bag. He nodded his head in approval, without removing the contents. The two of them disappeared from sight as they shifted away from the window. Marco could no longer see any activity. He decided to call it a day and let Flores know what he'd witnessed.

"Something seemed to be bulging on the sides of the bag they exchanged, like more than one object was inside," Marco said.

"Looks like they may be transporting something. It may be perfectly legit for all we know, but it's curious; their movements seem odd. Why is she taking something from the museum? Nothing we can do without a warrant, though. We don't have enough right now to ask the prosecutor for one. Let's keep our eyes on them," Flores said.

Chapter Fourteen

arco headed to the beach as the sun, the color of the Spanish flag, slowly rose over the horizon. Due to the early hour, only one or two stragglers milled about the deserted playa. Marco dropped his towel on the sand; his skin shone a yellow hue in the early light. He let himself be submerged in the emerald-colored water. It felt warm. He moved back and forth, completing laps like a fish. Once he finished, he emerged, like Poseidon, water dripping off him. Reaching for his towel, he jumped back, startled. Farah Zine stood staring at him, smiling.

She lifted her eyebrows. "No wonder you're in such good shape," she said.

Marco began to towel off. "What are you doing here? How did you know where to find me?"

"I hate to admit, I followed you. I didn't want that cute little girlfriend of yours to see me. I don't think she liked me too much," Farah said.

Marco smiled wryly. He finished drying himself and shook his hair. "I see. What's so urgent that you couldn't wait until I got to the office?"

Farah wore a white sundress and dark shades. Her hair glistened in the sun like a Pantene commercial model. She'd taken off her heeled sandals, which she carried to walk on the sand. "I think someone's trying to kill me."

Marco stopped drying himself. "Trying to kill you? What makes you think that?"

"Someone's been following me for the last week or so. I can sense them everywhere. I told my husband, but he said I'm just paranoid because of what happened to Addison. I'm sure, though. I see the shadows, silhouettes of a person near me. When I'm walking, I can feel them behind me. When I turn, they're gone."

Marco slipped on his beach shoes and walked towards the paseo. Farah followed. He remembered that same feeling when someone tried to attack him, though he didn't tell Farah.

"Why would someone be following you?"

She adjusted her large Jackie O frames. "I have no idea, that's why I came to you. I heard you're a great private investigator."

A glamorous woman like Farah attracted a lot of fans and gawkers. Whatever she wore looked expensive on her, and she walked with the posture of a runway model, exuding poise and confidence.

"Maybe it's just a fan or an admirer. You've been in a lot of magazines and on television. If you have visibility, you can become a target. You do need to be careful, though; an admirer could become obsessive. They can even develop an imaginary relationship in their mind," Marco said.

"Yeah, I know. I've had the stalker situation before. I'm careful about that. My husband keeps an eye on things too, which helps. This feels different somehow, more sinister, more determined."

"Do you think they followed you here?" Marco asked.

She looked around the beach. "I don't think so. I slipped out of the house from a different entrance and took one of our other cars."

Farah lived in a large house on the Golden Mile, where many of the wealthiest lived, in the hills of Vivirrambla. According to what Marco had read in magazines, she and her husband met at one of the fabulous White Parties held once a year at the Don Carlos hotel in Elviria. In an interview for one of the gossip rags, Bernard, a wealthy executive, said he'd been smitten right away. The two were pictured being snuggly and cozy. They hadn't had any children, as her new husband already had adult children from a previous marriage and didn't want any more. Farah didn't want children either, the column said.

"You have no idea who it could be or what they want?" Marco asked.

"No. I don't know. I'm getting a bit scared, though. I've been avoiding going out and not taking appointments or interviews."

"I can ask Detective Flores to send someone to keep an eye on you. I'm working on Addison's case. It would be hard for me to give you the attention you need on my own. Detective Flores can get an officer to protect you," Marco said.

"I know you're busy. I'd appreciate it if you get me someone. I was hoping you'd have time to see what you can find out, also," Farah said.

They'd reached the boardwalk. Marco turned towards his house. "I'll see what I can do."

"Okay. I'd really appreciate your help," she said.

"Glad to help, Farah. I won't let anything happen to you," Marco said.

Farah smiled a crooked smile. "I'll try not to worry," she said putting her shoes back on. "I'd better get back before my husband wonders where I've gone."

Chapter Fifteen

Before jumping in the shower, Marco phoned Flores to tell him what Farah Zine had said. Flores agreed to send an officer over to her home.

"Good excuse to keep an eye out for her in case she becomes a suspect. I can justify the manpower then. Also, if anything happened to her, the Chief'd have me demoted; she's a local celebrity. I'll get on it right away. In the meantime, see what else you can find out about Amy and her mysterious bag," Flores said.

"Just about to head that way," Marco said.

Marco got dressed and ready to continue his surveillance gig. Amy's car hadn't moved from the parking lot when Marco arrived at her building. The museum remained closed. So, he knew she wouldn't be going to work. Marco pushed his seat back and opened his iPad to scroll through the latest news as he watched her apartment for activity. After several hours, nothing happened. Amy hadn't left, and no one had come to see her. Marco stayed for a couple more hours, reading a book about the Medici in Florence. Then decided to go back to his office.

When he returned, he found Eva cleaning her desk. "Hola jefe, I thought you were gone for the day," she said.

"Yeah, not much going on with my surveillance target. So, I came back to work. Did I miss anything?"

Eva continued to rub the desktop with the bleached cloth. When she finished wiping, she tossed it in the trash. Her area smelled of cleaning solution. "Not really, some lady named Farah Vine or something like that, called. She said she's from the museum."

"Ah, yes, Farah Zine, she's one of the members of the board of the museum. Did she say what she wanted?" Marco asked.

Eva shook her head. "She said she'd rather talk to you directly. She left her cell."

"Okay, I'll call her back. Anything else?"

"Nope, pretty quiet otherwise," Eva said, eyeing him.

Marco switched on his office light and powered up his computer. By now, Flores should have gotten one of his officers to guard Farah. He felt assured she was safe. He dialed the number Eva had given him.

"I just wanted to let you know your detective called. He said an officer would be sent over this afternoon. I think the creep's still watching my house. I sensed his presence when I got home from meeting you," Farah said.

"Call me if you need anything else," Marco said.

When the call finished, he opened the Excel sheet he started, which contained information on museum personnel and board members. He added a note to Farah Zine's section about the stalker.

Then he turned back to internet searching. As he scrolled through stories, he ran across an article in an online magazine called "Arts and Antiques." The magazine had a feature story about an antique store in London. It had pictures of Amy Bloom and Oliver Hall. Looks like they knew each other before they arrived in Spain. The article, an extensive spread from two years ago, centered on an upscale antique shop called **Jules Moore Antiques, LTD**. Pictures of the inside of the shop revealed a store filled with expensive antique furniture, paintings, silver, and jewelry. A decorative curio cabinet, described as Louis XIV, displayed silver flatware, cream and sugar bowls, tea pots, and other shiny objects. The reporter spoke to an older man with slicked-back white hair and bushy white eyebrows that stood out on the sides, and a sagging chin. He sat perched in a French Louis XVI chair behind a white marble table. He wore a blue velvet jacket and grinned through large false teeth. The proprietor described the silver pieces in the pictures. Some, he said, were from the famous Gorham silver maker. The oldest pieces were seventeenth-century English silver.

A smiling Oliver Hall stood beside the chair, wearing khakis and a bow tie. Paintings of instant ancestors, as well as prints from Asia, hung behind him. The article noted that Hall was an antiques expert. Oliver told the interviewer that he assisted Jules in finding items for the store and helped to ensure the authenticity of paintings and silver. Amy Bloom stood next to a red cabinet with a glass top that contained highly polished silver spoons and flatware. She was identified as Moore's assistant in charge of sales and the day-to-day running of the shop. Jules said he didn't know anyone who knew more about silver than Amy. Amy responded, saying her boss, Jules Moore, was the real genius when it came to antiques. He taught her all she knew about silver.

Marco had no idea that silver could be so expensive and have such an interesting history. He knew, of course, that sterling silver was of better quality than silver plate, but according to the article, there was much more to it than that. Marco kept reading. He learned that old silver had hallmarks that identified the year it was made and its place of origin. Old English and American silver hollowware, assayed in Britain or in the New World, could be rare and valuable. *Very interesting,* he thought. *Why would Amy leave such a good job in the UK?*

Chapter Sixteen

"The Arabs...brought many musical instruments into Europe, including the lute...and the oval guitar."
—Spain the Root and the Flower, John A. Crow

Erudite poets and writers over the centuries have tried to tackle the complexities of love. Yet, beautiful sonnets and poems have failed to explain how feelings of happiness, eroticism, and hopefulness can so quickly turn to confusion, hurt, and pain.

"You're home early? I thought you were going to be late," Belen said, when Marco walked in the door.

He kissed her as he entered the room. "I wrapped up early. I wanted to see you," he said.

"I'm so glad you're home, honey," she said, smiling.

They decided to have an early dinner before Belen went to work. They had some leftover pasta in the refrigerator. With it, Belen whipped up a meal of pasta and fresh gambas. Marco thought it was genius that she could make a quick and delicious meal out of leftovers. Everything she did amazed him. He opened a bottle of Faustino V, Rioja, and poured them each a glass.

They took their plates out onto the patio. The sun still sat high in the sky, as it didn't get dark until ten in the evening. Yet, it felt cool, as they sat looking over the balcony surrounded by sweet-smelling honeysuckles. Lively waves danced a pirouette in the sea a few feet from them. They ate pasta con gambas and a spinach salad. Marco took a sip of wine and sat back in his chair.

"That was delicious, sweetie," Marco said.

Belen smiled. "Thank you. I'm glad you liked it. I wanted to talk to you anyway, babe."

Marco sighed. Whenever she said that, something was usually afoot. He braced himself for what she had to say. "Okay," he said.

"Remember that audition I had a couple of months ago to dance at the anniversary celebration for seven hundred years of flamenco?" Belen asked.

Marco hesitated and knitted his brow. "Yes, I remember."

Belen spoke rapidly. "Well…I got it. I'm going on a month-long tour through Spain to celebrate this anniversary of Spanish Flamenco. Can you believe it? It started off as a local program. That's when I first auditioned. I thought we'd have a one-night show here or in Malaga, but it's since grown into a larger tribute, a full-blown tour. I'm still stunned they chose me as one of the principal dancers. This is great for my career."

Marco frowned. "A month-long tour? You're going to be going all around Spain for a month?"

She took a sip of wine. "Yep. We start rehearsals tonight. We're leaving in a couple of weeks for Madrid as the first leg," Belen said.

"You'll be gone all that time? Does the show stop here?" Marco asked.

"Vivirrambla is the last stop before the tour ends. I know it'll be hard for us to be apart for so long, but aren't you happy for me? It's a great opportunity. My parents were thrilled when I told them we'd be coming to Madrid."

"So, your parents already know about it?" Marco asked.

Belen picked up the plates they'd been using and sashayed into the house to put them in the dishwasher. She returned a few minutes later, carrying a creamy flan and refilled each of their glasses with more Rioja. "Yeah, I had to call them to see how many tickets they wanted for the performance. I knew you'd understand. I wanted to tell you when we were alone. They picked us only a few days ago. You can join me on the tour at some point if you want to."

Belen took a bite of dessert. "It's a huge honor to be chosen for something this important. There'll be a lot of publicity surrounding the tour. The director's already been interviewed by a national magazine."

Marco took another sip of his wine. "I'd love to join you, but I don't know if I can with this murder investigation going on, honey."

"I figured you'd say that. You know I can't just sit around here and let my career go. When something this big comes up. I have to take it," Belen said.

In truth, Marco understood, but he still felt disappointed. The house always seemed empty when she left. He knew that at times she felt frustrated and unsure of his commitment. He had no right to hold her back if he wasn't willing to take a more permanent step. He loved her. He didn't want anyone else. Yet, he didn't feel ready to get married.

Marco walked over and put his arms around her and kissed her on the cheek. "Of course I'm happy for you, honey. It just that I'm going to miss you."

"I know. I'll miss you too. I'll give you my itinerary. See if you can join me at some point, even for the weekend," Belen said.

"Okay," Marco said, putting a spoonful of flan in his mouth.

Once they'd finished, Belen cleared the rest of the dishes and recorked the wine bottle. "I've told you before, if you can't make a commitment to me, then I feel that I'm free to do whatever I wish."

Marco could feel the marriage conversation rising like a storm cloud gathering strength in the ocean. It always seemed to come down to this: Belen wanted to get married. Her cultural upbringing and conservative parents demanded it. It'd always been the biggest tension in their relationship.

"I'm committed to you," Marco said.

"You say that, but it's only talk." Belen looked at her cell phone resting on the table beside her. "Oh, look at the time. I've got to get going to rehearsal. We'll have to talk about this later."

Marco watched her as she walked to the bedroom to get ready. He rose from the table, went into the living room, and sat down on the couch. Belen's news had thrown him. He picked up the remote and channel surfed. No futbol matches were listed. So, he turned to a movie, Director Pedro Almodóvar's classic "*Volver*," about relationships and the complexities of women popped up. How apropos, he thought. He got off the couch to get a beer.

Chapter Seventeen

arco spent the whole day drinking coffee and doing research on those associated with the museum. He turned his attention to board member, Oliver Hall. So far, he'd learned that Hall graduated from University with a degree in art and antiquities. He'd gone to school with Addison Mason. Halls' peers, including Addison, touted Oliver as being brilliant. He'd received numerous awards for merit in school. He'd even been an assistant to one of the school's most well-respected history professors. Articles from his university said he'd graduated with the highest honors. After graduation, Hall pursued a career in antiques and appraisals. He'd become certified, a recognized expert for museums, antique dealers, and auction houses. Hall provided advice, counseling, and appraisal services to clients like Jules Moore.

Marco couldn't see any reason for Hall to want to kill Addison Mason. All the evidence indicated they'd been good friends for years. Hall had a good career, which complemented Addison's, and which benefited the museum. Hall had no motive. Marco struck him off the list of potential suspects along with several others who had no motive or reason to kill Addison.

Marco made no progress with any of the other names he researched. As evening approached, he decided to close up and go home. He walked via the Casco Antigua, Old Town. The sun still felt warm on his skin, but not oppressive, as it could be with average temperatures over thirty-five degrees Celsius in the summer. He walked past souvenir shops with the doors open, advertising colorful flamenco dresses, decorative fans, and Spanish tile, amongst their wares. Marco greeted proprietors, who stood in front of their shops, hoping for one last sale.

Belen spoke to him as he entered the door. They hadn't resolved their differences from the evening before, but they both decided just to drop it and enjoy the time they had together before she went off on her month-long tour.

"How was your day?" Belen asked. "Do you want to go out to eat before I have to go to work?"

Marco walked over to the living room couch where she sat reading a magazine. He bent over and kissed her. "I'm still doing some surveillance on one of the museum employees."

"Then you're probably up for a nice dinner," Belen said.

"I am. Just let me get changed," Marco said.

Belen wore workout pants and a bright orange top. "I need to get changed too," she said.

"I'm in the mood for something casual, a good home-cooked meal," Marco said.

They chose *Restaurante Cafeteria, El Chef y la Pastelera,* a cafeteria-style eatery in the center of town. It served the locals and tourists who stumbled upon it, home-cooked meals and a variety of fresh desserts.

They walked into a crowded restaurant. As they waited for a table to clear, Marco spotted Amy Bloom and Nicholas Thompson having dessert.

Belen followed Marco over to their table to say hello.

The two looked up, startled.

"Marco, good to see you," Thompson said, standing up.

"Please sit down. Don't let us disturb you," Marco said.

Amy nodded and shifted back and forth in her chair. "Yes, good to see you both again. Belen, with everything that happened, I never had the chance to tell you how wonderful your flamenco was at the museum. I admire flamenco dancers."

"Thank you," said Belen.

"Nicholas and I needed to meet about some museum business. We thought we'd grab a quick dinner in the cafeteria," Amy said.

"Yeah, you can't beat it. Cheap and the food is good. I'd ask you guys to join us, but we're about to leave," Thompson said.

"Oh, of course. Amy, I need to get those emails from you that we spoke about," Marco said.

"Amy turned up her lip. "Which emails?"

"The emails discussed at the meeting with the board," Marco said.

"Oh, yes, I'll forward them to you tomorrow," Amy said.

"Great, well, don't let us keep you. Enjoy your dessert. They have the best flan in town," Marco said.

Belen and Marco found a table and ordered dinner. They both ordered pollo con patatas fritas. Belen gave most of her fries to Marco. "I've got to watch my figure," she said.

Marco flashed his eyebrows up and down. "I'll watch it for you," he said, grinning.

Belen laughed. "By the way, that couple we just saw from the museum, I remember Amy from the opening. She was Addison Mason's assistant, wasn't she? Was that her husband with her?"

Marco had to measure his words. He couldn't discuss his surveillance work. "I believe Thompson's married. I think they're working together at the museum to keep it running until Addison is replaced."

"Oh, they seemed very close." She finished chewing her chicken. "They're going to go ahead and reopen the museum then?" Belen asked.

"That's the plan, from what I've heard. I don't think we'll know for sure until the investigation into Addison's death is complete," Marco said.

Belen scrunched her face. "Are you sure those two aren't dating?"

"Why do you ask?" Marco said.

Belen shrugged her shoulders. "I just sensed something between them, women's intuition."

Belen had a knack for body language. She'd developed it dancing flamenco, which used the whole body to tell a story. Marco learned to listen to her intuition. Her instincts had helped him to solve cases in the past.

Chapter Eighteen

arco peered out of his office door to tell Eva that he didn't want to be disturbed. Flores had called and given him an earful. Flores said the Chief of Police had threatened him, that if they hadn't arrested a suspect for Addison's murder soon, he'd hand the case over to another homicide unit. For Flores, that may have meant a demotion. For Marco, though, it meant the end of his consulting contract, and it lessened the possibility of him getting future work. It didn't matter that he'd helped them solve complex cases in the past. *You're only as good as your last arrest*, a motto he'd heard the Chief say when Marco was on the force. Marco knew they needed to make measurable progress quickly.

"Eva, I need more liquid gold today. I'm going to get another cup of coffee before I knuckle down," he said.

"I'll bring you some," Eva said.

Marco thanked her and went back to his desk. He opened the emails Amy had finally forwarded to him. The emails written over a span of six months contained several admonitions and warnings to Addison Mason that if his museum featured Islamic art, he'd ruin Vivirrambla as a European city. Marco spotted no direct threats of harm to Addison or anyone on the Board though.

Sven Bjorgen had been emailing Addison several days before the murder. Though the emails seemed cordial, Sven talked about his preference for European art in many of them. It seemed apparent from his terse responses that Addison didn't want to keep up the correspondence. Marco had met that type before. The type that couldn't read the room. That couldn't tell when someone wanted to end a conversation with them. That type of person was annoying, but usually harmless. Still, Marco decided to mentally file the information.

He decided next to dig more into Farah Zine. Maybe if he could figure out who'd been following her, it could lead to pinpointing a suspect. He found more information on her in an article in one of those high-end fashion magazines, *Vivirrambla Ella*. Farah had been born in Tangier to a middle-class family. She'd been discovered by a Spanish photographer on vacation and brought to Spain as a young woman of twenty. She'd had a successful modeling career prior to her marriage to Bernard. She continued to model. She was in demand as a spokeswoman for various businesses, including the new museum.

Marco found news clips about the museum opening, depicting a smiling Farah, her straight white teeth gracing the cover, with her arm around Addison. For his part, Addison gushed beside her like a small child with a crush on his first-grade teacher. Addison told the reporter that he'd struck gold when Señora Zine accepted his invitation to join the Board of his new museum.

Addison was quoted as saying. "She's not only beautiful, but being Moroccan, she's the perfect spokesperson for her own cultural heritage. I'm hopeful she'll draw in visitors from all over Europe, Africa, and Arabia."

"I'm the one that's lucky," Farah said. "My husband, Bernard, and I are honored to be a part of this tribute to underrepresented Islamic art."

Marco took out his cell and placed a video call to his cousin, Karim, who lived in Tangier and worked part-time for the Tangier police. He often collaborated with Karim on cases. The two had been close since they were young when Marco went to Tangier to visit his grandmother, Jaddah, during the summers. As a young boy, he spent many days playing futbol in the dirt with Karim in front of Jaddah's home, pretending they were Pele or other famous players. They'd remained close over the years, though Marco lived in Spain. Marco saw Karim as a brother.

Karim, shaking his wet, dark, shaggy hair, appeared on Marco's phone screen. "Hola, Karim, como estas?" Marco said.

"Assalamu alaykum," Karim said.

"Wa alaykumu salaam, how is Jaddah?" Marco asked.

"I just got out of the shower. Jaddah just asked about you yesterday. I told her I hadn't heard from you in a while," Karim said.

Marco didn't see his grandmother much these days, which made him feel guilty. Karim said that his own family and all Marco's cousins were doing well. Marco wouldn't recognize some of the children, Karim told him.

"Everyone been asking me when you're coming to Tangier. When are you getting married to that cute girlfriend? We could use a big wedding," Karim said.

Marco could feel himself blushing. "I'll let you know."

A few years ago, Marco had had a rift with his Moroccan cousins, who'd accused him of caring only about his Spanish relatives and looking down on them. They'd reconciled after his grandmother had had a heart attack. Shock brought them back together. It made them all close again. Marco remembered feeling lost and bereft during those days when he visited her in the hospital. When Jaddah recovered, Marco promised himself that he'd never desert his family again.

"Karim, I need you to see what you can find out about a Moroccan model who lives in Vivirrambla."

"A model, huh? Does Belen know about this?" Karim asked, snickering.

Marco chuckled. "It's business, hombre." He explained the case he'd been working on about Farah Zine, a member of the museum's board of directors, and her fear that someone's following her. Karim said he'd look into it and see if he could find any information.

"Should I tell everyone that you'll be coming to see us soon?" Karim asked.

"Yes. Please tell Jaddah I'll see her soon," Marco said.

Marco disconnected the call and checked his calendar to see when he could make a visit to Tangier. Then he went back to work.

Several hours later, he realized he hadn't moved for some time. His back felt stiff. He stretched his spine and looked at the time. "Wow, it's getting late," he said. He shut down the computer. On his way home, as he walked through the Casco Antigua, the pungent smell of floral and orange prompted him to stop at one of the flower shops in the alley. He purchased a dozen claveles rojos, red carnations. Belen often wore them in her hair when she danced.

He found Belen in the kitchen when he arrived home, wearing a light blue top and white caprice pants. Her hair was pinned up, and her face—bare. She always looked beautiful, but he thought she looked radiant with the sunlight from the kitchen window streaming across her face.

He handed her the flowers. Their fragrance permeated the room, overtaking the smell of cooking.

She took the bouquet from him and sniffed it. "What's this for?"

"Can't I just bring my beautiful girlfriend flowers?" Marco asked.

Belen lifted her eyebrow. She put down the spoon she'd been using to stir dinner. "Hmmmm, I guess so," she said, kissing him. She pulled out a vase from the cabinet and arranged the flowers in it. That night, they felt the closest they had in a while.

Chapter Nineteen

The bright sun had risen high as it did in the days of summer. Its rays beamed down on the white stucco homes, making them gleam like a set of false pearly white teeth. When Marco stopped at the restaurant, Alvarez seemed subdued, not as chatty as usual. He stood opposite Marco at the bar, wiping the glass counter in front of him. Then he shifted over to the coffee machine.

"Anything wrong, amigo? You aren't your usual chippy self," Marco asked.

Alvarez shook his head. "No, not really. I'm just a bit worried. My daughter's baby is a few days late, and we're all concerned."

Marco took a sip of the café con leche Alvarez had made for him. "I see, there's something my Jaddah grandmother used to always say: 'Have faith. Don't worry until it's time to worry.' I'm sure it'll be okay. How's your daughter feeling?"

"She's got gestational diabetes, something that happens to pregnant women. They put her on bed rest, but my wife says she's bored and miserable. It breaks my heart, but my wife says the diabetes will go away as soon as she has the baby. She's usually right about these things," Alvarez said.

"I'm sure your wife is right this time too. I know you all are taking good care of her," Marco said.

Alvarez took a rag and wiped the area in front of Marco in a circular motion. He furrowed his brow. "It took her long enough to get married. She dated her husband for ten years. He kept saying he wasn't ready to commit. Finally, she told him she couldn't wait much longer. I felt so proud of her standing up for herself."

Marco felt his heart skip a beat. He wiggled in his seat.

"We'd all but given up hope of having a grandchild. This baby's a big blessing to us." Alvarez said, making the sign of the cross on his chest. "We can't lose this baby."

"Don't worry. You'll soon have a beautiful, healthy grandbaby," Marco said.

"When are you going to settle down with that pretty girlfriend?" Alvarez asked.

Marco shrugged his shoulders. "I don't know. I'm not ready yet."

"Well, I'd think about it if I were you before she finds someone else. I understand where you're coming from as a man, but women don't like to wait forever. My daughter may be sick, but I've never seen her happier than right now, knowing she's about to be a mother. Take a break from sleuthing and marry her," Alvarez said.

Alvarez sounded exactly like his mother. "Belen's been saying the same thing. She would love that you said that."

Marco finished his café con leche and hopped off the stool. He walked back to his office, still thinking about Alvarez's daughter's pregnancy and what Alvarez had said. He'd grown very fond of Alvarez, and he hoped it worked out well. He knew he needed to conquer his own leeriness of commitment. He and Belen had been living together for over five years. She should know he's faithful. On the other hand, Alvarez was right, women need to be shown that you love them. He couldn't risk losing Belen to someone else. He'd talk to her again after her dancing tour. He reached the door, still deep in thought, when he ran into none other than Farah Zine, who seemed to have developed a habit of appearing like Casper the friendly ghost.

"Señora Zine, Bienvenido, what are you doing here?"

"Excuse me for just barging in on you like this without an appointment, but I needed to talk to you."

"Of course, please come in."

Marco opened the door and allowed Farah to pass in front of him. Eva looked up from her computer, frowning. *"Jefe, buenas dias."* She addressed Farah Zine. "Señora, did you have an appointment today? I don't see anything on the calendar for this morning."

"Buenas dia, Eva. Don't worry, she didn't have an appointment. I ran into Señora Zine outside."

Eva narrowed her eyes. "Oh. Okay, jefe, I'll make you all some coffee."

"Thanks, Eva."

Marco turned to Farah, "Follow me," he said, leading her into his office.

Farah stood as tall as Marco. She wore black heels, which made her appear even taller. Her dangling silver earrings swung as she walked. She was thin, yet curvy and not boyish. Her white cotton dress, which exposed her décolletage, also accented her hips.

Marco gestured to a chair opposite his desk. "Please sit, Señora Zine."

"Please, Farah, call me Farah," she said.

Marco smiled. "Okay. Farah, what can I do for you?"

Eva came in carrying coffee. She put it down on a side table along with various creams, Almond milk, Oat milk, and sugar. She glanced side-eyed at Marco before walking out the door. Marco ignored Eva's stares and turned his attention to Farah.

"Help yourself," Marco said, pointing to the coffee.

Farah poured a cup from the pot and cream from the carton and stirred it. Her hands were dainty, her fingers long. Her nails were long, yet well-groomed and painted pale pink.

She sat down, crossed her long legs, and took a sip of coffee. "I'm sorry again for coming unannounced, but I couldn't sleep last night. I need to talk to you about one of the board members."

"Why, what happened?" Marco asked.

Everyone on the Board isn't as friendly as they first appeared."

"I thought the board members got along well, according to Señor Thompson."

Farah took another sip of coffee. "We had a meeting last night, and it got very heated."

"Really, What about?"

"I've never trusted Nicholas Thompson. I ask a lot of questions, which Nicholas doesn't like. He got very angry with me last night. He started shaking his fist at my face. Luis Castillo had to calm him down."

"Oh wow. What got him so upset? "Marco asked.

Farah drank the last of her coffee. "Questions about certain political views I consider extreme, and the motivations of some of the board members."

"What kind of questions?" Marco asked.

Farah put her cup down. "I think Nicholas's a member of Vox. I wanted to know if the museum's Board had been giving money to an ultra-right-wing organization. When I brought it up, Nicholas turned bright red and became defensive. I said belonging to a right-wing group, such as Vox, was incompatible with supporting an ethno-centric museum. I said we could be violating several laws. Attorney Luis Castillo agreed with me. He said it was an excellent point. Nicholas Thompson's face turned deep red. That's when he started shaking his fist and telling me I was out of order."

Marco leaned back in his chair. He was familiar with Vox, the extreme right-wing party of Spain. It was a part of a worldwide movement to end democracies in favor of authoritarian government. Vox was a neo-Franco movement that wanted to return Spain to the days of Franco-like control.

"That's a serious accusation. What made you think Thompson's involved in Vox?"

Farah looked at Marco. "I can't talk too much about it, but my husband's politically very well-connected. He's the one who told me about Nicholas Thompson's possible association with the group. There are people on the inside who keep track of membership."

"I see, internal spies. Do you think Nicholas could be diverting museum money to Vox?"

Farah shook her head, yes. "Our donations could be funding Vox if one of our Board members is a part of it."

"Señor Thomas is an Englishman, isn't he? Why would he be a part of a right-wing Spanish movement?" Marco asked.

"It's a worldwide movement. I believe he is involved in the British right wing, which is aligned with Vox," she said.

"Did Addison know about all this?" Marco asked.

Farah uncrossed her legs and shook her head. "No. I don't think so. My husband told me about this after Addison died. I doubt he had any idea."

"Why would Vox want to associate with a museum that specializes in Islamic art?" Marco asked.

"This sect of Vox believes in fundamentalism. Fundamentalists want to return to the past. They support art that glorifies the rule of the Caliphate, only they want people like you and me to be deported back to Morocco. They need money from wealthy sympathizers for their cause. Nicholas could be a big catch for them, especially with his legal skills."

"Do you think this could have had anything to do with Addison's murder?" Marco asked.

Farah leaned forward. Marco got a whiff of Chanel No 5, which he recognized as Belen wore it on special occasions.

"I honestly doubt it. Like I said, Addison didn't know anything about it. Nicholas Thompson was a good friend of his. Addison had no reason to suspect him of anything."

"Do you feel like you're in any danger?" Marco asked.

Farah hunched her shoulders. "I don't know. It's possible that's who's been following me. Nicholas could have sent someone to scare me into resigning from the board. If Thompson puts himself in a position to take over, the museum could divert a great deal of funding to his cause."

"Thanks for telling me this, Farah. I'll check it out. In the meantime, we'll make sure Detective Flores still has someone protecting you at all times," Marco said.

"Thank you." Farah stood and headed towards the door but turned back. "Whew. It's a relief to talk to you. I really care about the museum. I refuse to be bullied into resigning."

"Good for you," Marco said.

Farah said. "For some reason, I feel better when I talk to you."

Marco smiled. "Let me know if you need anything."

As soon as Farah left, Marco picked up his cell to update Flores on his unexpected interview.

"Hmmm. That's the second shady thing we've heard about this Nicholas Thompson guy. I'll see what we can find out about his association with

Vox. I'll ask upstairs. I know Señora Zine told you she doesn't think it had anything to do with Addison's death, but we need to look into all possible connections."

"I agree completely," Marco said.

"I was going to call you anyway. We saw Amy Bloom leaving the museum again at midnight, carrying that same bag. My officer said it seemed full and awkward to maneuver. Amy had difficulty getting it into her car. Can you check on that? I'm going to speak to Nicholas Thompson. He may be the key to a lot of locked doors," Flores said.

Chapter Twenty

Looking in retrospect can help us to see more clearly, like a mirror to the conscience. Since his visit to Alvarez, Marco couldn't stop thinking of his conversation with Belen. He'd felt bitter about her leaving. On reflection, Marco concluded he'd been selfish to want to stop Belen from pursuing her highest calling as a flamenco artist. She'd done nothing but support his career when he left the police force. He decided to give her a surprise send-off.

***

The day of the party, Marco's mother came over early to help him set up for the luncheon. She decorated the apartment and put flowers on the tables along with the table settings. The fragrant bouquets scented the house. Marco's mother had always been good at entertaining and making things beautiful. He recalled that his family always enjoyed gathering in their home: the beauty of the decorations, the food made with love, and the warmth.

Marco had to admit it all looked nice. Belen, expected to be home at any moment, would be pleased. Her friends had done well in keeping the surprise. Marco placed bottles of wine on the dining room table and on the outside patio. He opened several bottles and offered the guests a glass. The atmosphere was festive. Several couples they hadn't seen in a while, as they'd had babies or become otherwise engaged, showed up to wish her good luck. Belen would be ecstatic to see them.

When they heard the key turn in the lock everyone stopped talking. Marco stood by the door waiting. Belen entered the house to shouts of 'Surprise!' Her eyes widened. She covered her mouth with her hand. "What's all this?" she asked.

"I wanted to send you off right," Marco said.

She hugged him. "Oh, Marco, this is wonderful."

Belen's friends rushed over to hug her and extend good luck wishes. She chatted and thanked them each for coming. Marco felt pleased she looked so happy and relaxed, surrounded by friends.

One of Belen's friends approached them, accompanied by a tall blond woman.

"Belen, I hope you don't mind that Ingrid tagged along. We had plans to spend the day together. Marco said you wouldn't mind."

"Of course, not."

"Ingrid," the woman said. "Mucho gusto."

"Bienvenido," Belen said, kissing her on the cheek.

Ingrid spoke with a Swedish accent. "Thank you so much. I remember you, actually. We met at the museum opening after you did that wonderful dance. I'm Sven Bjorgen's wife. He owns the modern art museum in Puerto Bella. It's a shame what happened to Addison."

"Oh yes, I remember you. You were searching for your husband for a while at the party. He'd wandered off somewhere. Did you ever find him?" Belen asked.

She laughed. "Yes, that's my husband. I eventually found him," Ingrid said.

"Marco and I visited your husband's museum," Belen said.

"I hope you enjoyed it. In truth, the museum's not doing too well. The only thing that sells are the Dala horses in the gift shop. We sell more of those than actual art," Ingrid said. "I don't know how much longer we can keep it open."

"Oh, yes, I saw the Dala horses, they're quite beautiful figurines," Belen said.

"Sven has them shipped from Sweden. We adore the decorative versions of the Swedish national symbol."

"Sven told us that. Please, enjoy the food and drink that Marco and his mom put together. I'm amazed at what they've done," Belen said.

It proved to be a wonderful afternoon. Marco's mother had prepared various tapas: croquetas, olives, patatas bravas, albondigas de corerdo, sliced lomo, chorizo, and tortilla Española. For dessert, there was a table of tartars and olive oil cake.

The celebration went on into the early evening. Guests replenished plates of tapas, shared stories, and rekindled old memories. Marco's mother made sure everyone was comfortable, pressing seconds and thirds on the stuffed guests. Belen began to cry when they asked her to say a few words. After the cake had been cut, they turned on the music and danced. Some of the guests lingered for several hours, drinking wine and vino tintos, and boogying to the beat.

At last, when everyone had gone, Marco and Belen helped his mother to finish cleaning up. With the kitchen gleamed, every dish stacked, counters wiped, the remnants of celebration cleared away, they went outside onto the patio. Marco's mother appeared at the door to say goodnight. Marco got up to walk her to her car.

"Belen loved it, you did a wonderful job," he said.

Once they reached her car, his mother kissed him on the cheek. "Of course, my love. It was wonderful of you to give her a party."

When Marco returned, he found Belen in the kitchen. He took her by the hand and pulled her out onto the patio. The air smelled of sea and honeysuckle. He wrapped his arms around her, and for a moment, they stood silent, listening to the distant sound of waves. He kissed her on the forehead. "You know I *am* proud of you," he whispered in her ear.

"I know," she said.

When night fell, they were too wound up to go to bed. They sat snuggled on the couch, Belen resting her head on Marco's shoulder, with a glass of wine. Her train was set to leave the following day in the afternoon. They only had the night left.

Belen turned to Marco. "I wish tonight could last a little longer," she whispered.

He brushed a strand of hair from her forehead. "Me too."

She looked up at him. "Honey, I know at first you were upset about my leaving. Thank you for putting your feelings aside and giving me such a nice send-off."

"I'm sorry I wasn't more supportive. I want you to have everything you want. I just didn't want you to leave," Marco said.

"I'll be back in no time. You and Oscar had better not be drinking beer and watching futbol in here every day," she said, chuckling.

Marco laughed. "We'll keep it to a minimum, I promise," he said, holding his two fingers up as a sign.

The next morning, the alarm went off sooner than expected. Belen rose to shower and gather her things. When she was ready, Marco drove her to the train station in Fuengirola. Marco walked her to her gate and kissed her goodbye. He watched her board the train and lingered as it chugged away.

When he returned home, the house already seemed empty, filled with silence. He ordered a pizza, grabbed a beer from the refrigerator, and plopped in front of the television.

He was glad the party had turned out well. *What a coincidence, Sven's wife showing up*, he thought. Then, his phone vibrated, jerking him back to reality.

Chapter Twenty-One

"To enter Cuerta, a Moroccan city occupied by the Spanish for five hundred years, the locals needed neither passport nor visa."
—*Leaving Tangier,* Tahar Ben Jelloun

A spectacular view of the Mediterranean isn't all one can see from Vivirrambla. On clear days, Tangier, North Africa, is visible as is Gibraltar, the great island rock founded in the eighth century, then known as the Mount of Tariq.

Flores filled his gas tank before hitting the highway en route to Gibraltar. He hadn't driven the seventy-three kilometers to the rock for some time. The promising bright sun had not yet reached its full capacity, and there was still a purplish hue over the sky, which made the sea appear a fluorescent emerald. Flores opened the window of his Citroën, and cruised down the coast on the A7 motorway, listening to Tom Jones on the radio. He hoped he'd left Malaga in time to avoid the long queues at the border. He had his badge, his police equipment, and other identification, should he need it, but he preferred not to have to cut in line.

He drove on singing to the music. His kids hated it when he listened to Tom Jones. He was happy to have the radio to himself. He cranked up the volume. Once Flores reached the end of the Spanish border, he felt relieved. He saw no one in front of him, except a couple of tourist buses. These buses passed through on a regular basis. So, the border patrol waved them through after a quick search. When it was Flores's turn, he flashed his Spanish police badge, and the border agent bid him good day.

Flores turned to the locator on his phone and punched in the address to an office building in the heart of town. The streets of Gibraltar buzzed with cars and yellow buses. Flores arrived at a red brick building with a white front and a sign that read **Gibraltar House**, the main building of the seat of government. He'd reached his intended location. He slowed the car as he neared the address and finally stopped in front of a white building designed in a geometric shape. The building, surrounded by large windows. had a cone-shaped figure in the middle of its six-storied frame. Flores turned into the underground parking garage and paid the attendant. He put the receipt in his wallet, reminding himself to hand it in for reimbursement.

He rode the garage elevator to the lobby of the building, then to the fourth floor and walked to the end of the hall to Suite 404. He pushed open the door to **Thompson Law LTD.** Flores showed his badge to the young woman seated at a desk in the lobby.

"Buenas dias. I'm here to speak to attorney Nicholas Thompson," he said.

The serious-looking woman, with shoulder-length hair, narrowed her eyes and surveyed the badge, then looked up at Flores. "Do you have an appointment, Detective?" she asked.

"Yes, I made an appointment to speak to Señor Thompson this morning at ten," Flores said.

The woman looked at her watch picked up the phone on her desk and pushed a button. "Just a moment, Sir. Please have a seat," she said, nodding her head in the direction of a group of chairs in the waiting room.

Flores sat on one of the chairs of cherry wood. *Thompson must be doing okay. These are some expensive-looking chairs*, he thought.

He'd been seated for only a moment when the young woman spoke. "Attorney Thompson will see you now."

"Thank you," Flores said, walking to the only office in Suite 404.

As he approached the door, Flores spotted Nicholas Thompson hurriedly tossing a folded velvet pouch into a trash can next to a shelf of books.

Thompson, his cheeks flushed, scurried over to greet his visitor. "Ah, Detective, good to see you again," he said, extending his hand to Flores and offering a limp handshake.

Flores shook his hand. "Good to see you too, *Señor Abogado*. Thank you for taking the time to talk to me. I'm sure you're quite busy."

"Not at all, Detective. Anything I can do to help find out who killed Addison. He was a good friend of mine."

"I understand, and I appreciate your cooperation, Señor. Has the board decided what's going to happen to the museum? Have you decided on a new director?" Flores asked.

Thompson wore a crisp navy suit and a white shirt. His hair fell to his face in the front. His angular chin had good structure. His large eyes sat under full eyebrows. He looked to be no more than forty-five.

"No, we haven't decided yet. It's still too raw. We want to take our time and get things right. We've all agreed, though, that we want to reopen the museum and keep Addison's legacy alive."

"That's good." Flores looked around the room. "I notice a lot of books on art and antiques next to the law books. How did you develop an interest in antiques?"

"Oh, antiques have been a passion of mine since I was young," Thompson said.

Thompson explained that he'd been interested in antiquities, old books, old art, silver, since he was a child. He attended Cambridge University, where he majored in art history. Addison had been his good friend and roommate in university. At his parents' urging, Thompson decided to go to law school instead of pursuing a career in antiquities. He'd studied law at Oxford. He'd moved to Gibraltar when the opportunity came to take over a law practice. Since Gibraltar's still the UK, he had all the qualifications he needed.

"I didn't want to work in my father's law firm and be under his shadow," Thompson said.

"I can understand that," Flores said.

"When my old university friend, Addison, asked me to serve on his new museum board, I jumped at the chance."

"I know it's been difficult having the museum closed. I think forensics has nearly finished going over everything. We can take down the tape soon.

CHAPTER TWENTY-ONE

We're sorry for the inconvenience."

Nicholas smiled, displaying straight white teeth. "Of course. I understand, Detective."

"Amy Bloom hasn't even been allowed to get in museum. We're going to lift that order today. I'm sure she needs to get in to get paperwork sorted," Flores said.

Thompson switched in his chair. "Uhm, yes, I do think she's been hoping to get back in there."

"I know it's been a while, but forensics had to do a thorough job," Flores said.

"I completely understand. I instructed Amy that we had to wait until the police gave us the all clear," Thompson said.

"I see. So, she hasn't tried to go into the museum at all since Señor Addison's death, then?" Flores asked.

Thompson furrowed his brow. "No, she's out of a job until it reopens."

"Is she being paid during this time?"

Thompson cleared his throat. "Yes, we have some reserve funds that we've been able to pay her with. She'll have a lot to do once we reopen. We didn't want to lose her."

"I see. Does the museum continue to receive donations?"

"We've received some monies. Will you excuse me for a moment, Detective? I need to take care of something with my secretary."

"Of course, I know you're busy," Flores said, standing.

When Thompson left the office, Flores went to the trash receptacle and retrieved the velvet pouch he'd seen Thompson throw away earlier. Flores wondered why Thompson had been so furtive in disposing of such a benign item like a small bag. Flores put the pouch in his coat pocket. Then he scooted back over to his place in front of Thompson's desk.

"I'm so sorry to keep you waiting, Detective, what is it you were asking?"

"No problem. I actually wanted to talk to you about the museum's funding now that Señor Addison is gone. Are you still raising funds?"

Thompsons sat up in his chair. "Yes, we are working on what is the best way to secure donations, and whether we need to hire a fundraiser."

"I see. How are your donations allocated when they come in? Who's in charge of seeing where the money goes?" Flores asked.

"The Board votes and determines how the museum uses its resources. Why do you ask?"

Flores's face grew serious. "I'm making general inquiries. I heard a rumor that the museum may be giving to some unsavory causes. I'd hate for it to be shut down for that reason."

Thompson fiddled with his pen. "Uh, I assure you nothing like that's happening at the museum."

"I'm glad to hear it. We hear these things sometimes and need to check them out. I wanted to warn you that the museum's under scrutiny," Flores said.

"Yes, of course. We do everything by the book. Listen, Detective, I just remembered. I need to take care of something urgently. Is that all you wanted to know?"

"Oh, I completely understand. I'll only take a few more minutes of your time."

Thompson let out a breath and leaned back in his chair.

"I recall you objected to the museum's main exhibits focusing on Islamic and African art rather than European art, didn't you?" Flores asked.

"I simply voiced the opinion of some that I heard that were against the museum. I thought all sides should be considered."

"Oh, I see. Did you object to the Runya painting being unveiled the night of the party? I understand it was an important work of Islamic art. I don't know that much about art," Flores said.

Thompson sneered. "I suppose police work doesn't require you to know a lot about art."

"You're right about that. The painting's very valuable, isn't it? Being lost makes it even more valuable, I understand."

"Yes, that's true. It was quite a coup for Addison to get it. A fantastic way to kick off the new museum. We got so much publicity from it."

"I'm sure a lot was involved in securing something like that," Flores said.

Thompson nodded. "Luis and I did all the necessary legal work to bring it to fruition. I brokered the auction with Oliver Hall to purchase the painting. It had been in England for some time, and it took some back and forth to get it back to Spain. I'd hardly be against Islamic art and do all that would I?"

"I suppose you wouldn't. How did Addison acquire such a rare painting?" Flores asked.

"I don't know all the details. I think we told you before that Carmela Sanchez had a big part in securing it. You need to ask her. What does all this have to do with Addison's death?" Thompson asked.

"We need to investigate every angle," Flores said.

Thompson turned up his lips in a half smile. "Of course, Detective. Is there anything else I can do for you?"

"Have you heard of an organization called Vox?" Flores asked.

Thompson's eyes grew wide. "Uh, yes, I've heard of them."

"Is the museum sending donations to them?"

"Uh, not that I'm aware of, one of our other members is in charge of donations. I don't have much to do with that," Thompson said.

Flores closed his notebook. "Oh, I see. Well, take my advice and vet your donors. You shouldn't be accepting or giving donations to any extremist or political groups."

Nicholas Thompson rose from his desk and walked over to shake Flores's hand. "Thank you for the sage advice. I'll keep it in mind. Is that all you wanted? Sorry to rush, but I've got other business to attend to."

"It's no problem, Señor. I understand," Flores said.

Flores retrieved one of his tattered business cards from his pocket, being careful not to disturb the pouch he'd taken from the wastebasket and handed it to Nicholas Thompson. "In case you lost my card. Please let me know if you think of anything else that might help in the investigation."

Thompson flipped the card between his fingers. "I will, Detective, and good luck."

"Gracias, Señor Thompson."

Flores took the elevator back to the parking garage. Back in his car, he took out the pouch he'd retrieved from Thompson's wastebasket. He noticed a rag inside. He placed the contents in a plastic bag. He'd been careful to only touch it with his fingertips so as not to contaminate it. He saw a dark substance on the rag, which he was sure was now all over his jacket pocket. He'd have to remember to get his jacket cleaned and send the bill to procurement. Once he returned to the station, he headed to the forensic lab and handed them the plastic bag. "See if you can analyze this and let me know what it is," he said.

"You couldn't tell what the pouch was used for, could it have been for carrying drugs?" Marco asked when Flores relayed his visit to Nicholas Thompson.

"I thought of that, but there was no drug residue that I saw. No. It was a red velvet pouch with a drawstring. It had some sort of rag inside," Flores said.

"Hmm. interesting. I wonder what he could be hiding in a velvet pouch," Marco said.

"We'll see what the forensic team says. I sent it to the lab."

Chapter Twenty-Two

A mother needs only glance at her child with a disappointing glare or speak in a certain tone to stir up feelings of guilt and shame. No one else could hold the same power and sway over the heart. Marco was cleaning the apartment when his mother rang his cell. She called to say his grandmother had been asking about him. She wanted to know why he hadn't gone to see her.

"Jaddah called me in tears, the other day," his mother said. "You haven't been to see her for months. You know she's getting old. You won't have much more time to spend with her. She's terribly upset and feels like you don't care about her. You need to make time to go to Tangier."

"Of course I care about her," Marco said. He tried to explain that he'd been tied up with a murder investigation and that he'd make every effort to go to Morocco soon.

"No murder investigation is more important than your grandmother."

He hated it when his mom spoke in that disappointed voice. Marco promised he would go and visit Jaddah soon.

He hung up the phone and finished cleaning, but he felt depressed, overwhelmed by guilt.

By evening, he needed to go out and relax. He phoned his buddy Oscar and invited him to go out to watch futbol. Their team, Barcelona, had advanced to number one in La Liga and would face Sevilla another good team. They decided to watch the match at Laila and Lar's bar, Townhome. Belen being gone, Marco could stay out as long as he wanted and celebrate what he hoped would be a glorious Barcelona victory.

He showered and changed into a pair of jeans and his favorite Barcelona shirt, which showed off the team tattoo on his left arm. He microwaved a quick dinner of lomo that Belen had left in the freezer for him. He scarfed it down and put the dishes in the dishwasher. Oscar arrived just as he'd finished, and the two headed out into the warm evening air like two school kids on their way to the playground. Oscar also wore his Barcelona shirt and carried a Barcelona flag and other paraphernalia. They reached Townhome and headed up the narrow stairs. The bar was already busy. Laila handed beers to patrons, while Leslie assured the television screens and sound functioned well.

Laila greeted Marco and Oscar and handed each cervezas as they found seats on stools in front of the large projector screen. They sat next to Sevilla fans, attired in clothing representing their favorite team. The bar had a joyful atmosphere. Marco could feel the excitement and anticipation. He grabbed a handful of nuts from one of the small cuencos placed in various locations around the bar and ate them with a swig of beer. He and Oscar toasted one another, clinking bottles for Barcelona futbol.

Everyone in Townhome chatted and made small talk until the game started. Then screams pierced the room with each goal or near goal. In the end, it was a tense ninety minutes decided by penalty points. "Penalty points!" Marco exclaimed. "Can you believe it?" They shouted when the final whistle of the game rang, and the score was still 2-2. The entire bar stood on edge when Marco's favorite player, Messi, scored, then a score from Sevilla. Then another score, and finally a blocked kick by the Barcelona goalie, who became an instant hero. Laila placed shots in front of them to celebrate the victory, which they each swallowed in one swig. Both Marco and Oscar grew louder with each shot, giddy with excitement. Marco soon forgot the guilt from his mother's phone call. He felt loose and happy.

As Marco gulped another shot, he looked down to see his phone flashing Flores's number. He checked the time on his phone. Eleven o'clock in the evening. What could Flores want?

"Darn. I've got to get this," Marco said, more loudly than he intended.

"Don't answer it," a drunken Oscar slurred.

Marco started to put the phone down and pretend he didn't see it, but his senses told him he'd better answer.

"Dime," he said, sounding curt.

"Marco, where are you? It sounds loud in there. You need to come to Sanchez's restaurant as soon as you can; there's been a death."

Marco stared at his phone in disbelief. A death? He must have heard that wrong after too many cervezas. Feeling himself sober up, he realized the call had been real. He made his apologies to Oscar and to Laila and Lars and told them he had to go.

"Go? You can't go now. We've just gotten another round of sho…t…s," said slurry Oscar, his head bobbing back and forth.

"*Lo siento*. Sorry, amigo. Emergency at work," Marco said. He hopped off his barstool and headed down the stairs to the Townhome exit.

Marco felt lightheaded as he walked through Casco Antiqua. He didn't feel himself swaying, but he could tell he wasn't walking straight. None of the others in the area seemed to notice. Luckily, no one stared at him, half-drunk, strolling through town. He only had to walk a few blocks from the Townhome bar to Sanchez's.

Marco opened the door to the restaurant. Instead of being greeted by a beckoning waiter, he saw police in uniform milling around and light bulbs flashing. Flores spotted him as he entered the dining area. The restaurant, with its tables set for the dinner service, had been roped off. Centerpieces of candles and flowers sat upon each table along with silverware and glassware. The candles created an ambiance of romance, though the scene Marco entered seemed more macabre than romantic. People stood around looking shocked, hoping for answers to what they'd witnessed. Police wearing booties and plastic gloves to keep from contaminating the scene, clashed with photographers who walked through the room taking pictures and speaking into microphones.

"The scene here at Sanchez's, one of Vivirrambla's most beloved restaurants, can only be described as bizarre. Tables of pasta sit cold and remain uneaten, bottles of wine unopened. It's not the typical Friday night out," one reporter said, holding a microphone and looking through a large television camera.

"Over here," Flores said, beckoning Marco over to him. Flores stood next to a thin man with a worn face wearing a tuxedo. "This gentleman is one of the waiters," Flores said. "He was just about to tell me what he witnessed."

The waiter blinked rapidly. His hands shook. "Si, si. It was a regular Friday night; we were fully booked and just starting service."

Dinner in Spain normally began at ten at night. Marco, almost sober now, looked at his watch.

The waiter pointed to the table next to them. "I was taking my table's order when this man stumbled into the dining room and collapsed right next to the table leg."

"He says the man almost fell on his foot," Flores said.

The waiter spoke with his hands waving about, like a conductor guiding the Nutcracker Suite.

"Si, si. We all stopped when we realized what had happened. *La sangre*, blood started gushing out of him. Some of it spilled on my customer's shoe," said the waiter. "She nearly fainted. That's when she screamed." The waiter pointed to his jacket, which had a large reddish-blue stain. "Some of the blood even splashed on me."

Flores looked at the pool of blood on the tile floor. He noticed that the trail ran to the kitchen door, a few steps away from them. "The blood's coming from the kitchen," he said.

Flores knelt closer to the body lying still on the floor, the man's eyes now shut forever, and his mouth open with a look of shock and pleading. "He's been stabbed. He must have tried to stumble out here to the dining room to get away."

He looked up to find the coroner Javier Bortello, who'd just arrived.

"Buenas tardes, what do we have here?" Bortello asked.

Bortello knelt next to Flores. "He's been stabbed several times," he said, shaking his head. "Tsk Tsk, look at all those wounds. Somebody must have been very angry at the deceased."

Chapter Twenty-Three

"Can you tell me anything more?" Flores asked the coroner. Bortello, who always looked as if he wished the world would stop bothering him, shook his head. "All I can tell you is he received five or six stab wounds. A couple to his neck that reached the arteries. The killer acted with precision. They knew what they were doing. The fatal wound appears to be here, right next to his heart. That's all I can tell you right now."

"Okay, let me know if you discover anything else. Marco, let's follow the trail that leads to the kitchen and see if we can figure out what happened," Flores said.

Flores pushed the heavy metal kitchen doors that swung open from both sides. Bewildered chefs, dishwashers, and stunned waiters stood around the kitchen. Flores asked them to remain until they spoke to one of the officers.

Police officers in lime green vests milled through the kitchen gathering evidence, taking pictures, checking for fingerprints, and spraying blue light of luminol, a water-based substance, used to detect blood. One test reported that the luminol revealed most of the blood to be near the freezer room.

An officer called for Flores and waved him over. "Look, Detective, over here."

The officer pointed to a large knife, which had the remnants of blood, sitting next to the oven.

"Get prints and bag the knife," Flores said.

He turned to Marco. "Looks like they left the murder weapon behind. Hopefully, we'll get some useable prints."

Then Flores addressed the assembled in the kitchen. "How could a person have been stabbed in here with all these people around and no one saw anything?"

A short, pudgy man with a round belly, wearing a stained white apron, spoke. "I'm Jesus, the head chef. None of us were in the kitchen at the time." Jesus pointed to a door that led to another room attached to the kitchen. "We were in there having our briefing. We always gather before meal service to go over things and ensure service runs well. We were in there, and the waiters were in the dining room. No one was in the kitchen for at least twenty minutes," the chef said.

"Do you always have these meetings? How long do they generally last?" Flores asked.

"We meet before every service. They last aaa….bout fifteen to twenty minutes or so. I like to hold the briefing in the other room, so my chefs won't be distracted by the wait staff asking them questions," the head chef said.

"So, no one was here in the kitchen when the man was stabbed?" Flores asked.

Jesus shook his head. "When we came back in, the Sous Chef spotted blood on the floor. That's when we heard the screams coming from the dining room. We all ran to see what happened."

"I see. Did anyone notice anything else unusual in the kitchen before then?" Flores asked.

One of the assistant chefs, a young woman, spoke. "I noticed earlier that one of the knives had been moved. I didn't think anything of it at the time. I thought someone had been filleting and forgot to put it away."

Another chef pointed at a wooden knife holder. "I noticed the Syosaku knife missing. It's one of our best knives. I also assumed someone had forgotten to return it after prepping, although we have strict rules about putting knives away," she said.

"It's a fireable offense," said the Sous Chef.

Flores held up the bag, holding a large knife with a sharpened blade. "Is this the missing knife?"

The head chef nodded. "Yes, that's the one. Did someone use it for murder?"

"It looks that way," Flores said.

They all gasped.

Flores asked them to remain until the officers released them. He and Marco went back into the dining room. They approached a man identified as the floor manager, who sat in a chair near the door, shaking his head.

"I can't believe this happened," the tall, olive-skinned man, said.

"Did you see anyone acting strangely come into the restaurant this evening?" Flores asked.

"The floor manager shook his head, no. "We'd just opened. We only had a few customers, though we're booked for the evening. I'd checked in two couples. An old white-haired English gentleman who wore a lot of cologne came in. He smelled like he used the whole bottle. Anyway, he didn't have a reservation. He told me he'd just arrived in town and heard we had one of the best restaurants in Vivirrambla. I told him he normally needed reservations, but since it was still early, I could probably seat him. I asked him to have a seat while I checked over the books. I stepped away for a minute. When I came back, the old man had gone. I figured he decided to go somewhere else."

"Did you get his name?" Flores asked.

The floor manager shook his head, no. "He'd gone before I could get any information."

"Do you know who the man was that was stabbed?" Flores asked.

"Si, si, of course. Diego Sanchez. The owner, Señora Sanchez's brother. He comes to the restaurant sometimes. He usually goes back into the kitchen to check the specials. He'd called earlier to say he'd be bringing a special guest for dinner."

"Is Señora Sanchez here? I haven't seen her," Marco said, looking around.

She mentioned that she had business to attend to and wouldn't be coming. She doesn't come into the restaurant every evening. The manager, Santiago, is in charge when she's not here. Santiago's been here for years. He knows everything about the restaurant," the floor manager said.

"What's Santiago's last name?" Flores asked.

"Gonzalez."

"Where can we find Señor Gonzalez?" Flores asked.

The floor manager pointed to a man with a full bushy head of black hair on the other side of the room. "He's talking to one of the other officers."

"I'll go and see if Señora Sanchez has arrived," Marco said. "I assumed someone called her."

"We called her right away," the floor manager said.

"I'll go and speak with Gonzalez," Flores said.

Flores walked over to Santiago Gonzalez, who was gesturing with his hands as he explained what he'd seen to the officer. "Thank you, Officer. I'll take it from here," Flores said.

"Yes Sir." The police officer bowed and walked away.

"Señor Gonzalez, did you see Señor Diego Sanchez come into the restaurant this evening?" Flores asked.

"Yes, I saw him for a few minutes. We spoke when he first came in. He doesn't come in too often. He usually comes over to speak to me when he's here. I've known him for many years. He told me he was nervous because he was having dinner with an old friend that he hadn't seen in over eighty years," Gonzalez said.

"Wow, eighty years. Did he say whom he was meeting?" Flores asked.

Gonzalez shook his head. "No. He was more dressed up than usual, I noticed and he did look nervous. So, it must have been someone special."

"Did anyone come in to ask for him?"

"No, not that I'm aware of, but then again, everything happened so fast."

"Did anyone come in asking for Diego?" Flores asked the floor manager.

"No, no one," the floor manager said.

Flores went to find Javier Bortello. He showed the coroner the bagged knife. "Looks like this is the murder weapon."

Bortello got up off his knees, where he'd still been scrutinizing the dead man's body. He put on a pair of black rimmed glasses and studied the large knife. "Yep, that would do it. I see all the blood around it," he said.

"Can you tell anything about what happened so far?" Flores asked.

"Well, from the state of the body, it seems he was stabbed about an hour or so ago. Rigor hasn't set in. The person seemed to be skilled with a knife and to know exactly what they were doing. This looks like hatred and revenge, almost like someone had a vendetta," Bortello said.

"Interesting. Thanks, Javier. I'll leave you to it," Flores said.

Bortello grunted.

Flores spotted Marco on the other side of the room, consoling Carmela Sanchez, who sat weeping in one of the plush velour chairs in the front of the restaurant. He walked over to them.

"I'm so sorry, Señora," Marco was saying. She heaved from weeping.

"Condolences, Señora," Flores said, bowing slightly.

Carmela shook her head, "Thank you." She took the tissue she held in her hand and wiped the tears from her face. "I can't believe it. My little brother's been murdered."

"If you're up to it, I'll come and see you tomorrow," Marco said.

Carmela sniffled. "Okay, that will be fine."

After speaking to Carmela for a time and a few more patrons, Flores determined that they'd done all they could do that evening. When he and Marco walked out of the restaurant, the sun had begun to rub the sleep from its eyes as daybreak dawned.

"I'll speak to Carmela first thing. I wonder if there's a connection to our museum murder," Marco said.

"It doesn't seem so from what I can see. The last death was a strangulation, and I don't know what connection Diego could have with the museum," Flores said.

The two parted for the evening.

Chapter Twenty-Four

Marco decided to go and speak to Carmela Sanchez before going to the office. He'd gone to bed late, too hyped to sleep when he got home. He slept only a few hours, and his head still pounded from drinking shots. Watching the game seemed like a lifetime ago now. He silenced the annoying buzzing sound of his alarm and crawled out of bed. He got up and went off to the bathroom to shower.

He made himself coffee before leaving home. He drank two cups, along with several ounces of Lanjaròn water from the mountains of Grenada, and two aspirina. By the time he pulled into Carmela Sanchez's driveway, he felt semi-alive. He parked next to the rectangular courtyard with a green topiary trimmed in the shape of a Spanish bull in the center.

He rang the bell. The door opened. A young woman ushered him into the drawing room with green furniture. He stood near a window as daylight poured through. The bright morning light stood in contrast to the bleak darkness in the atmosphere of the house.

Carmela Sanchez entered wearing black pants and an emerald, green shirt that matched the furniture. Her face seemed more aged, her eyes red and puffy from crying. Yet, she moved with the grace of a swan. She suggested they go out onto the patio.

"I can use some fresh air. This is all so surreal," Carmela said.

Marco followed her through the French doors to a brick courtyard that overlooked the sea of turquoise. They ambled over to a white metal table with white chairs. If the area hadn't been walled off by a bevy of palm trees, a clear view of the beach would have been visible. Carmela sat at the head of the table. Marco sat next to her in one of the outdoor chairs. Coffee in an ornate silver pot rested on a matching silver platter along with an assortment of pastries. Marco eyed the coffee as Carmela gestured for him to partake.

"Please help yourself to some," she said.

Marco poured himself a cup of the steaming brown liquid and helped himself to leche, which sat on the side in a small silver creamer. He picked up the sterling silver spoon next to him and stirred in the creamy substance. He noticed that all the silver was highly polished and had the same pattern.

"Thank you for agreeing to see me this morning. I know it's difficult for you," Marco said.

Carmela poured herself a cup of coffee, plopping in a lump of sugar using small silver tongs of the same ilk. "I don't understand why the police need to speak to me. I wasn't even at the restaurant when my brother was killed."

"We generally speak to family members and those connected to the victim to get as much background information as possible. You may have some other useful information," Marco said.

Carmela nodded. "Oh, I see. How could this have happened? My brother had some problems. But who'd want to kill him?"

Marco looked out onto the clay tennis court, which was just beyond them to the right. So much wealth hadn't shielded Carmela from this loss. "That's why I'm here. To see if we can find out what happened."

Carmela's voice shook. "I can't imagine why anyone would kill him, and so brutally."

"Did your brother have any enemies? Had he received any threats from anyone?"

Carmela shook her head, no. "Not that I know about."

"I believe I read that your brother was an alcoholic at one time. Could he have had any outstanding debts from gambling or drinking? Could he have owed anyone a lot of money?"

"Yes, it's true. Diego went to rehab a while ago. He seemed better after a month in a facility. Our father left me very well off. More than I can spend in one lifetime. I can't imagine Diego being in debt. He knew he could come to me. I never refused him anything. I always felt guilty that Papa left everything to me and shut him out."

Pointing to the silver pot, Marco asked. "May I, Señora? So, he was no longer drinking that you knew about?"

Carmela nodded. "Yes, of course. Help yourself. As far as I know he was clean. He had to hit rock bottom first. He did have some trouble once, but I took care of it. That's when he agreed to go to a facility."

"How long ago was that?"

Carmela twisted her lip. "About a year ago. He'd gotten himself into some debt and he owed his ex-wife some money. Like I said, I took care of it. I always took care of my little brother."

Marco poured himself more coffee and spooned in creamer. *"Gracias, Señora.* He held up the spoon and looked at it in the sunlight. What a beautiful spoon. What's the writing on the back?"

"It's the Hanoverian silver mark. It's from the time of King George I. I have a whole set. The hallmarks on the back indicate the year it was made and the place. This was made in the British Isle. The pattern is called Fiddle, early nineteenth century, one of my favorites. My father had a passion for sterling silver, especially English silver. He left quite a collection."

"That's really interesting. How did he acquire such a lovely collection?"

"My father traveled to England quite a lot before and during *la guerra civil.* He befriended an English antiques dealer during the war, who sold him this collection. Of course, we'd always had our own family Spanish pieces, but Papa became almost obsessed. I've had to replace some flatware here and there, as they got lost over the years."

"Your father was able to travel during the war? Marco asked. "I remember my parents told me that Spain was isolated. They said it was difficult to get out of the country."

Carmela arched her back and took a dainty sip of coffee. "That may have been true for some, but my father was able to travel anywhere without any trouble. He went to Europe and Morocco quite often; he always came back with beautiful things."

Carmela's eyes turned moist. "Now I'm all alone."

"There's no one left in your immediate family?" Marco asked.

"No, I come from a small family. Most of my relatives died in the war. My husband died a few years ago. We'd been divorced for several years. We never had children. Diego may not have been perfect, but he was all that I had left."

"You said your father left everything to you? He and Diego didn't get along? I remember sensing tension between them when I used to come to the restaurant," Marco said.

"Ever since I could remember, there'd been quite a bit of tension between the two of them. I honestly think my father hated Diego. I believe that's why my brother started drinking. He could never reconcile his relationship with Papa."

"That's really sad. Can you think of anyone who'd want to kill him, even after you paid off his debts?" Marco asked.

Carmela sat back in her chair and remained quiet for a time. Then she spoke. "He had some enemies, I suppose, but he never spoke to me about anyone who hated him enough to want to kill him."

"What about his ex-wife?" Marco asked.

"She moved to the States. We haven't seen her in years. They never had any children, thankfully," Carmela said.

Was your brother involved in the business at all?" Marco asked.

"No. He had no interest in restaurants. Besides, I'd never let him get close to the money."

"Did he do any kind of work for a living?" Marco asked.

"He wanted to be an artist. He painted from time to time, but he never took it seriously. I gave him money, a generous allowance to dabble in his art. In turn, he let me do whatever I wanted with the restaurant. One of the art pieces in the house went missing a few years ago. I honestly thought my brother sold it. I didn't do anything about it at the time. I figured he needed the money. So, I let it go."

"I see. Do you think someone could have been blackmailing him, for gambling debts, for example?"

"He never told me anything about that. I would have paid it off."

"Did Diego have anything to do with the recent painting, the Runya that was going to the museum?" Marco asked.

Carmela knitted her eyebrows. "No, that painting was my passion. Diego could have cared less about it. He could be cold, like our father."

Marco sat up in his chair. "I'm not sure I understand, Señora. Your father owned a very popular restaurant. Everyone loved him and your family."

Carmela looked straight at Marco. "That's just what you saw on the surface. You don't know what went on in our household. You were only there for a few hours. I'm afraid I'm left to clean up the mess."

She looked around at her surroundings, "I'm left here in this large estate alone. Don't get me wrong, I'm not lonely. "I have plenty of friends, and a few," she paused and looked down. "a few suitors, even at my advanced age. I guess I don't look too bad," she said, batting her eyelashes.

Marco smiled. "You look great, Señora."

"Wealth comes with a great price. As you see, I'm devoid of close family. Diego was named after my father, you know."

"Yes, but you were married at one time, you said."

Carmela rolled her eyes. "Yes, but as I said, we never had any children. Paco couldn't stop having affairs long enough for us to have children."

"I'm sorry, Señora, I didn't mean to bring up painful memories."

She fanned her hand in dismissal. "Oh, don't worry about it. I've long gotten over Paco. May God have mercy on his soul," she said, making the sign of the cross on her chest. "He was an abusive conman. My father would have killed him himself if he'd lived long enough to really know him."

"I don't want to make you uncomfortable, Señora. If it's not too painful, tell me what else you think might be helpful about your family," Marco said.

"It doesn't matter. It's old news now. If you'd asked me ten years ago, when it was all raw, I'm not so sure I could have told you everything. There was much about my family that I didn't know about until many years later."

"Only what you feel comfortable talking about," Marco said, biting into the last of his pastry.

"Let me say, despite it all, I still loved my father. Towards the end of his life, he told me he'd left Sánchez's to me. He cut Diego out of his will. My father said times had changed, and he didn't have to leave his legacy to the boy child he hated. He could leave what he wanted to his Carmelita, as he called me. I never said anything to Diego. I made him believe he'd be getting half the estate. He never found out the truth until Papa died."

"I'm sure he was upset once he found out," Marco said.

"He went on a drinking binge that lasted a week. He wouldn't speak to me for over a year. Sanchez's was thriving. Diego wanted to manage it. I wanted to let him, but he couldn't be trusted due to his drinking. He'd been angry for a while about that," she said.

Marco looked at his watch. He'd cleared the morning for this appointment. Carmela's story fascinated him, but he needed to tell Eva that he'd be in later in the day. "Perdona, Señora, I must call my office," Marco said.

"Of course," Carmela said. She poured herself another cup of coffee.

Marco poured himself another cup.

"If that's cold, Margarita can make us a fresh pot," Carmela said.

"It's fine, Señora." Marco texted Eva that he didn't know what time he'd be in the office. Everything's fine here. She texted back.

"Now what were you saying, Señora?" Marco asked, putting his phone down.

"What was I saying?" Carmela asked.

"You were telling me about your life, and about Diego," Marco said.

"Ah, yes. It might be easier if I go back to the beginning." She smiled. "Forgive me as I tend to go off on tangents. It comes with age."

"Take as much time as you need, Señora."

"You really have turned into a fine young man."

Carmela began her soliloquy. "I was a little girl when my father opened the restaurant. Diego was only a baby. My father worked hard and travelled a lot. Sometimes we didn't see him for months. My brother wanted to be a pilot once he heard about war beginning in Spain. He saw himself as a great pilot off to save the world. My father said he couldn't, that he needed him at home to work in the restaurant. I think that's what first led Diego down the wrong path.

I often accompanied my father to the restaurant. He'd take me around and introduce me to the chefs and waiters. Unlike Diego, I loved it. Things went well for a time. As you know, Marco, we became one of the most famous restaurants in Vivirrambla. But things changed over time. I grew into a teenager. My brother grew into an angry adult and started hanging around angry friends. Right before the war, my father changed. A lot of strange men started coming to the restaurant. My father began to have secret meetings with these people. He'd say to me, '*Hija*, go and do something for a while.'"

"Who were these strange men?" Marco asked.

Carmela looked over at Marco. He noticed her cabochon sapphire earrings reflected the light as she spoke. "Eventually. When the war started. I found out they were Fascist supporters of Franco."

Marco suppressed the urge to gasp aloud. "Fascists, what did they want with your father and his restaurant?"

"They used the restaurant as a front for planning and mounting an army against the Republic. Father would tell me to stay away when the men came. When I got older, I'd just started going home when I saw them. One of the men tried to touch me once. My father would have killed him had he known."

Marco frowned.

"My brother told me Papa was conspiring to help them hide things and store away money to build up for an uprising against the monarchy. I didn't believe him at first, but Diego was right. You see, Marco, my father was in essence a traitor."

Marco tried to hide his shock. "What about your brother? Did he help your father with the Fascists?"

"My father forced him to; he gave him no choice. Diego started running errands for them. That's when he really started drinking."

"I remember your father being a kind but stern man. He was always nice to me," Marco said.

Carmela nodded. "Yes, people are complex. Papa could be kind. He treated me like a princess. He loved me. The same man was cruel to my brother and a traitor to his country. Still, even after I found out what he'd done, I loved him."

Marco saw a tear drop on Carmela's cheek. "It must have been hard for you to find all this out about someone you admired."

Carmela put her hand to her heart. "It's still hard whenever I think about it. I've always been realistic, though. I know that I must carry on."

Carmela stopped talking and looked at Marco. "I don't know if any of this will help you to find out who killed my brother and Addison."

Marco said. "Your information may prove to be very helpful, even if we can't see it now. I hope I haven't caused you too much distress dredging up the past."

"It's okay. I'm glad to talk to someone who remembers the restaurant from the old days. At least there's some joy and delectation in the early memories of my father," Carmela said.

Marco put his cup down on the table. The flavor of coffee lingered in his mouth. "It helps to recall the good times." Marco stood up. "*Gracias, Señora Sanchez, para todos.* You've been very generous with your time. Thank you for the delicious coffee and pastries. I will let you know when we've found out anything."

Carmela escorted Marco back into the house. When they reached the front door, she said. "By the way, you may want to speak to Oliver Hall about the painting. He helped me to acquire it. Please let me know if you find out anything about Addison, and of course, any news about Diego."

"I will," Marco said.

As he strolled down the driveway to his car, the sun slanted through the trees. Marco reflected on the conversation. The Sanchez family's saga bore notes of sorrow, regret, and tenderness played together like an etude. He wondered if, somewhere in the tragedy and the drama, he'd find the answer to who killed Carmela's brother.

Chapter Twenty-Five

"[C]ircumstances were different. Franco just wouldn't die."
—*Leaving Tangier,* Tahar Ben Jelloun

Unlike Flores, Marco believed the Runya painting, Amy Bloom and Nicholas Thompson's odd behavior, as well as Diego's murder, had to somehow be connected. He phoned Oliver Hall, as Carmela had suggested. He also wanted to ask him about Amy Bloom and her previous job in London to see if he had any information. When he called him, Hall said he couldn't meet in person because he'd flown back to London to be with his family for the holidays.

"You're from London. Did you know Amy Bloom before she came here?" Marco asked him.

"I knew her. Why do you want to know?" Hall asked.

"Just getting a profile on everyone who worked in the museum," Marco said.

Hall said Amy used to work for a mutual friend, Jules Moore, an antique dealer who had a shop in London. She worked there for several years before moving to Spain. She'd been Jules's trusted assistant. Jules was distraught when she told him she intended to move to Vivirrambla.

"How do you know Jules Moore?" Marco asked.

"Jules is an old client of mine. I authenticated some paintings for him, as well as doing some appraisals. I still see him from time to time. In fact, he's asked me to come and see him while I'm in London. Wait, I have an idea, why don't you come over here to London and talk to Jules in person? He can tell you what you need about Amy. He's older now and doesn't travel much, but I'm sure he'll be glad to talk to you if I recommend it," Hall said.

Marco hesitated. He didn't know if he should leave town, or if Flores would let him.

"Jules is a character. I'm sure he'd love to talk to you about all this stuff. He's knowledgeable about paintings and antiques," Hall said.

Marco thought about it for a moment. He decided a trip might be what he needed to escape the loneliness of home, even for a few days.

Flores's immediate reaction was a vehement no when Marco proposed the trip to London to him.

"We don't have the resources for you to be jetting over to the UK."

After a lot of explaining, Marco finally convinced Flores that the trip could be useful if it could help to connect the dots. "Perhaps we'll find a motive for at least one of the murders," Marco said.

Flores finally relented on condition that Marco paid for his own hotel room.

* * *

As it neared Christmas, Vivirrambla had begun to decorate. Large white angel figures flew over the streets and dangled from light poles, red and green swag ran down the buildings. Decorated wreaths graced doors and old-fashioned streetlights down each avenue. Marco loved this time of year. London would also be decorated, he reasoned, and he'd get a bit of chilly winter weather, making it seem even more like Christmas.

He found a cheap round-trip flight to London on Air Portugal and booked for three days. He packed his bags and drove to Malaga airport, where he left his car. The flight board said the plane was leaving on time. He walked through the airport in search of coffee before he boarded the plane for the two-hour trip.

After ascending, the pilot announced that they'd reached a steady altitude of thirty-five thousand feet. It was safe to turn off your seat belt and use electronic equipment, the flight attendant said over the speakers. Marco switched on his phone to airplane mode to find a message from Flores.

The Chief's in a tizzy about the latest murder, and everyone wants to know if Diego Sanchez's murder is related to Addison Mason's death. He said the public believes murderers are running amok, and the police haven't been doing anything. You'd better come up with something while you're gone."

The flight was uneventful, except for a slight bit of turbulence. Marco had just finished a beer when the attendant came back to the microphone to advise everyone to put up their food trays, raise their seats to the upright position, and turn off all electronic equipment. Marco braced himself. A few minutes later, the plane's wheels hit the tarmac with a thud.

Marco hadn't been to London in quite some time. He'd forgotten how crowded Heathrow airport could be with passengers scurrying back and forth like wound-up action figures searching for their gates and trying to collect their luggage. He'd carried on his bag. So, Marco joined those searching for an exit that would take them to an Uber or taxicab. When he got outside, the air felt chilly. He'd expected rain, but the sun shone. Marco spotted a line of taxis waiting for anxious customers. He jumped into the cab that was first in line rather than waiting for an Uber. The driver, an elderly Englishman with graying hair and bushy eyebrows that curled upwards, placed Marco's bag in the trunk.

"Where you from?" he asked.

"Vivirrambla," Marco answered.

"Ah, Malaga, I go there at least three times a year when I can. Beautiful weather," he said. "Today's nice, but as you probably know, we get a lot of rain here."

"So, I hear," Marco said.

"Had an old gentleman in my cab not too long ago for an airport run. About my age, ha, ha, ha. Well-dressed. Said he was headed to Malaga. Said he hadn't been there in years. I told him life's too short. You need to go while you still can. Nice fella. He had on a lot of cologne, though. Had to air out my cab before I picked up another fare," the driver said, laughing.

The driver stopped in front of the hotel Lassett near Kensington Palace, a white structure with iron railings and floor-to-ceiling windows. Marco retrieved his bag and walked up to the front entrance. He checked in and found his room, which had a large king-size bed. Bright light penetrated through the blue drapes, hanging from floor to ceiling.

After unpacking and getting a sandwich, Marco got an Uber to the address he'd been given for Oliver's home, which was near his hotel. Oliver and his partner occupied a two-bedroom apartment in a scenic area of town. The lush green neighborhood surrounded by trees looked picturesque, with many of the homes decorated for the holiday. The front of Oliver's façade was brick. Strings of white lights surrounded the door, lighting up the green swag. A wreath hung on a nail on the door. Marco opened the door and walked up a flight of stairs to Apartment 10 and knocked on the door. A young man with light brown hair wearing a Christmas sweater of little elves opened the door.

"Hello," he said in a strong British accent. I suppose you're here to see Oliver. Come right in. He'll be back soon."

Marco stepped inside the flat to a spacious room decorated in classic tastes with a modern feel. The wooden floors were covered with old rugs like the ones in his native Morocco. Marco recognized the patterns he'd seen many times on his visits to family and in his own home. A cream-colored silk sofa and two antique chairs sat in front of the walls painted cream. Several large paintings hung strategically placed on the walls. A blue and white tile piece, depicting an Islamic Mosque, hung over the sofa. A big screen television had been mounted above a fireplace. Next to it were comfortable-looking lounge chairs. A tall Christmas tree, emitting the scent of pine, stood in the corner, decorated with white ribbons and bows. Ornaments with scenes hung from the tree. Miniature white lights, the same type as were on the door, strung around the tree, made the room feel ethereal.

Josh, the young man who'd opened the door, gestured for Marco to sit. "Nice tree, huh? Oliver and I walked all the way home with it," Josh said.

"It's beautiful. You guys go all out."

Belen would have loved the decorations. Their apartment always looked like a showroom during the holidays. Marco stayed out of her way when she got into decorating mode.

"Oliver's brilliant at decorating," his roommate said. "Make yourself at home. He should be here soon. He had to go to Mapperton estates in Dorset for an appointment with the Viscountess of Montagu and her husband, Luke, the Earl of Sandwich. They're wonderful people. The Earl's married to a rather funny and clever American by the name of Julie. She and Luke work to keep up their estate. Oliver's been helping them with some art restorations, pieces that have been around for hundreds of years. He also appraised some pieces for them."

"That sounds really interesting," Marco said.

The click of a key turning the lock interrupted them. They both turned their heads. "Hello," a voice echoed from the front hall.

"We're in here, Oliver. Your visitor's here."

"Oh, great, I'll be right in."

Oliver Hall dashed into the room and extended his hand to Marco. "My gosh, sorry to keep you waiting. Dorset was quite a hike. Well worth it though. Good to see you again, Marco. Did Josh tell you where I've been? I love visiting the Viscountess and Luke, they're great people. Did he offer you anything to drink? Josh, be a love and bring us some tea, would you?"

"Of course, it would be my pleasure," Josh said as he left the room.

Oliver rubbed his two hands together. "It's getting chilly out there, a lot different than Spain. Thanks so much for hopping over here to England. I only get to see my parents once a year."

"Gave me an excuse to get away. I haven't been to London for a while. I've been looking at all your wonderful paintings. I can see you know a lot about art. I understand you assisted in obtaining the Runya painting," Marco said.

Josh returned bearing a silver tray with a decorated silver teapot, two blue and white China cups, and a small silver vessel of milk, sugar, and lemon. Like Oliver, he had deep-set blue eyes. His tall, thin body could be described as lanky. He set the tea on a side table and lifted the pot. Then he turned to Marco. "How do you like your tea?"

"Milk and sugar, please," Marco said, accepting the cup. "Oliver, Carmela Sanchez suggested I speak to you. We've got two murders now, as you know, Carmela's brother was stabbed."

"Oh yes, I couldn't believe what happened to Carmela's brother. Do the police have any idea who did it?" Oliver asked.

"They're working on it," Marco said. "During a discussion I had with her, Carmela told me that you helped to secure the Runya painting."

Oliver took a sip of tea and crossed his legs. He wore an oxford shirt with a bow tie, decorated with Christmas bells. "Yes, I brokered the deal with the auction house, and I did the work to authenticate the painting."

"Who paid for the authentication? That must have been expensive," Marco said.

"The Board paid for it. They okayed the restoration. People like Carmela donated the money."

Josh tipped back into the room. It was evident that he doted on Oliver. "Can I get you anything else?" he asked, looking at Marco.

"No, thank you, the tea was really good."

"There's nothing like a good cuppa," Oliver said. "Now, where were we? Ah, yes, the painting. Jules Moore, whom you're going to meet, called me one day. I hadn't heard from him in some time. He told me that he's been ill. He has cancer and, at eighty-six, he doesn't expect to live long. He wanted me to help liquidate some of his paintings and other things. He's never married or had children. He decided he wanted to spend most of his money while he was still alive."

Oliver took a sip of tea then continued. "Jules sounded resigned. I'd never heard him sound like that before. He spoke in a whisper. I had to keep asking him to repeat himself. He told me he needed to get something off his chest before he died. He'd acquired a work of Islamic art from Spain several years ago. He wouldn't say how he got it, though he admitted it had been by dubious means. Now that he neared death, he wanted to clear his conscience and return the painting to Spain. He knew I was a friend of Addison's. So, he said he contacted me when he read I was on the Board of a new museum that would feature Arabesque paintings. He wanted to sell the painting to them. I put the idea to the Board. They agreed when I showed them the pictures Jules sent. Addison in particular was keen to have the painting. Then, Carmela got involved to help with the negotiations and purchase."

"So, Jules sold the painting to the museum?" Marco asked.

Oliver leaned forward. "Yes, of course. Well, technically, Jules sold it to Carmela, and she sold it to the museum. They worked that out somehow. Addison scored a real coup. He couldn't believe his fortune, having a lost painting to exhibit at the same time as he opened his museum. The intrigue of a lost painting brought publicity and sparked a lot of interest. Addison took it as a sign the museum would be a success."

"What about Amy Bloom. Was she involved at all in the acquisition?" Marco asked.

"No, other than paperwork, typing up contracts, that sort of thing. Amy knows a lot about antiques, silver. She doesn't know much about art."

"How did she end up coming to Spain and working for Addison?"

"Through Nicholas Thompson. I only knew her from seeing her in Jules's shop. I think she was friends with Nicholas. Are you ready to go and meet Jules?" Oliver asked.

Marco put his teacup down and stood up. "Yep, let's go."

As they put on their coats, Oliver shouted out to Josh, "We're leaving now. I don't know when I'll be back."

Josh peeked his head in. "Ok, take your time. I've got a lot of work to catch up on. Good to meet you, Marco. I hope you enjoy your stay in London."

"Thanks, pleasure meeting you as well," Marco said.

"Shall we?" Oliver said, gesturing with his hand towards the exit.

Marco and Oliver headed outside. It had gotten colder than when Marco landed in London; a misty rain fell.

"Jule's shop is right around the corner. He still opens it every day despite being sick. His new assistant runs things, but he still likes to come in and talk to the customers. I think he still misses Amy."

Marco shivered. He and Oliver quickened their pace to get out of the chill.

"Not used to this cold, huh?" Oliver said, laughing.

"Not really. If it's below twenty degrees, I'm shivering," Marco said.

Oliver chuckled. "It took me a while to get used to the heat of Spain in the summer."

A few steps further, they reached the door of what appeared to be a townhouse, except that the sign painted royal blue read **JULES ANTIQUES** in calligraphic gold lettering. The red and white brick structure had a Victorian roof attached. Once inside, the store, crowded with antiques and old furniture, had cabinets with glass tops displaying antique silver and jewelry. There was little room to walk. A large Rose Medallion vase sat precariously in the corner of the room. It looked much like the store Marco had seen in the newspaper article he'd read. The computer couldn't capture the musty smell of old, undusted antiques. A scent of cologne also hung in the air.

At a Louis XVI table near the front entrance of the store, an old man sat on a Louis IX chair behind a table with a glass top that displayed old diamonds, rubies, and gold. Though seated, it was apparent that the old man had osteoporosis as his back was stooped and hunched over. His ears were large, which reminded Marco of Detective Flores. He had bushy white eyebrows and a mass of white hair. He looked as if the wind blew, he'd topple over and snap in two. The man rose from his chair to greet Marco and Oliver.

"Detective Marco, so nice of you to come all this way to see me and Oliver."

Marco wrinkled his nose. "Just Marco, I'm a police consultant, not a detective. This is a beautiful shop you own, sir."

"Thank you. I've worked hard over the years. Luckily, I've always had an eye for antiques. I've been able to acquire some good pieces over the years."

Jules wore a black velvet dinner jacket and black trousers. He had a gold earring in his left ear. He also wore several gold chain bracelets, a gold chain necklace, and gold rings, one with a large square diamond. The cologne emanated from seemingly his every pore.

"It's more than luck. Jules really knows his stuff," Oliver said.

Oliver picked up a spoon from an open display case and examined it, turning it over and putting it closer to his eyes to see the hallmarks. He nodded his approval. "Coin silver, really nice," he said, turning to Jules. "I see you still acquire wonderful pieces."

"That's from the nineteenth century in America, made after the Civil War.

It's a rare piece," Jules said.

Marco nodded his head, impressed. He had no idea.

"You've come to talk about the Runya. I acquired that painting nearly eighty years ago." He paused, as if measuring how much of the story to reveal. He picked up a pen with a shaky left hand filled with age spots and tapped it on the glass table. "Buying that painting, I must say it wasn't the most ethical thing I've ever done, but I couldn't resist it," Jules said.

"How did you acquire it?" Marco asked.

The old man scrunched his eyes. Fine lines formed tiny webs in each corner. He stared intently at Marco. "Are you of gypsy descent?" he asked.

Marco grimaced, surprised at the man's upfrontness. He was routinely asked that question at home in Spain. He didn't expect this man from London to ask his origin. "No, Señor, I'm half Spanish and half Moroccan. I was born in Spain."

"Ah, I see. I didn't mean to offend you. Some of the most beautiful people I've met are gypsies and Moroccans," he said.

Marco squirmed.

"Ah, please, forgive an old man. I can be blunt at times. It's just that I'm curious about people, always have been."

"He's always been that way with me, too," Oliver said. "Jules, you were saying about the painting."

"Ah, an art dealer I knew to be unscrupulous offered it to me many years ago. Paintings like that don't come up too often. I decided on a whim to buy it, even though I knew it couldn't have been obtained legally. Now that I'm going to meet my maker, I decided to return the Runya to Spain. Coincidentally, a new museum was opening in Vivirrambla that featured that kind of art. I found out that Oliver was on the Board of Directors. So, I called him and offered to sell the painting, if we could go through an auction house. I didn't want to sell it directly to the museum in case there were questions."

"He called me out of the blue. I couldn't believe it. Like he said, lost paintings by famous artists are rare," Oliver said.

"I'm sorry I won't see it when it's hung in the museum. I assume it will be after all that murder stuff is over. Oliver told me about Addison Mason. So Sad. I haven't been to Vivirrambla for quite some time. Too many bad memories," Jules said.

Both Marco and Oliver stared at him.

"Forgive me for going on tangents, I'm an old man. I can't remember what I was doing a moment ago, but the past haunts me like the Ghost of Christmas Past," Jules said, laughing.

"You didn't know how the person who sold the Runya to you acquired it, is that right?" Marco asked.

Jules shook his head, "No, I and I didn't ask." A shock of white hair fell forward towards his face. "The painting added prestige to my collection. I wanted to make a success of my antique business. It's no big deal now, but being gay during that time, I could only gain acceptance in a few places, and the art world was one of those places. So, I gravitated to arts and antiques. I don't regret my choice, though I have other regrets."

Jules looked over at Oliver. "Things have changed now of course. Back then, during the war years, it was dangerous to be the type of man that I was. I felt angry at society for not accepting me."

Oliver nodded his head in understanding.

"Is that why you didn't you report the stolen painting to the police?" Marco asked.

Jules shrugged his shoulders. "I was giving the middle finger to societal rules. I kept the painting here in England hanging in my house for years." Jules said.

"You should see Jules's home. It's filled with wonderful art and antiquities. I salivate every time I go over. He has so much silver, I don't believe he even knows what he has," Oliver said.

"I'm liquidating everything before I go. I need to clean house, physically and spiritually. Perhaps it's a metaphor for cleansing my soul. I don't have any children, and most of my family is dead. I don't have anyone to leave the things I've collected. I have a brother who lives in America, but we don't speak. He's never been interested in antiques. He called it 'my gay thing.' He has children, but I barely have a relationship with my niece and nephew. I haven't seen any of them for over thirty years."

"Jules has been generous in offering his things. He's even given me some rare books," Oliver said.

"I wanted them to go where they'd be appreciated." Jules looked over at Marco. "Listen, I just had a thought. Why don't you both come over for dinner this evening? I've invited a few friends. I'm sure they'll enjoy meeting you. My friends are quite entertaining."

Marco noted a twinkle in Jules's crinkled eyes as he talked about his friends."

"Thank you, what a kind invitation. I look forward to it. I understand Amy Bloom used to work for you," Marco said.

"Yes, Amy was a great assistant. She's like a daughter to me. She got a fantastic opportunity to work in that new museum, something she'd always wanted. I hated to see her go, but I had to let her. We still keep in touch. She stays in my place sometimes when she's back in the UK. I intend to give her some of my jewelry and several silver pieces once I'm gone," Jules said.

"Have you spoken to her recently?" Marco asked.

Jules began to cough, a deep-sounding cough that caused his body to jerk. "Forgive me. I suppose Oliver told you I'm sick."

"Yes, he mentioned it. I'm sorry you aren't well," Marco said.

Jules waved it off with his hand.

"It's ok. Can't live forever can you? I haven't seen Amy for several months. I take it she's busy, especially after the tragic death of that museum owner. I hope Amy won't be out of a job," Jules said.

"We're still working all that out," Oliver said. "Marco, we'd better get going. I have to make a few calls before we go to dinner."

"Okay. Jules, thank you for taking the time to speak to me. I'm looking forward to seeing your home later." Marco said.

"It'll be great to have some young people around. If you have a few minutes. Look around the shop and see if there's anything you like. I'll give you a deal," Jules said.

Oliver looked at his watch. "I suppose we could stay for a few more minutes."

Marco perused the jewelry while Jules and Oliver continued to talk. He paused at a velvet-lined tray of jewelry. He selected a pair of antique white-gold earrings with a sapphire in the middle for Belen.

"Those earrings once belonged to a Russian ballerina," Jules's assistant said.

Belen would appreciate their history as much as their beauty. Jules's assistant wrapped them in white tissue and a small velvet pouch and then in a decorative box. Marco tucked it in his jacket.

Chapter Twenty-Six

Marco returned to his hotel and changed into black trousers and a white shirt. He dabbed on a bit of Lowe Aqua for men. The hotel concierge secured him an Uber, which whisked him off to the address Oliver had given him for Jules's home. He experienced real London as the rain started to fall as he got into the cab. The driver stopped in front of a red brick duplex with a large bay window. Marco opened the black golf umbrella he'd purchased at the hotel and stepped out into the rain. A fog had rolled in, making visibility difficult.

When Jules opened the door his cologne scent arrived even before he did. He wore a red velvet silk flowing robe over his neon blue pants. His white hair had been combed and slicked back on his head. His ears were already beginning to turn red from too much drink. "Come in, come in out of the rain," he said, waving Marco into his house.

Marco shook his umbrella and dropped it in the majolica umbrella stand next to the door, while Jules took his coat. He walked into the massive living room with soaring ceilings and a low-hanging chandelier over top of a plush multicolored sofa. Fine art filled every inch of the walls with large abstracts positioned next to old paintings, which were later identified as seventeenth-century Flemish.

Other guests stood around sipping champagne from flutes. Jules introduced his guests to Marco. First, he met an older couple from England, whom Jules said he'd known for over forty years. The woman had dyed blond hair done up in a beehive. Her skin was lined, but her eyes danced and twinkled. Her husband was stooped, but it was apparent that he'd been a tall man. He'd dyed his hair jet black, which was a mismatch to his face, which looked shriveled and freckled. They both smiled and extended their hands to Marco.

"What a handsome young man," the woman said.

"Yes, he reminds me of someone," Jules said with a glint in his eye.

Marco blushed.

"These are my friends Naomi and Charles Johnson. Naomi's American, and Charles is from South London," Jules said, whooshing Marco over to another couple.

"Mucha gusto," Marco said to the couple.

A young man with dark hair down to his shoulders stood alone in the corner, looking at his phone. "This is Andrew. He's an art student and a friend of mine," Jules said, leading Marco over to the man.

The young man shook Marco's hand. "Pleased to meet you. Can you believe it? I met Jules over ten years ago, when I walked into his shop one day searching for a present. We started talking, and we've been friends ever since."

Jules turned to his right to another guest standing beside him. "This is Ian. He's another great friend and smart. He's finishing his first term at Oxford."

Marco extended his hand to the pasty-faced young man. "That's wonderful."

Ian brushed a section of hair behind his head. "I hope I can have a career nearly as successful as Jules."

"You will, of course."

Jules escorted Marco over to meet other guests that had arrived. He introduced him to a portly middle-aged woman named Maureen with pink hair, who wore a bright colored caftan, dangling silver earrings, and a turquoise squash blossom necklace. Another flamboyant elderly gentleman, named James, wore a red checkered jacket. James and Jules exchanged knowing looks. From time to time, Jules sidled over to him and whispered in his ear, at which point James giggled like a schoolgirl.

Left on his own as Jules went off to talk to his guests, Marco stood near the fireplace. He spotted Oliver Hall, wearing a light blue shirt with a bow tie and creased black pants, standing with Josh near a wall."

Marco sidled over to them.

"So glad you made it, Marco. Jules really piled on the cologne, huh," Oliver said in a low voice, laughing.

"It's Hugo Boss," Josh said. "I'm afraid 'the Boss,' not Springsteen, enters the room before he does."

All three of them laughed.

They each reached for a drink from the tray of a passing waiter. Oliver and Josh each took a glass of champagne. Marco grabbed a beer and thanked the waiter.

Jules made his way over to the trio. "I hope you're enjoying yourselves."

"Yes, of course. It's a great party. When's the last time you were in Vivirrambla?" Marco asked, spotting an Islamic ceramic piece on a table in the corner.

Jules took a swig of champagne. "Oh, it's been many years. I used to fly over there often. I haven't been in some time, though."

Before they could engage further, a voice announced dinner. All the guests meandered into the dining room, where an elaborate tablecloth covered the table. Each of the dinner guests had personalized place cards with bird designs on one side that instructed them where to sit. Waterford crystal glasses had been filled with water. Place settings of fine silver rested on designer napkins.

Oliver noticed one of the silver settings. He turned to Josh. "Nice. Eighteenth-century English," he said.

Other fine pieces of silver had been laid out. Oliver's face lit up as he examined each piece.

In the center of the table were large vases containing flowers. This ensured that those at the table couldn't see or talk to the person across from them. Jules sat at the head of the table, making a grand gesture with his robe before sitting down. A fire flickered and crackled behind Marco, emanating from a fireplace surrounded by green marble.

As soon as they were seated, a waiter entered with bowls of soup. The potato leek bouillabaisse was warm and soothing on the cold evening. The main course was duck, garnished with fresh herbs and an apple. The bird's brown skin glistened presented on a silver tray. Fluffy rice and green beans, accompanied as side dishes. Each course was served to be accompanied by a piece of fine sterling .

"He does have a lot of silver," Marco said to Oliver, who was seated next to him.

"You haven't seen anything yet. He has so much, he'd never know if anything went missing," Josh said.

The dinner conversation turned to travel. As the fireplace crackled, guests shared stories of humorous adventures. Marco had to admit the group, though odd, was entertaining and interesting. Oliver and Josh recounted trips to Italy and nights on the gondola. More wine meant greater laughter and loosened tongues. Jules regaled stories of trips to Paris, Amsterdam, and America, visiting famous museums, and meeting musicians like Jimi Hendrix in the sixties. He told how he picked up various pieces from his travels and pointed out some that were in the dining room: antique vases, silver, and paintings on the wall.

"I must say, my favorite though was Spain and Vivirrambla." He pointed to Marco. "Our new friend here reminds me of someone I knew there," Jules said.

"I remember that Arabesque Islamic painting you used to have. What happened to it? What was it called? Something about justice, I think. Did you move it? Where did you get it? I'd never seen a painting like it before," The American, Naomi said.

Jules coughed, a wretched-sounding cough that rattled, nearly choking on his food. His face turned the color of the ash in the fireplace. Everyone rushed to his aid.

Chapter Twenty-Seven

Marco flew back to Spain early the next morning and headed straight to work.

"Did I miss anything?" he asked Eva when he arrived at his office.

"Not much. You had another message from that Farah Zine woman," Eva said.

He could feel Eva's disapproving eye following him. He went into his office and phoned Farah. "Como estas? Any updates on the stalker? Has anything else happened?" he asked.

"Not so far. I still get that creepy feeling that someone's watching me, but I haven't seen anything for the last few days. I'm calling you about something else. I thought about calling Detective Flores, but somehow I relate more to you."

Marco smiled, though she couldn't see him on the phone. "I'm glad you feel you can talk to me."

"I had a call the other day from Morocco. An old friend of my parents' whom I haven't seen in years. My friend said he and his wife had been following my career, which was sweet. Anyway, he said he'd been reading about the museum opening since I became a member of the board. He'd heard about Addison's death."

"What's your friend's name?" Marco asked, grabbing his pen to take notes.

"Emir Mohamed. He and his wife, Azela, were best friends with my parents when I was a child. They saw me as one of their own. I hadn't seen them since they came to my wedding, and I moved to Vivirrambla."

"What did Señor Mohamed want?" Marco asked.

"He called about the Runya painting, *The Gates of Justice*. The one Addison had intended to unveil the night he was killed."

"Yes, what about it," Marco asked.

"As you may know, the painting had been lost since the Spanish Civil War."

"Yes, I'd heard that, fascinating story," Marco said.

"Well, Emir says the painting was stolen from his family in Morocco in 1937. They never caught the thief. They suspected a former servant of Emir's family, but they never had proof and the guy disappeared. Emir said they never thought the painting would resurface. They'd were shocked to see it turn up in Spain at an art museum opening."

Marco thought about his discussion with Jules, and how Jules had said he'd gotten the painting by dubious means. "That's really interesting, especially in light of what I heard this weekend," Marco said.

He relayed his visit to London. That Jules had purchased a painting from a scrupulous seller. He told Farah that Jules had almost passed out at dinner when asked where he got the painting.

"Wow, I didn't know any of that. It has to be the same painting. Emir says he wants me to see what I can do to get the painting back to them. I know the Board would object, as that painting's the star piece of the museum. I told you my husband was building an immersive interactive exhibit of the artist, Runya. It'd be a shame to have to give it back at this stage," Farah said.

"Yes, I recall. I believe he's also working on filing a patent for the 3D software," Marco said.

"Yes, that's right, Bernard and Addison had been working closely on it. Emir did say his family would be willing to discuss the matter with the Board, as they are getting old and they don't want a big court battle," Farah said.

"Yeah, something like this could drag on for years in court," Marco said.

"The Board's going to look bad if this gets out, especially if there's a dispute as to the ownership of the painting, right after Addison's death. That could cause many of our investors to pull out. Some are already questioning their investment in the museum, after the murder, from what I've heard. That could be it for them. The museum would have to close."

"That would be a real shame. It's a beautiful museum. How do we know your friend's telling the truth?" Marco asked.

"I know them. They're honest people. The family's always had a lot of money. They've had close connections to monarchy for ages. Emir says that the painting had been commissioned by Boadil, the last ruling Caliphate before La Reconquista, and given to his family directly by the king. It'd been passed down to each generation until it was stolen in 1937. They claim they can prove its provenance. I believe them. I remember seeing a painting in their house when I was a child, and then hearing that it had been stolen," Farah said.

Jaddah had told Marco the history of Boabdil. She had taken him and his cousin, Karim, on trips to museums and heritage sites. "I want you boys to be proud your history," Jaddah had said to them. She'd instilled an appreciation of their heritage in them.

King Boabdil had a vibrant court in the Alhambra palace. All types of artisans, as well as Arabian nights and dancers, surrounded him. Like the Medici family during the Renaissance, preferred artists lived and worked in the ruler's court. Runya lived and painted in Granada in the Alhambra for Boabdil.

Marco, lost in thought, realized Farah was still speaking. She'd asked him a question, which he had to ask her to repeat.

"Would you be willing to go to Morocco with me to meet with Emir and his wife? I'm hoping we can reach some sort of agreement with them. The museum has a duty to verify Emir's claim that the painting belonged to them before the war. That's why I'd like to have someone affiliated with the police to tag along," Farah said.

"Sure, that makes good sense. I'm due to visit my grandmother anyway. I'm happy to go to Morocco to talk to Emir. I'll also speak to my cousin, Karim, who works for the police in Morocco, to see if he can find out any information."

"That would be great. Like I said, they were friends of my parents, but I haven't seen them for some time. So, a background investigation before we meet is a good idea. When can you go to Tangier? I'll inform the family that we're coming and set up a meeting with them," Farah said.

"Let's give Karim a little time to investigate. Would a week from now be convenient for you?" Marco asked.

"That's perfect. Bernard will be out of town on a business trip then," Farah said.

"Great, shoot me an email with all the information you have about Emir and his wife, and I'll get in touch with Karim right away," Marco said.

Once he disconnected from Farah, Marco Face Timed Karim, who was working out lifting weights.

"Assylam alakum, keeping in shape, I see. Looks like I'll be coming to see Jaddah soon," Marco said.

Karim put down the weight he'd been lifting. He wore a ripped black tee-shirt, which showed off his halal tattoo. "That's great news. By the way, that model you texted me about, Farah Zine. I couldn't find anything on her. Looks like she's lived a clean life. She's married and has no children. You weren't kidding. She's been in a lot of articles and on the cover of some magazines. Quite a beauty, huh?" Karim said.

"Marco laughed. "She is. I have another project for you."

Marco explained what had transpired with the painting and that he needed Karim to look into Emir and Azela Mohamed, who claimed to be the rightful owners of the Runya work. He needed to get some background information before he and Farah Zine set up a meeting with Emir.

"Sure, I'd be happy to investigate it. I can't believe they owned that Runya painting. Jaddah's going to be overjoyed to see you and hear about the painting," Karim said.

Chapter Twenty-Eight

Murder was like a chess game. Each piece moves forward and back, hoping to block the path of the opponent, until someone reaches checkmate and hopefully, the perpetrator is identified. Marco asked Eva to do some research on Runya and his work, as well as the history of the stolen painting. Eva was an excellent researcher. Her meticulous attention to detail had been crucial to solving cases in the past. He trusted her instincts. If there was more to unearth, she'd find it.

"I'll get right on it, jefe," she'd said.

* * *

Karim had an update a few days later when he called Marco. "Hey, I've finished researching that couple you wanted me to look into. The family's legit. They are an old established Moroccan family with a history with the royals."

Karim said that one key piece of evidence he'd found was a feature story in an old local paper from the nineteen fifties about a family trying to track down the stolen Ruyna painting. The article explained how it'd been stolen from the family after several generations. Emir and Azela's picture appeared in the article.

Karim agreed to broker a meeting with the family. Marco asked him to set up something for next week. Travelling to Morocco in search of lost art, art that he knew meant so much to Jaddah, galvanized him. He confirmed his itinerary then phoned his grandmother. He could hear her joy over the phone. She seemed intrigued by the story of the Runya painting.

"Allah has command over all things precious; nothing can disappear forever from him," she said, her voice carrying a knowing lilt. "Sooner or later, they return like bees to the honeycomb."

Marco pinged Detective Flores to inform him of what had transpired.

"You just got back from London. You say you found out that the painting had been acquired by dubious means, but is that connected to Addison's death? The only way I can get the chief to requisition your travel is if you can show some kind of causal link to our murder investigations. The Chief's been harping on me about the budget shortfall, lately," Flores said.

"If Addison's death is related to the painting, it's probably got something to do with the fact that the Runya was stolen. I may get some answers from the original owners who can tell us more about the painting," Marco said.

"Okay. I'll see if the Chief approves it. We haven't ruled out any of the Board members, which means Farah is a potential suspect. You need to be careful what you say to her. Meanwhile, let's not say anything to the rest of the Board. If one of them is guilty, we don't want them hiding evidence," Flores said.

"I really don't think Farah had anything to do with Addison's death. Someone's been following her, as you know. I'll instruct her not to mention our trip to anyone," Marco said.

Once he'd gotten Flores's approval, Marco let Farah know that their trip to Morocco had been arranged. He planned to leave a couple of days earlier to visit his grandmother. They agreed to meet at the Fairmont Tazi Plaza hotel to discuss strategy before the meeting with Emir.

"That's a charming hotel. I'll see you there," Farah said.

Chapter Twenty-Nine

Marco felt happy to be leaving his empty house again. He stopped off at Alvarez's to let him know he'd be gone for a few days. He also wanted coffee before heading to the ferry. Alvarez seemed in a lighter mood. He said his daughter was doing better and the baby was out of danger.

"That's great news," Marco said.

"My wife and I are so relieved," Alvarez said, his hand on the ubiquitous cleaning rag thrown over his shoulder.

Marco told him how happy he was for him and that he couldn't wait for the baby to be born.

"Have a safe trip and don't get yourself into any trouble," Alvarez said, winking.

* * *

Marco arrived in Algeciras port just in time for the ferry to Tangier. He'd have two whole days to spend with Jaddah and the family before meeting Farah. He embarked and took a seat near the front of the boat. As the ferry left the shore, Marco walked back to the eating area and ordered a sandwich. He took out his iPad and scrolled for some entertainment. He landed on *Scarface*, starring Al Pacino, a movie Belen always objected to him watching. It was a guy thing. None of his friends' significant others let them watch it either. Marco reclined his seat back and settled in to watch the movie. A tall, lanky white-blond figure, wearing plaid pants and a lime green shirt, materialized over him like a phantasm. Marco looked up. Sven, the owner of the modern art museum in Puerto Bella, grinned at him.

"Hello, fancy meeting you on the ferry? Are you on your way to Tangier?" Sven asked.

Marco furrowed his brow and smiled back at him. "Yeah, I'm on my way to see some family," Marco said.

"Ah, cool. I've got a business meeting for the museum," Sven said.

Marco wondered what kind of business Sven could be doing. His museum was the worst Marco had ever seen, with its strange portraits and weird abstract art. Perhaps he'd found some more strange pictures to hang.

Sven verified his supposition. "I've got some people interested in donating some pieces to us."

"I thought I read that you opposed Addison's Museum featuring Moroccan art?" Marco asked.

"Oh, you know how the media exaggerates. I simply expressed concern that people would be so entranced by Addison's art that they'd stop looking at European art. I wanted to make sure museums like mine weren't forgotten. I'm going to feature a few pieces of Moroccan art by some modern artist I know. I don't want to steal Addison's vibe, but I'm sure we can both feature *some* Arabic art."

"I see. I hope it works out for you." Marco said, anxious to get back to the movie.

Sven nodded. "I do, too; it's no secret I need to attract more visitors. The museum's been a bit empty these days."

Marco lifted his lip in a half-smile. "I'm sure you can turn it around."

"Any word on Addison's killer. Have the police found any suspects?" Sven asked.

"The police are still looking into evidence and following up on every possible lead," Marco said.

"Well, let me know if there's anything I can do. I'm happy to help in any way I can."

"Thank you. I'll pass that along to the police," Marco said.

"Good to see you, amigo," Sven said, sounding overly friendly. He pulled out his pen and a sheet of paper and began writing. "Here's my private number if you need anything. The police can reach me directly."

Once Sven finally left, Marco enjoyed the movie. Before he knew it, the ferry had landed on the docks of Tangier. The ride had been calm, and the boat hadn't swayed. When he stepped off the pier, the weather in Tangier felt just as oppressive as in Vivirrambla. Marco spotted Karim waiting for him, wearing a white shirt and shorts. Marco always marveled at how much they looked alike, even though they had different parents. They'd often been mistaken for brothers as young boys. When Marco jumped into Karim's car, Karim caught him up on what the rest of the family had been doing as they made their way through town, past the medina where peddlers stood offering goods and rugs like the ones Marco had seen in London.

Jaddah's house, made of white brick and surrounded by a patio, was typical of the homes in the area. She stood outside waiting for him. Her lined face shone with glee as Marco emerged from Karim's car. Marco noticed that she'd aged. She seemed to have shrunk in stature. Her once smooth, bronze, velvety skin had developed wrinkles that marked the passage of time. He felt the usual guilt, multiplied, for not spending more time with her as she got older.

When Marco reached the door, she hugged him tightly. Marco could feel the love radiating from her tiny body. They walked into the home arm in arm. The aromas of cumin, cinnamon, and ginger wafted from the kitchen. The familiar smell of spices, the foundation of Moroccan cooking, always brought him back to his roots.

Marco walked into the red tiled kitchen with white cupboards. It looked just the same as it was when he was a child. The familiarity comforted him.

Some of Marco's cousins who'd come over, greeted Marco when he went into the living area where the TV blasted a futbol match.

"Jaddah has prepared a feast for your arrival," one of his cousins said. "Like the prodigal son."

Marco and his cousins shouted at the TV and rooted for Morocco, known as one of Africa's greatest futbol teams, until Marco's grandmother announced that the meal was ready. His cousin hadn't exaggerated. Jaddah had spent all day preparing a meal fit for a Caliphate. He grabbed some of the bread being passed around and dipped it into the bissara. The spiced bean paste was as flavorful as he remembered. Tagines filled with lamb stew, made with saffron and chickpeas, were shared around the table, along with dishes of couscous and spinach with raisins. Jaddah had also made a savory bastille pie.

"It's the best meal you've ever made," Marco gushed.

His grandmother blushed and looked down at the table. Servings of Atay, Chinese green tea made with mint leaves and sugar in decorative handmade glass tumblers, were being passed around. The tea soothed him. After dinner, exhausted, he went to his room ready for a sound sleep.

As night fell, the next evening after a day of activity and another shared meal, Marco announced that he had to leave. He saw his grandmother's face fall. He felt his heart break. He turned down Karim's offer of a ride to his hotel. He decided to take a taxi. Karim had spent two days with him. He needed to get back to his family. He also turned down Jaddah's offer of leftovers to take back with him to Spain.

He finally reached his hotel room in Fairmont Palace. He kicked his shoes off and put his bag down. The plush room had a king-sized bed. The lights hanging above were in an Arabesque shape. A tan settee sat at the end of the bed with a headboard decorated in a geometric design. An Arabesque chandelier with tassels hung over the bed. He wanted to dive into the beckoning bed, but he had an appointment to meet Farah. He'd found out from the front desk that Farah had checked in a few hours earlier. He phoned her room. She said she'd be ready to meet with him in an hour. Marco agreed to go to her suite then.

Marco showered and put on a pair of clean slacks. For reasons he couldn't explain, he splashed on cologne, careful not to overdo it like Jules Moore. He took the elevator to Farah's room. He felt somewhat nervous. Farah opened the door wearing a flowing white pants outfit with bell sleeves and dangling gold earrings. Her thick hair had been set free in a mass of curls. Marco stepped inside her suite. It was more spacious than his, with the same Arabesque design, but with a separate room with a table and chairs. Farah invited Marco to join her in what she called the meeting room.

"Can I offer you some tea?" she asked.

Marco rubbed his stomach. "Oh no, not right now." He recounted the big meal he'd eaten at his grandmother's house. Farah laughed and told him it sounded like her own relatives when they got together.

"I thought you could help me figure out how best to approach Emir and Azela. It's such a delicate subject," Farah said.

"Yeah, if we want them to agree to not pursue ownership of the painting. We need to be careful how we approach them," Marco said.

The two discussed strategy and rehearsed what to say. After a couple of hours, the conversation lulled. They realized there was silence between them.

"Are you sure you don't want that tea?" Farah asked.

"Sure, I'll have a cup. Some mint might be good for my stomach," Marco said, rubbing his tummy area. His mind told him that he should leave and go back to his own room. Yet he didn't move.

Farah returned a few moments later with two glasses of hot tea with mint in ornate glasses ringed in gold, and a small plate of shortbread cookies. She handed a cup to Marco. He noticed her perfume had a rose scent. Their eyes met as she passed the tea.

Marco fidgeted in his chair. "Uh-hum, thanks for the tea. It's delicious."

"You know my husband is a really great guy, but sometimes it bothers me that he's so old. There's thirty years between us. He travels a lot, too," Farah said.

Marco took a sip of tea. "You've been married for a long time, haven't you?"

Farah chuckled. "Ah, I see you've been looking into me, Mr. Investigator. Yes, we've been married for quite a while. Naturally, he's aged during that time. Tell me more about your girlfriend."

Marco told her that they'd been together for several years. He'd dated a Moroccan woman before that, that his family wanted him to marry, but he loved Belen. Belen wanted to get married but have a child and he wasn't ready.

"I'm sure I'll marry her someday. I can't see myself loving anyone else," Marco said.

Farah scooted her chair closer to his. "It sounds as if you're unsure about your relationship, or are you just one of those men who fear commitment?"

Marco was silent for some time. He sat staring into his cup, searching for answers in the tea leaves. "Honestly, it may be a little bit of both," he said.

Her scent made him feel intoxicated, like in that Sting "Desert Rose" song. He looked up into her eyes. She moved closer and kissed him. The tea, forgotten, they explored one another's mouths and tongues for a time. Marco began to feel dizzy. He jerked away from her.

"I think we'd better keep it professional," he said.

"Sorry. You're right." She smiled. "One of the good guys. You don't give that impression at first. I'd pegged you for a bad boy. That girlfriend of yours doesn't know what a good thing she's got," Farah said.

Marco blushed. "I have my moments." He stood up and walked to the door. "Let's get a good night's sleep, so we're fresh for tomorrow."

Marco left her room and headed for the elevator. The smell of her rose perfume lingered. He could feel his heart pounding with regret. He walked down the hallway, lit with more lights in Arabesque design. He thought he saw a shadow behind him. He looked around, but saw no one.

Chapter Thirty

Two unsolved murder investigations had started to wear on Flores. The Chief had threatened him with demotion again. The Chief had unrealistic expectations that cases should be solved in a few days with little expense to the budget. Of course, Flores realized that was the nature of the Chief's job. He answered to the mayor, and city government. Flores had never wanted to be beholden to anyone like that. He'd been satisfied with his middle management position. Some days, though, he didn't know why he just didn't quit and do something else with his life.

Flores hoped Marco's Tangier excursion would lead to some useful information, especially since he'd agreed to pay for the trip from his own budget. He'd been reluctant, as he often didn't like Marco's swashbuckler tactics, but Marco had gotten results on some important cases. Flores walked down the hall to the vending machine and purchased a cup of lukewarm coffee that purported to be a café latte. He'd been out interviewing the staff at Restaurante Sanchez all day, fishing for information that could help to solve Diego's murder. When interviewing the restaurant staff, he looked for nervous glances, rapid blinking, or half-truths. He noted if anyone's hand trembled when mentioning Diego's name. None of the staff displayed obvious signs of guilt. No one seemed to have a motive for killing their boss, Carmela's brother, Diego. To make matters worse, forensics hadn't found any fingerprints on the knife or any useful DNA.

He'd fared no better on Addison Mason's case. Both investigations had stalled. He carried his cold coffee back to his office and sat at his desk and stared at his computer screen. He pondered whether he'd missed something.

Perhaps, a thread running through both murders would soon unravel the truth.

One of the guys from forensics, Jose Garcia, knocked at his door. "I've got those results you're waiting for," he said.

Flores gestured for Garcia to enter. "Great, come on in. I hope you have some good news for me."

Garcia had worked at the station for over fifteen years, examining forensic evidence. His colleagues respected him and said he was the best at evidence interpretation.

"That velvet pouch you gave me to look at; it's used for carrying silver or small jewelry."

"Silver, what kind of silver?" Flores asked.

"Silver as in hollowware. The rag had traces of silver polish. The pouch could hold small items like flatware or silver creamers and sugars, that kind of thing," Garcia said.

"I see," Flores said. Seems innocuous enough. I wonder why Nicholas would need to dispose of something like that in a secretive manner." In Flores's experience, when someone went out of their way to hide something, they had a reason.

Garcia shrugged his shoulders. "A pouch like that would be easy for transport," he said, handing Flores his report along with items in a plastic bag, marked police evidence.

"You're right. Gracias, Jose, good work," Flores said.

Flores picked up the items and studied them. He flipped through Garcia's report. Was Nicholas Thompson guilty of murder? What could the connection to silver be?

When Flores explained the evidence to the prosecutor. The prosecutor agreed it seemed suspicious enough to subpoena Amy and Nicholas's electronic bank records as well as their cell phone records. A few days later, when he received the information, Flores took the phone and bank records upstairs to the cyber unit, a new unit in the department that dissected computers, cryptology, and communications information from devices such as phones, laptops, and iPads. The Cyber Unit or CU as they called it, told

Flores they'd put his request at the top of the list. They'd have something for him soon.

Flores decided to go out to lunch. He normally ate at his desk, tuna con acieta y tomato sandwiches his wife made for him each morning. He'd leave that in the fridge for the next day. He deserved a nice lunch after the day he'd had. He walked over to the restaurant nearest to the station, La Rincon, and ordered *polo con fritas*, chicken and fries, and a coffee. The meal felt decadent compared to his usual fare. As he sipped a café con leche, he heard the table next to him discussing the museum murder.

"I wonder who killed that museum guy?" one of them said.

"I heard they don't have any suspects. The police don't seem to know what they're doing from what I hear."

"Then that other guy, Carmela Sanchez's brother, one of the museum's trustees, got murdered at Sanchez's restaurant. They had to be related," the other diner said.

As Flores wore plain clothes as a detective, the diners had no way of knowing they'd been discussing his cases. Though criticism came with the job, and Flores had become used to it, he felt hurt by their comments. Marco thought the murders were related. Now, these people who weren't even working on the cases came to the same conclusion. He gulped down his espresso and walked back to the precinct. He went back to his desk and looked through his notes and the other evidence he'd gathered so far. He pledged to untangle the web of any connection.

CU buzzed him a few days later. They'd found information he may be interested in knowing.

Flores rushed upstairs. "Thanks for making this a priority."

"You happened to catch us when not much is going on," Garcia said.

Garcia opened a folder with several documents inside. "I reviewed the digital and computer records we pulled up in the search to see what kind of digital footprint they made. Whether the two target individuals, Nicholas Thompson, and Amy Bloom, showed signs of a digital relationship, meaning did they frequently communicate with one another."

"What did you find out?" Flores asked.

"Let me show you," Garcia said, gesturing Flores over to his desk.

Flores sat in a chair next to Garcia's desk and looked at his computer as he navigated through online folders. "I checked computer records, including cryptology, encrypted information such as phone calls on WhatsApp or Viber, and social media presence, looking for activity. I mapped every digital connection they had. I checked for shared clouds and overlapping logins, anything that could suggest collaboration. Using the records from Cellbrite, I found they'd made over six hundred calls and texts to one another in just the last month. I printed out the messages for you," he said.

Garcia clicked open a spreadsheet. "A few interesting spikes showed up from the last ten days: shared calendar events, location pings late at night, and some Venmo activity in varying amounts."

Flores scooted his chair closer and peered at the screen. "Oh really,"

"I'll print it out for you so you can look at the activity chronologically."

"Were you able to retrieve any messages from WhatsApp?" Flores asked.

Flores knew that criminals used WhatsApp or Viber as it was encrypted technology, difficult for the police to trace.

"We could only capture a couple of messages. We got all the messages from the regular cell towers, though. I tracked down a joint computer IP address created by Thompson a couple of months ago. It looks like a front for some kind of commodities exchange for silver. Nicholas Thompson and Amy Bloom are identified as sellers on all platforms. As far as social media is concerned, they're on Facebook, although they don't seem to have a lot of interaction on the platform. I found more interaction on Instagram and TikTok, where they set up seller sites under the pseudonym *Silverbloom*.

I've made copies of the online exchange and all the other information we found." He pointed to the folder he'd handed Flores. "It's all in there."

"Thanks so much, Jose. This is really helpful."

Flores took the information back to his office. He spent the rest of the afternoon going through messages and social media. He called his wife to let her know he wouldn't be home for dinner. At nine o'clock in the evening, as dusk fell, Flores was still reviewing documents. They showed incriminating information against the two, as well as a connection. Cell calls exposed Nicholas's and Amy's romantic relationship. Amy left numerous love messages to Thompson, a married man. He responded the same to her. One set of text messages alluded to large sums of money they expected to make.

To Nicholas from Amy: I finished setting everything up for Silverbloom. Thanks to Addison, I'm pretty good at setting up websites. Smile emoji.

To Amy from Nicholas: Ha ha ha, that job was good for something. Make sure the IP address can't be traced.

To Nicholas from Amy: Don't worry, love, everything's taken care of. I've made a list of possible clients. I'll tell them the sales are private and exclusive, that's why we can't give the email address out.

To Amy from Nicholas: Great. If we can get it in the hands of the right people, we should be able to unload it all in no time. Have you decided where we should go?

To Nicholas from Amy: Smile. I've been looking at Bermuda. There are a lot of English there, and we should be able to get there pretty easily.

To Amy from Nicholas: What about your law practice?

To Nicholas from Amy: I can do my business online from Bermuda. I don't have to shut down my practice. It's all working. We're going to make it.

From Amy to Nicholas: I'm so excited. I can't wait. I love you.

From Nicholas to Amy: I love you too, it won't be long, baby. We should make enough from the silver in no time.

The rest of the messages contained several hearts and love emojis.

Flores had to give them points for originality. He'd never pursued criminals with a bogus business selling silver.

Despite C U's findings, Flores still worried he didn't have enough to give to the prosecutor. Nicholas, being a shrewd lawyer, knew how to manipulate the legal system. It wasn't illegal to have an affair, nor was an online exchange, per se, illegal. He needed to show that they'd sold stolen silver, and he needed to show a nexus between the stolen silver and Addison's murder.

Perhaps Addison had found out what they were doing and threatened to go to police. Flores stared at the whiteboard he'd developed, with the lines drawn between motive and possible suspects. He pondered how he could make the connections.

As night fell, Flores sat in his office with only a table lamp and the light from his computer. He stared out his window at the clear, dark sky. Flores rested his hand on his chin. The sound of cars going up and down the street gave him an idea. He'd place trackers on Amy's and Nicholas's cars. Maybe they'd incriminate themselves in real time. He knew it'd be expensive. He'd likely get reamed out for going over budget. The Chief couldn't have it both ways; if he wanted the cases solved, he'd have to spend money. Flores wrote up the necessary paperwork and went home.

One of his officers reported to him the next day that listening devices had successfully been installed under each of their vehicles. Video cameras had been attached for live feed. It'd all been connected to a surveillance van.

Chapter Thirty-One

arco tossed and turned all night. He wasn't used to a hard bed. More than that, he felt guilty about what had almost happened—well, actually did happen with Farah Zine. He rose with the sunrise, showered, and shaved. While he waited for room service to bring tea and breakfast, he dressed in a white Oxford shirt and navy trousers. He decided to use the extra time to go over what he and Farah had discussed before he'd become enraptured in her kiss.

When it was time, he went to the lobby, where he found Farah talking to someone at the desk. She spotted him and waved. She seemed perky and chipper. The opposite of how he felt.

"Ah, Marco, are you ready to go?" she asked.

Farah and Marco headed out of the lobby. Farah said she'd drive as she'd just verified the address and information with the front desk. The day was warm, and the cloudless sky was crystal blue. Farah wore a light blue maxi dress. She looked breezy and carefree. The air conditioner in her sports car worked well. Marco soon felt cool despite the Tangier heat, as they rode past white houses with iron balconies. The navigator led them to a neighborhood of villas, such as those where the painter, Matisse, once lived.

Farah parked in the driveway of the house indicated. She and Marco walked to the door and knocked. A male servant answered.

"We're expected," Farah said.

The man stood tall and erect. He wore a serious expression, as if he dared anyone to challenge him about anything. "Just a moment, please," he said.

Marco and Farah looked at one another. The man escorted them through a hallway with checkered black and white floors and large white columns. He led them to a sitting room with a green marble fireplace and chairs of chintz in a flower design. A chandelier hung from the ceiling over the sofa. The stiff man gestured for them to sit.

A brown-skinned man with white wavy hair entered the room, followed by an older gray-haired woman wearing a tan dress. Farah and Marco rose from their seats.

The man spoke first. "Assalamu alaikum. I'm Emir Mohamed," he said to Marco. He looked over to Farah and bowed. "Good to see you, Farah. It's been a long time," he said, placing his right hand over his heart.

"Wa-Alaikum-Salaam," Farah responded.

Marco bowed and introduced himself in Arabic. "I'm Marco, a police consultant with the Malaga Police. Señora Zine has asked me to accompany her to discuss the painting."

Grace exuded from every pore of Emir's brown skin. "Thank you for taking the time to come here to see us. Farah, we haven't seen you for so long. You look wonderful. Life in Spain must be good for you," Emir said. "We've been fortunate enough to keep up with your career from your mother."

"You're married, I understand," Emir's wife, Azela, said.

Emir and his wife had the appearance of one of those couples who'd been together so long that they shared the same essence.

Farah shifted in her chair. "Yes, I've been married to my husband, Bernard, for several years. He's away on business and couldn't join us for this trip."

"I see. I hope we can meet him one day soon," Emir said.

Then he addressed Marco. "Ah, and you, young man, you're from Tangier?"

Marco sat up straight. "I'm from Vivirrambla, but my mother's from Tangier and much of my family's here."

"I see, quite a cultural mix," the man said, smiling.

"We appreciate your willingness to talk to us about the painting. As you know, the museum's had quite a shock with the death of our founder," Farah said.

Emir and Azela took seats next to one another on silk chairs across from the sofa. A tall green candle stood on the table beside them. Farah and Marco also sat down across from them.

"Yes, I've been reading about it. I was surprised to learn that our family's lost painting would be the main exhibition at a museum opening." Emir said.

"I've read all the documentation you sent us. It's a remarkable story," Marco said.

The stiff servant returned with a gold tray containing mint tea in glass tumblers decorated with Arabesque shapes and outlined in gold leaf. Small white cookies on little plates also sat on the tray. The room took on the fragrance of mint.

Emir turned to Marco. "It's remarkable indeed. I'd heard about that painting since I was a child. My family was immensely proud of its connection to the last ruler of Spain from our people."

"How did your family acquire the painting?" Marco asked.

Emir arched his back. "The Mohameds have always been in service to the royal family. My ancestor served his majesty, Boabdil, as a negotiator emissary between Boabdil and other kings of Africa. Family lore has it that my ancestor prevented a war with our neighbor. He reportedly saved Boabdil's life when he uncovered a plot by the neighboring country to assassinate him. As a thank you, the Caliphate commissioned the painting, *The Gates of Justice*, for my foregoer as a thank you, and to express the king's openness to our neighbors. At the fall of Grenada, my forefather took the painting with him when he fled for his life. It'd been in our family ever since the fifteenth century until it was stolen."

Emir's wife moved closer to him and patted her husband's hand. Emir's eyes grew moist. He took a sip of tea. No one had moved since he spoke.

"The painting had been passed down to your family all of that time?" Marco asked.

Emir nodded. "From generation to generation. It went to the eldest male, up till 1937 right before the war. Then one day, the painting just disappeared."

"Amazing, where was the painting when it was stolen?" Marco asked.

Farah Zine sat up in her chair and perked up her ears.

"As I said, it'd been passed down to the eldest son; indeed that was to my father, and then it was intended to come to me."

Emir pointed to a section of the wall which held a large modern abstract painting. "The Runya painting hung here on this wall. I was a baby when it was stolen. I never got to see it in person."

"How could the painting have been stolen from your house?" Marco asked.

"According to my father, one spring day, the family had gone on an outing to an Amazigh folk music concert. Spain was on the verge of a civil war, and the rest of Europe feared a conflagration. The world was in turmoil. People clamored for entertainment as an escape. My family returned home that night to find a hole in the wall, where the painting had been, as if someone had just ripped it off the wall. A few hours later, we found out that one of the servants had disappeared."

"Wow, the servant was able to just run off with a huge painting?" Farah Zine asked.

Marco heard the vibration of his phone in his pants pocket. He pulled it out to see who'd called. Belen had left him a text message to call her. He put the phone back. He'd call her later.

"We believe he had help. He found a time when none of the other servants would be around, and that servant and his accomplice, no one knows how many there were, took the painting and simply disappeared off the grounds. My parents returned home too late," Emir said. "He could have been anywhere."

"Did they figure out who it was right away?" Marco asked.

Emir shook his head yes. "His name's Abdul. The police tried everything, but Abdul was long gone. We believe he escaped to Spain. As Spain was on the brink of war, they had little time to worry about a lost Moroccan painting. Over the years, we've heard rumors about its whereabouts." Emir chuckled. "We've even heard some ridiculous stories like it's hung in Elvis's mansion in the US. Until we discovered it was going to the new museum, nothing panned out."

"We once saw another Runya for sale, and we got all excited, but it was one of his earlier works, and much less valuable and without the same meaning as *The Gates of Justice*. That painting was done especially for Emir's family," Azela said.

Emir nodded. He looked at Azela as a husband looks at his wife of many years, like their hearts beat in symbiotic rhythm. "I think one of the reasons my father died at such a young age, he was only forty, was his heartbreak in losing that precious painting, which had been entrusted to him. I don't think he could live with the guilt of having lost it. Even though it wasn't his fault."

"Times were much simpler then. No one dreamed of locking their houses or securing such valuables as paintings. Everyone assumed that they'd be safe," Azela said.

"Do you have any idea how much the painting's worth?" Marco asked.

Emir's voice cracked. "We have only vague estimates. It's valuable due to its rarity. Over four million Euros at least."

"Wow, four million euros," Marco said.

Emir shook his head, yes.

Azela picked up the teapot on the gold tray. "Would anyone like more tea?"

Both Marco and Farah held up their glasses for more of the refreshing golden tan liquid. "Several years ago, it had an appraised value of five hundred thousand dollars, because of its rarity. The equivalent today would be four million Euros," Azela said.

Emir shook his head. "Here we are, after all this time, the painting happens to surface at a museum opening."

"It's unbelievable," Azela said.

"The Runya was to be the centerpiece of the museum opening. I understand that it belongs to your family but considering the shock of Addison's death. Addison was a good friend of mine. We worry that returning the painting under these circumstances or even letting the press find out that it had been stolen would close the museum before it's even open," Farah said.

"Yes, I see your dilemma, but you understand I have a duty to return my family's painting for the next generation. I'm almost ninety years old. I would like to see it in my lifetime. I have a son of my own, and he should inherit the painting and know the greatness of his heritage."

Marco understood Emir's point. He himself always felt conflicted. La Reconquista was considered a great European achievement to Spaniards like his father. For Moroccans, like his mom, it represented loss and defeat of an ancient rule.

"Señor Mohamed, a man's been murdered at the museum. We don't know if the painting had anything to do with it. The police are still investigating. If the painting is gone, it may hamper our investigation," Marco said.

Farah sat forward in her chair. "Perhaps there's something we can work out, at least until the murder is solved. None of the other trustees knows about your ownership claim. We wanted to speak to you first."

The room remained quiet for a time. The tick-tock of a clock in a white case over the mantel was the only sound in the room, except for the periodic clink of teacups.

After a time, Emir cleared his throat. "Okay, I'll give it some thought. In the meantime, I will let the painting stay with the museum for six months. That should give us all time to figure out a solution."

"What if Addison's murder isn't solved in six more months?" Marco asked.

Emir sat up in his chair and looked at Marco. "Then the police aren't doing a very good job. We'll see what happens after that time. That's all I'm prepared to do right now. I'm sure you understand."

"I understand. It's a difficult case, but the police have dedicated a lot of resources to solving it," Marco said.

"My husband's been working on a 3-D immersive exhibit on the life of Runya, based on *The Gates of Justice*. The visitor will feel like they are in that time period and that Boabdil and Runya had come back to life. I've seen my husband's work. It's amazing. He did some work in America at the African American Museum in Washington, D.C.," Farah said.

Emir sniffed and pulled a handkerchief from his shirt pocket and wiped his nose with his bony fingers. "That sounds just wonderful. Runya's works have never been properly celebrated. This could be the perfect way to honor him. Let's see if the police can solve this case. We'll re-evaluate in six months as to what to do about the painting. In the meantime, I'm going to need something in writing acknowledging that it's my painting. My lawyer insists on it. I don't want it stolen from my family again."

"Of course, Emir, I'll have to speak to the Board's lawyer. We'll get you something by the end of the week," Farah said.

Emir's eyes narrowed, and the tiny creases on his face turned down. "If it weren't for you, Farah, I wouldn't even consider this proposal. I'd have my lawyers in Spain right now demanding the courts order the painting to be returned to us."

Chapter Thirty-Two

Marco decided he still had time to catch the last ferry back to Vivirrambla and not wait until morning to get back home. He checked out of the hotel and went to see Farah to say goodbye. He couldn't trust himself to stay alone with her in the hotel any longer. Marco could hear Farah talking on the phone when he knocked on her door. She opened it and gestured for Marco to come inside. She'd changed into a comfortable-looking tracksuit, and her hair was in a bun.

"I was just about to go to the spa. Do you want to get some dinner later?" she asked.

"I'm going to head back home on the ferry. I've got a lot of work to do," Marco said.

Farah said she understood. She said she intended to stay in Tangier for a couple more days and visit with friends.

"Thanks for all your help, Marco. We did a good job keeping Emir from taking the painting back, at least for now."

"Of course. You need to talk to the Board, though. You should tell them what's going on in case word gets out in the media. Everything you all do is being scrutinized right now," Marco said.

"Yes, of course you're right."

Marco said his goodbye to Farah and took the elevator to the lobby. He asked the desk to call a taxi for him. While he waited for the cab, he phoned Karim to thank him for his help and to ask him to thank Jaddah for the great visit. The cab soon arrived. He made it to the ferry as the dock was about to close. He grabbed his bag and sprinted to the door. He found a seat and caught his breath. As the ferry began rolling across the sea, he checked in with Eva to see if he'd missed anything at the office. Eva messaged back that nothing had been going on. She'd been working on the assignment he'd given her before he left for Morocco, researching art from the Runya period.

"This is so fascinating," she wrote. "I had no idea of this rich Moroccan art history in Spain. We didn't learn anything about it at school in Britain," she said.

When Marco finished conversing with Eva, he ordered a beer from the bar. He took it back to his seat and reclined his chair for the trip home. This time, though, the boat rocked along choppy seas. Marco felt himself swaying back and forth. He closed his eyes and tried to a nap. He awakened when they reached Tarifa. Once the boat docked at the ferry terminal, Marco disembarked and walked off the port to his car, which he'd left in the lot.

When he neared the area where he'd parked, he beeped his car door open and threw his bag in the back seat. He turned his body to get into the driver's seat. A car, driving at top speed, like an invisible bullet train, swooped past his car door and missed him by a millimeter. Had he not jumped onto the car seat, landing on the steering wheel, and shut the door, the car would have struck him. He had no doubt he could have been seriously injured or worse. He caught a glimpse of what looked like a white car speeding away, but it all happened too fast. Marco felt his heart's rapid beat. He got out of the car and looked around the parking lot. No one else in sight, only rows of empty cars. He felt too shaken to move. He sat frozen for a time, his hands trembling. When he gathered himself, he phoned Flores.

"Someone just tried to kill me," he said.

He relayed what had happened. Flores asked him if he'd be okay to drive home. Marco told him that he felt shaken, but that he hadn't been physically hurt.

"That car missed me by a quarter of an inch," Marco said, demonstrating with his index finger over his thumb, though Flores couldn't see him through the phone.

"Do you have any idea who could be after you?" Flores asked.

"Not a clue," Marco said. He felt a sharp pain in his arm.

"This case gets crazier and crazier," Flores said.

Once Marco's hands stopped shaking enough for him to grip the wheel, he headed home. He turned the key to his door and started to call for Belen. Then he remembered. He recalled she'd left him a message while he was meeting with Emir Mohamed. He tapped the dial sign for her number. She sounded excited to hear his voice.

"Marco, how are you? I'm having a wonderful time on the tour. I hope you're making out okay without me. I called you a while ago. I was starting to worry," Belen said.

Marco said everything was fine. He told Belen about his trip to Tangier, though he didn't tell her about Farah. Nor did he mention that someone had just tried to kill him.

"Honey, my tour's going to be in Campillos this weekend. I wanted to ask you if you could take the train and meet me there. We'll be performing at Tablao El Arenal. I even have a solo. We can stay with Lourdes. I called her. She said she'd love to see us. We can stay with her both days," Belen said.

Marco and Belen's friend, Lourdes, had moved back to her hometown of Campillos from Vivirrambla a year ago. Lourdes had been upset she couldn't make it to Belen's surprise party. Marco thought it would be good to see Lourdes. She'd just gone through a painful divorce. Their son, Juan, now a teenager, had really taken to Marco, who'd taught him how to play futbol.

"It's a good idea, but I'm not sure I can take the time," Marco said.

Belen sighed. "You can't afford one weekend away with me? I've been gone for weeks, and I really want to see you." Her voice dropped. "Don't you miss me?"

"Of course I do. I really want to see you, too, honey. I just have a lot on," Marco said.

"Is something wrong? You sound different," Belen said.

Marco lied. "Everything's fine, sweetie. I've just got a lot on my plate. Let me get back to you. I'm tired after a long trip. I can't think straight right now."

Marco could hear the disappointment in Belen's voice. He needed to hang up before he said too much.

Belen sighed "Okay, I don't know what's going on. I hope everything's okay. I'd really like it if you could meet me. Let me know by tomorrow, so I can call Lourdes," she said, disconnecting the call.

Marco went into the kitchen to find something to eat. He rummaged through the refrigerator and found some bread and a can of tuna in the cabinet. He made himself a sandwich of tuna *con aciete* y tomato and grabbed a beer. He plopped on the sofa and flipped on the television to an American crime show, *CSI,* which showed slick cops solving crimes with fancy equipment. *If only,* he thought. As he sat staring through, and not looking at the television, he began to think. He called Flores.

"Did you make it home ok? We're sending men to see if there are any cameras near the port parking lot that may have spotted the car that tried to hit you," Flores said.

"Yeah, thanks, I finally made it home. Listen, my girlfriend wants me to meet her in Campillos this weekend. She's dancing in a show. I haven't seen her in a couple of weeks. I thought about it, and it would be good to get away to clear my head. I don't know if I can afford the time off, though," Marco said.

"You know, I think it's a good idea. Someone's trying to kill you. It's probably good for you to leave town for a few days," Flores said.

Marco hung up the phone. Flores was right. He texted Belen that he'd meet her in Campillos for the weekend. He still didn't mention that someone had tried to kill him.

"I can't wait to see you, babe," Belen replied. She admonished him in the meantime to get some groceries and to make sure the house was clean.

Marco chuckled to himself and went back into the kitchen to wash his dish. He got another beer from the fridge. Before he knew it, he'd fallen asleep on the sofa with the television blaring and half the beer consumed.

When he woke up, groggy and dazed, it had become dark. His body still had the sensation of being on the ferry, like he was swaying. He wandered off to his room and went to bed. At night, he dreamed that someone was trying to kill him as he ran through the ferry boat, which was sinking like the Titanic.

The next morning, Belen's words echoed inside him. He tidied up the house. He tossed a load of laundry in the washer and tried to dust and mop the kitchen floor. He packed his weekend bags of clothes and some aftershave. Before leaving, he double-checked all the windows and locked the door behind him. He still had no idea who was after him, or if they intended to kill him.

Chapter Thirty-Three

Marco took the bus to the station in the center of Vivirrambla. The midday sun was hot. He felt glad for the cool air once the bus arrived. He found an empty seat, though the bus was crowded, and put his bag overhead. He arrived at the train station in Fuengirola in good time for the one o'clock train. He boarded the train for the one-hour and fifty-minute ride. He pushed his seat back and leaned against the headrest. He watched the olive trees pass along the hills. Sheep and cattle grazed nonchalantly on the pastures as the train rattled on. Soon, the conductor announced their arrival at Campillos station.

The train came to a halt. Lourdes and her son, Juan, stood waving at Marco on the platform. Belen had arranged for them to meet him. They all hugged.

"I'm so glad you're here, Marco. We'll have dinner, then go to the show. I can't wait to see Belen dance again," Lourdes said.

Lourdes had purchased a large house with a wooden door that looked like a church door. They entered the foyer, a spacious room with a flood of light. Lourdes showed Marco to his room. He unpacked and then went out into the living room. Juan asked him if he wanted to kick around a football until dinner was ready. Marco agreed and followed Juan outside to the courtyard.

"I've been waiting for you to visit so we could play. I'm supporting Barcelona like you," Juan said.

Marco smiled and patted Juan on the back. It reminded him of his days playing futbol with his cousin Karim in Jaddah's yard. The sun blazed. It beat down on them. Still, Marco and Juan, drenched in sweat, kicked the ball, shouting *"Goal,"* when their shot landed the ball inside the makeshift goal post. They played until their energy started to wane. Then they went inside to shower before dinner.

The three gathered around the wooden table that seated twelve. Juan's cheeks were still flushed from the heat. Lourdes had prepared a delicious meal of lomo and potatoes. The house smelled of oregano and rosemary. Each of them took their seats, assigned by Lourdes. Marco was placed across from a large abstract painting with hues of orange and blue and a blurred human figure in the middle. It hung in a gold antique frame that highlighted the colors.

Marco found himself drawn to the striking work. "That's a wonderful painting. I don't remember seeing it before."

"Lourdes looked up at the painting. "Oh yes, don't you love it? I just got it a few weeks ago. A friend helped me get it," she said.

"Really? It's beautiful. Is your friend an artist? I've been working on this case that centers around a painting. So, I've started to notice paintings more."

"No, he's an art dealer. His client wanted him to take the painting to auction, but he offered it to me first. He knew I needed something for that large wall. We thought the painting would be perfect. My friend arranged the sale with an auction house. They sold it to me directly, at what they called a closed auction. I got it for much less than if I'd bought it on the open market," Lourdes said.

"Wow. The colors add character to the whole room," Marco said.

"It's an original work by an emerging Spanish painter. The bright colors reminded me of flamenco," Lourdes said.

"It reminds me of one of Belen's Flamenco dresses," Marco said, snickering. Lourdes laughed.

"I didn't know you could acquire art directly from a dealer at an auction," Marco said.

"Yeah, according to my friend, if you know the right art dealer, you can," Lourdes said.

Marco twisted his lips. "Interesting."

When they finished dinner, Marco said goodbye to Juan, who was going to stay with friends for the rest of the weekend. Then, Marco and Lourdes walked out into the warm air of the evening and huddled into a taxi as Lourdes didn't want to drive as they'd be drinking.

The cab let them out at the door of Tablao El Arenal. They walked into a venue awash in hues of pink and blue lighting. Marco and Lourdes went over to the seats reserved for them in front of the stage. They ordered a bottle of wine as the lights dimmed, and the performers appeared. Belen stood in the center of the stage, surrounded by a male singer with long hair and a dark olive-skinned guitarist seated on a stool. Marco thought Belen looked innocent, like a nymph, in a black and white ruffled dress, a large white shawl, and black shoes. Her hair was in a bun. She wore a red flower near her ear. She began to move in the graceful movement of a ballerina, while playing castanets, tapping with her fingers to the rhythm, as the singer crooned next to her and the guitar strummed a tune of love and longing. Marco could feel the emotion in her dance. *No wonder she's always picked as one of the top dancers*, he thought. Another male dancer joined her on stage, moving in the same rhythm to the soulful sound. The performance ended to thunderous applause.

Marco knew a woman like Farah could never stir his heart like Belen could. He regretted having kissed Farah in Tangier. He willed his thoughts elsewhere as Belen joined them at their table. She'd changed into a blue dress. Her cheeks were still flushed.

"So good to see you, honey. I really missed you," Marco said, kissing her on her cheek.

"I missed you, too," Belen said.

Marco squeezed her hand under the table. The three of them, Marco, Belen, and Lourdes, hung out at the table and talked for a couple of hours, drinking wine and laughing. Then they piled into the taxi, giddy with drink and joy, and rode back to Lourdes's home. Marco and Belen went off to their designated room. The two undressed, under the soft lamplight with urgency of two lovers who hadn't seen one another for some time. When Belen touched his arm, Marco let out a screech.

"Ouch," he said, squirming and moving his arm away.

Belen narrowed her eyes, "What's wrong?" she asked.

"I bruised my arm, working out," he said.

He didn't tell her that he'd nearly broken it on the steering wheel of his car when he landed on it to avoid being killed. The swelling had died down, though it still felt sore to the touch. Good thing Belen hadn't seen it earlier.

Belen looked at him with concern.

"I'm ok, really," Marco said.

Marco made love to her with the passion of a dying man. Then he fell into a deep sleep, feeling the safest he had in some time.

* * *

"You were really snoring, honey" Belen said when they woke up the next day.

"I haven't been sleeping well without you," he said.

Belen smiled and kissed him.

Belen had the next day off from dancing. Once everyone had dressed and eaten breakfast, they decided to go shopping for leather goods in the shops of the small town known for its fine leather products. Marco purchased a new leather jacket, which Belen said made him look like a stud. After shopping, they enjoyed lunch at Taberna de Ni, where the round-bellied owner, with a wisp of hair flying from his bald head, cooked them a special pork dish. Back at Lourdes's full, and satiated, they sipped sherry from Jerez until late in the evening, when finally, everyone tipped off to their rooms.

Just as he and Belen had gotten undressed to get in bed, Marco's phone began to beep.

Belen looked over. "Ignore it. You're not working right now."

"I can't. It's Flores," Marco said. "Si, Flores, *dime.*"

Belen rolled her eyes and hopped into bed.

"We've just arrested Amy Bloom and Nicholas Thompson for theft and the murder of Addison Mason. I know you're on a mini holiday, but we need you back here right away. I'm going to interview them tomorrow," Flores said.

Chapter Thirty-Four

Flores didn't often want to pat himself on the back. He deserved it this time. His team's long hours of research and surveillance of Amy Bloom and Nicholas Thompson had paid off. During the surveillance period, his officers reported several instances of Amy carrying a large, bulky bag back and forth from the museum. Thompson then appeared at her apartment the next day to retrieve the bag. With the help of the forensic evidence, and the velvet pouch Flores took from Thompson's office, they'd been able to piece it all together. The duo had been engaged in the illegal trading and selling of stolen antique silver.

A break in the case came when police intercepted a conversation between Amy and Nicholas. Nicholas spoke on his car phone, hooked to his cell. They discussed their future wedding plans. Then they evaluated their silver operation and talked about a potential new client. Nicholas said the client wanted to replace several pieces of English silver flatware in a pattern called *Silver Thread*.

Flores flipped through his silver book. He'd had a crash course through books suggested to him, about silver and silver patterns. *Silver Thread* was made in the time of William IV, and hallmarked London, 1831. The flatware had been priced at over five thousand euros for an entire set. Individual pieces sold for as much as two hundred euros each. These sums were staggering. Flores had a hunch, but he wasn't sure where they obtained the silver for their clients. It was the one wrinkle in the case needed to tie it all together.

Flores worked with his team to set up a rouse. He felt sure Amy and

Nicholas had no inkling the police were on to them. Flores asked Amy to meet him at the museum under the guise that police needed a tour of the layout to help track Addison's murderer and trace his steps. He told Amy that they'd surmised the perpetrator had hidden out somewhere in the basement in wait for his prey. They needed Amy to make sure they didn't miss any inch in their search of the museum.

Flores and his officers met Amy at the door.

"Come in. I've missed the museum. I haven't been here in a long time," Amy said.

She led them through the exhibit rooms, down the steps to the basement level. It smelled musty and felt cold and eerie, like being buried in a crypt in an Edgar Allan Poe novel. Dust particles had formed in corners, as the museum had been closed and no one had cleaned it. Amy, wearing a ponytail that bounced when she moved, pointed out an alcove in the back of one of the rooms that had a stone circular staircase. Flores took out his flashlight and lit the way up the winding, narrow stairs, through dark space, casting shadows until they reached a hidden door.

Flores turned the handle. The unlocked door led right to Addison's office.

"The killer could have definitely come this way without being noticed. Can you show us the rest of the museum? I need to trace all of his possible footsteps," Flores said.

"Sure," Amy said. "I doubt if you'll find anything else, though."

They toured various rooms with paintings and others that remained empty. Some rooms appeared to be storage. Amy told them a little about the history of the art in each room. Flores had to admit it was interesting. He knew little about art.

As they continued through the basement, Flores's attention was drawn to a door painted mustard yellow at the end of a long narrow hallway. He sniffed in the air. The paint smelled fresh. Flores pointed his flashlight at the door. He turned to Amy. "What's this room?" he asked.

Amy's face reddened, as if she'd grabbed a handful of red rouge and patted it on her pale English cheeks. "Oh, that's nothing. It's a storage room we never use. There are a lot of those little rooms around here," she said.

"I see," Flores said. "It smells freshly painted. Has anyone been using this room?

Amy stammered. "Uh, no. I think the museum had started to do some painting down here before all this happened. Addison had requisitioned that the basement be repainted so that the walls were fresh and the musty air wouldn't harm the paintings."

Flores turned up his nose. "This paint smells new."

Amy shrugged and looked down at her shoes.

"Let me just take a quick look around," Flores said, waving his flashlight in a circular motion around the door. Then he turned to Amy. "Okay, let's keep going."

Amy sighed. Flores saw the relief in her eyes. They continued the journey until they'd seen all of the museum. Flores escorted Amy outside when they were done and instructed her to lock up. He thanked her for her cooperation. He said they'd let her know if the police needed anything else. He watched as she got into her car. Then he directed his officers to keep an eye on her.

"Don't lose her under any conditions."

Flores contacted the prosecutor as soon as he returned to his office. He obtained a search warrant for the freshly painted yellow room. Police went back to the museum to inspect the room.

A crew of police in uniform banged on Amy's door at seven in the morning. She poked her head out, confused, still half asleep.

Her voice sounded dreamy. "What's all this banging? What do you want?" she asked.

"Buenas dia, Señorita. Sorry to disturb you so early. We need you to come back with us to the museum. There's something I need to check," Flores said.

Amy's voice sounded sharp. "What? Now? We went over the whole museum yesterday."

"Si, Señorita. I need you to come with me right now. Bring any keys you have to the museum," Flores said.

Amy looked around as if searching for an escape. As none of the officers moved, Her face dropped as if to concede she had no option.

CHAPTER THIRTY-FOUR

"At least let me change. I was sleeping," she said.

Flores and his officers waited at the door for some time until Amy had changed. Other officers were stationed around the building. So, she couldn't escape. Amy finally emerged wearing the same ponytail, jeans, and a top bearing the logo bearing the face of Britney Spears. She began to shake as the officers grabbed her arm and escorted her to a waiting car.

When they reached the museum, they went straight down to the mustard yellow room. Flores tried the door. It was locked. He turned to Amy, who stood shaking next to an officer.

"Señorita, do you have the key to this door?"

Amy fiddled with a set of keys for a time. Eventually, she handed Flores the key to the mustard yellow door. As soon as one of the police guys opened it, a large clanging occurred as silver pots, creamers, trays, and various pieces of silver tumbled out of the closet. Inside, they found stacks of boxes containing silver, flatware, including *Silver Fiddle Thread,* the pattern Flores had researched. They confiscated a variety of other items. The team on-site gathered and tagged each item. It took several hours to bag everything. Amy and Nicholas had fully stocked an entire antique store in the basement of the museum.

Amy hunched her shoulders and backed up behind one of his officers and tried to exit the room. When she noticed Flores had seen her, she took off running.

"Amy, stop! There's no use in trying to outrun us," Flores said.

Amy looked around and accelerated her speed. One of the officers sprinted after her. He returned fifteen minutes later, panting out of breath, holding Amy's arm. He said he had to run through the entire museum to catch her. Amy stood before Flores, looking like a young girl who'd disobeyed her parents.

Flores reproached her. "I could add resisting arrest and fleeing an officer to your already serious charges."

Amy remained silent. Flores forced her to sit on the ground under guard until the police had finished gathering evidence from the room. Once they'd completed securing all of the items, Flores walked over to her.

"Señorita Bloom, you're under arrest under Spanish Penal code Article 234 for aggravated theft of stolen goods of high cultural value and for operating an illegal exchange.

Amy hung her head and looked down at the museum floor as Officer DeLuca snapped handcuffs on her and led her away.

Flores had gathered intelligence from Thompson's phone that Nicholas and Amy intended to rendezvous at her apartment later in the afternoon. Flores staked out officers around her building. When Thompson showed up, instead of Amy, he found a group of Malaga police waiting for him. Thompson spotted them and tried to flee down a set of stairs to an exit. His attempt at flight, futile. Officers brought him into the police station.

Chapter Thirty-Five

Marco exited the train at the station in Malaga, the stop before Vivirrambla. He put on his police Visitor badge and went straight to the interrogation room, wearing jeans and a light tan polo shirt. Flores sat at the head of the metal table in one of the uncomfortable green metal chairs. Marco sat next to him across from a small window. A flat screen television hung on the wall behind them, mounted to the, dull gray wall.

Detective DeLuca led Amy through a security door into the room. She kept her head down as DeLuca ushered her to one of the chairs across from them. DeLuca stood behind Amy with her arms crossed. Flores read Amy the required rights under Spanish law.

"Señorita, you're here on charges of aggravated theft. We have reason to believe you have been selling stolen antique silver here in Spain. I also believe you are guilty of murder," Flores said.

Amy jumped up from her seat. "Murder? No, no," she screamed, startling everyone in the room. Detective DeLuca pushed her back down in chair.

Marco noticed that Flores seemed more confident than usual in the interrogation. Marco respected Flores as a dedicated and thorough officer, but his experience with him had been that Flores closed cases too soon, missing signs and subtle pieces of evidence in his rush to please the Chief. The two of them didn't operate in the same way. Flores, a rigid rule follower, let the rules strangle his imagination and intuition. In Flores's mind, he'd gather enough evidence to charge Amy.

Amy straight ahead with a dazed look. She'd been crying, and her eyes were puffy and red.

Flores snapped on the recorder next to him. "Do you have anything you want to say before we begin, Señorita, Bloom?" he asked.

Amy shifted in her chair. "No, not really."

"As I told you, we have evidence that you've been selling stolen silver over here in Spain."

"Stolen silver? I don't know what you're talking about," Amy said.

Flores extracted several documents from a folder he carried, and photos on a computer in the room. "Remember the room in the museum where all the silver fell out?"

"You have no proof that that silver belonged to me. Plus, you tricked me into opening the door," Amy said.

Flores shoved several papers in front of Amy; printouts of text messages between Amy and Nicholas Thompson, cellular phone call records from Cellbrite, and a printout of a website advertising the sale of silver.

Amy's eyes widened. "Where did you get all of this?"

"We've been watching you for some time, Señorita Bloom, ever since we first saw you sneaking out of the museum late at night carrying a large bag," Flores said.

Amy squirmed in her chair. "I went to the museum to get some stuff. I brought my work home since you wouldn't let us back in the building."

"We initially thought you could be taking out work. Then, my officers noticed you dragging out an odd sized bag containing unidentified contents."

Amy squiggled. Detective DeLuca touched her shoulders to signal for her to relax. Amy sunk down in her chair. "I don't have any idea what you're talking about. I'm afraid you've made a mistake." She spoke under her breath. Of course, I wouldn't expect much from the Spanish police," she said, turning up her nose.

Flores ignored her insult and continued. "Our surveillance spotted you and Señor Nicholas Thompson together on several occasions. You'd transport a bag containing unidentified contents to your home. Thompson would pick it up from you the next day at your apartment."

Flores handed her surveillance pictures and took out another printout that displayed text conversations. "We've reviewed your text messages. Seems as if you were engaged in more than business."

"That's not illegal," Amy said.

"You're right, your seedy affair's your business. Conspiring to sell stolen goods and planning escape with the money is *our* business. Even we Spanish police know that," Flores said.

Detective DeLuca chuckled.

Marco looked over at Amy, who clenched her fist.

A slight smile suddenly shone on Amy's face. "So, what. We fell in love. We were planning to go to Bermuda and get married," Amy said.

"One problem. Señor Thompson is already married," Flores said.

Amy shrugged her shoulders. "He doesn't love her. He's going to get a divorce, and we're going to go away and start again."

"So, you were planning to leave the museum?" Marco asked.

"Sure, I considered it a temporary gig. I wanted to get out of England. I found out Nicholas was coming over here. So, I applied for the job with Addison, and I got it."

"You worked in an antique store owned by a man named Jules before moving to Spain, didn't you?" Marco asked.

Amy studied Marco. Then she looked away as if his eyes had penetrated her heart. "Yes, I worked for Jules Moore Antiques."

"You had a good job. You practically ran the shop in London. Why would you want to leave?" Marco asked.

Her eyes narrowed like a cat ready to pounce. "Yes, it's true, but Jules was getting old. I didn't know how much longer he'd keep the shop open."

"You mean you followed your lover," Marco said.

Amy slouched down in her chair. DeLuca watched her every move.

"What did Jules think of you leaving?" Marco asked.

"He said he understood. There wasn't much he could do. He said that I should travel while I was young, or I'd regret it later."

"You and Thompson decided to come to Spain to be together. You opted to sell silver to finance your tryst. Thompson must not have been earning enough as a lawyer," Marco said.

"Nick's a great lawyer," she said.

"Where did you and Thompson get the silver you sold?" Flores asked.

"I have nothing more to say," she said.

Amy refused to answer any further questions. She said she wanted an English lawyer to talk to her in addition to the Spanish counsel she'd been assigned. Flores informed her that they'd also brought in Nicholas Thompson. They surmised he'd be willing to give them more information.

Amy sneered. "Nick won't tell you anything."

Flores hunched his shoulders. "He has more to lose than you do."

"Nick will never betray me. I don't have anything else to say. Can I go now?"

"Of course," Flores said.

Detective DeLuca escorted Amy out of the interrogation room. She refused to look at either Flores or Marco in the eye on her way out.

Flores and Marco debriefed after Amy had gone. "I'm glad you visited that antiques store in London. I argued against it at first, but I see you have helpful background information on Amy," Flores said.

Marco nodded. "When I went to her old antique shop with Oliver Hall, I saw it for myself. The owner, Jules Moore, could be described as a hoarder. He had sterling silver pieces and art all over the place. His home had even more. I suspect that's where Amy and Nicholas got a lot of their bounty. Jules is old and frail. He told me Amy still comes to stay with him sometimes. She stays at his house and swipes the silver. He doesn't even notice. Oliver Hall said Jules had no idea of how much he had in the way of antiques."

"Maybe Jules is the mastermind and is pretending not to know anything," Flores said.

Marco cocked his head. "I didn't get that vibe from him. Although he could be trying to avoid taxes by selling off things in Spain, Jules told me he had no relatives. No one to leave his estate to. I'm not sure the taxes would matter that much to him."

"You could be right. I'll have someone run a background check on Jules Moore. We need to make sure we don't miss any red flags."

"It's a good idea. Jules said he hadn't been to Spain for years, but he could have business connections here to help facilitate the silver trade," Marco said.

A uniformed officer walked into the room. He nodded to Flores, signaling that Nicholas Thompson had arrived.

"Good. Thompson can give us more insight," Flores said.

The detective motioned to the officer to bring Nicholas Thompson into the interrogation room. Flores switched on the recorder again, as Thompson sat in the same chair Amy vacated.

The sophisticated Thompson no longer wore a designer suit or silk tie. His sandy hair looked disheveled. He sat in a metal chair, his thin lips pursed.

"Señor Thompson, we had a lovely conversation with Señorita Bloom. Seems you two were close. You even had business together. She gave us some good information," Flores said.

Thompson narrowed his eyes. "I don't believe she told you anything."

"Still, we have mounting evidence of your conspiracy to sell stolen goods. We're working on murder charges as well. They would probably hurt your law career," Flores said.

Thompson turned his body in his chair and crossed his legs.

Flores shot pictures and text messages, the same information he'd shared with Amy, across the table to Thompson.

Thompson shrugged and sent the documents back down the table. "You're wasting your time. I have nothing to say to you. My lawyer should be here soon."

Flores leaned over the table. "Okay, you don't want to talk. Then just listen. Here's what I think happened. You and Amy Bloom came up with this scheme to make some quick money so you could leave your wife and the two of you could run off and get married."

Nicholas Thompson grunted. "You don't know what you're talking about."

Flores continued. "Señor Addison found out about your little silver treasure plot and threatened to turn you in. So, you decided to kill him, or did he ask you for a cut? Where did you get the silver? Did Addison know you were storing silver in his museum?"

"Do you know a man named Jules Moore?" Marco asked.

Thompson twisted his face and looked over at Marco. "Who?"

"The antiques dealer in London. Amy used to work for him," Marco said.

"Never heard of him," Thompson said.

"Somehow I don't believe you," Flores said.

"I want to go back to my cell," Thompson said.

As Thompson refused to answer questions it was futile to further interrogate him. Detective DeLuca escorted him out of the room.

Flores picked up the evidence he'd shown Nicholas and Amy, now spread out, and scattered along the table. He organized it and put it back in the evidence folders. "We've got motive and opportunity. They were both in the museum that night. Addison must have found out about their enterprise and threatened them. They killed him that night because they knew the museum would be crowded and they thought they could slip away unnoticed."

"We've definitely got enough to charge them for the silver theft, but I don't see where we have enough to tie them to murder. I think you'd need a lot more to make that connection," Marco said.

Chapter Thirty-Six

One who thinks he knows seldom has the answers. Jaddah had given Marco that pearl of wisdom many years ago.

Flores seemed almost giddy. He'd solved Addison's murder. Marco, for his part, wasn't convinced. The stolen painting still loomed in the shadows. How did the Runya fit into the scheme he wondered. It seemed unlikely the stolen painting played no part in it.

Marco shared with Eva that he didn't think the cases had been solved. "We're missing something, a piece of yarn that knits things together."

"I agree with you," Eva said. "How does the painting fit into it? Amy and Nicholas didn't seem to have much to do with it."

Marco shook his head. "Exactly."

Marco sat on the edge of Eva's desk for a few more minutes, conversing. Then he went back to his office, where he stared at his computer, strumming his fingers on his desk. He needed more information as to how the museum acquired the painting. Therein could lay the key to finding a motive. He recalled the dinner conversation he'd had with Lourdes when he visited her home and saw her beautiful painting. Lourdes had explained that original art could be acquired in several ways, including at a private auction.

He swiveled around in his chair and telephoned Camela Sanchez.

"I'm still so upset about my brother. I can hardly think, but I'll help you as much as I can," Carmela said, when Marco told her what he wanted.

"Yes, of course I understand," Marco said. "The police are doing all they can to find out who killed your brother."

"Thank you," she said.

Marco asked Carmela for all the auction papers and the bill of sale for the Runya painting. She sent him all the information the following day. Marco spent the afternoon reviewing the paperwork. He noticed the bill of sale referenced **Tuille House**, a British-based auction house with offices in Spain and the United States. Tuille specialized in high-end paintings, antiques, and unique goods. Their website *www.tuillehouse.com*, indicated that Tuille offered private auctions, which they claimed allowed them to discretely obtain world-class art and objects, based on client need. They touted that their extensive knowledge of fine art and antiques enabled them to secure even the hardest-to-find pieces. The final sale of the Runya painting was signed by John H. Tuille, Managing Director, Tuille House, Spain and Europe.

Marco buzzed Eva. "Yes," she said.

"I need you to do research on auctions and auction houses, especially private sales. See if you can look more into a company called Tulle House. I've already started looking. I'll bring you what I've found."

"Happy to, jefe."

Eva popped into his office later in the day.

"The auction house never disclosed the seller of the *Gates of Justice*. John Tuilles represented the seller's interest. You can be anonymous, I read. On the bill of sale I have, Carmela's listed as the buyer, with Nicholas Thompson as her representative," Eva said.

"That's interesting. Thanks, Eva," Marco said.

Marco decided to walk over to the ayuntamiento to check with the Chattel Registry to see if he could find information on the seller. His shirt was soaked by the time he reached the building, as the day was steamy and sunny. The municipal building had little air conditioning. So, Marco stood around, uncomfortable, while he waited for the clerk to look up the requested information. When the registry clerk finally returned—she could only confirm the sale of the painting to Addison Mason. She found no further information.

Marco asked Eva to make an appointment for him with John Tuille at the Auction House, located in Puerto Bella.

"I told him you were working with the Malaga police. He sounded surprised but agreed to meet with you tomorrow morning," Eva said.

Marco continued to review Eva's findings on the auction process. He wanted to at least—sound like he knew what he was talking about at his meeting with John Tuille. When he felt well-versed enough, he closed down the office and headed home. He'd been cautious walking home since the various attacks. He'd changed his route and left at different times of the day. The police hadn't yet identified a suspect. The perpetrator always managed to avoid cameras. For all Marco knew, someone still wanted him dead.

The temperature hadn't lowered much by the time he went home. Marco changed from his work attire into his swim gear and walked down to the beach. Children and families still reveled and played in the sand, though it was early evening. Others sat in beach chairs on the sandy shore or strolled the paseo. Marco dived into the sea. He navigated the waves bobbing up and down in the cool water like an Olympian. When he emerged to towel off, he sensed someone had been watching him. He stopped toweling and looked around. He saw only children playing in the sand, and a couple walking along the beach.

"I'm getting paranoid," he said to himself. He dressed in his shorts, slipped on his sandals, and walked back to his apartment.

*　*　*

Once home, he foraged through the refrigerator for dinner. The house seemed even more lonely after he'd spent the weekend with Belen. He found a package of pre-cooked croqueta and made himself a salad. He decided to turn in early. As he dressed for bed, his phone buzzed. Belen had sent him a text message, wishing him a good night with a heart emoji. Marco smiled and replied with a moon and a heart. He checked his remaining voice messages before getting into bed. There were several messages on his phone from the same number. A number he didn't recognize. It was like someone kept calling then hanging up, then calling again, over twenty times. He tried calling the number back, but it said out of service. He put the phone on his dresser. He'd see if Flores's forensic department could trace the calls. He hopped into bed. The swim had relaxed him. He drifted right to sleep.

The next day, he rose craving coffee and a pastry from Alvarez. He stopped at the cafe before heading to Puerto Bella for his meeting with John Tuille of the auction house. Alvarez was in a cheery mood, humming a nameless tune as he wiped down the counters. He put a steaming café con leche in front of Marco once it had finished perking.

"My daughter's doing much better. The doctor said she can come off bed rest," Alvarez said, sliding a pastry in front of Marco.

"That's wonderful news, amigo. I'll bet you and your wife are relieved," Marco said.

Alvarez's pudgy cheeks turned deep red. "We are, we were worried there for a bit."

Marco talked for a while longer to Alvarez before hopping off the bench.

"I've got to get to an appointment. I'm so glad you had good news," Marco said.

Alvarez beamed. "*Gracias, amigo. Hasta pronto.*"

When he reached his car, Marco found a note under the windshield wiper. "Great, just what I needed today," he said, pulling the note off and unfolding it.

The note typed on white paper, written in broken Spanish read:

> *Moroccan Gypsy, you think you some kind of hot lover boy. Remember you ferry from Tangier? You got lucky in that parking lot. I missed the last time, but I won't miss again I try. I give you this last one time.*

The author wasn't a native Spanish speaker. At least now he had one clue. Marco looked around but saw no one except some students going into Enforex, the Spanish language school. He threw the note on the car seat and drove to Puerto Bella. He parked and took the escalator up to a building with a blue and white sign that read: **TUILLE AUCTION HOUSE: FINE GOODS.** He walked up to the impressive steel and glass door and pulled the handle. It didn't open. Then he noticed the call button. Marco pushed it and spoke to the intercom.

"I have an appointment with Mr. Tuille." A buzzing noise sounded, and the door clicked.

A distinguished, pale-faced man with gray hair and crystal blue eyes greeted him. He shook Marco's hand with a firm grip. Marco recognized his posh English accent. "Good morning, sir. I'm John Tuille. Welcome to our auction house."

The aging man wore a dark grey suit with a white blouse and a maroon tie. His black round-toed shoes were highly polished, and a crisp white kerchief hung from the breast pocket of his jacket.

"Good morning, thank you for taking the time to meet with me. I'm here on an important police matter. I'm a consulting for the Malaga police," Marco said, handing him his card.

"I see. Please follow me," Tuille said.

Tuille escorted Marco into an office with an antique wooden desk and a wooden cabinet against the wall. The floor had white carpeting, and fine grain leather chairs. Tuille gestured for Marco to sit in one of the chairs near his desk.

"May I offer you a cup of tea?"

"No, thank you," Marco said.

"How may I help you?" Tuille asked, taking a seat in a tall chair behind his desk.

"I'm assisting police in the investigation of the murder of Addison Mason. I'm sure you heard about it."

John Tuille took a deep breath before speaking. "Yes, I read about it in the newspaper." He shook his head. "Very sad. What does this have to do with our auction house?"

"Someone murdered Mason on the night he intended to unveil a painting purchased through your auction house."

Marco opened the portfolio Eva had prepared for him and sat several papers on Tuille's hand-crafted antique desk.

John Tuille put on a set of dark-rimmed square glasses and flipped through the papers.

"Page 16 is the bill of sale for the painting, *The Gates of Justice,* by Sumaya Runya from the fifteenth century," Marco said.

Tuille picked up the paper and examined it. Then he nodded. "Yes, we facilitated that transaction. We represented the seller's interest."

Marco pulled out another set of papers. "It looks like you had an arrangement with Carmela Sanchez as the sole bidder for the initial sale. A second transaction with Señora Sanchez, also a private sale, transferred the painting to the museum," Marco said.

Tuille paused to look at the second group of papers. "Yes, that seems to be correct."

Marco tilted his head. "Is that normal? Two buyers of the same item at the same time? Why didn't the museum just purchase the painting as the initial sole bidder?"

Tuille revved back in his chair. "I believe it had something to do with transfer taxes," he said.

"I see, can you give me the name of the original seller?" Marco asked.

"I'm afraid not. The seller requested anonymity. I won't be able to give you that information. I can only tell you that the seller was from the UK," Tuille said.

"This is a murder investigation. It's especially important that you cooperate," Marco said.

Tuille cleared his throat. "I appreciate the predicament you're in, but our clients rely on our discretion, or they won't trust us to do business."

"Did you disclose the name of the seller to Señora Sanchez?" Marco asked.

"Certainly not, we take anonymity seriously," Tuille said.

"The police will likely come back with a subpoena for all of your sales and records, including the name of anonymous sellers," Marco said.

Tuille furrowed his brow. "In my thirty-five years here, I've never been threatened by law enforcement. Our company prides itself on its high standards and ethical dealings."

"This is not to question your personal integrity, Señor. This is about finding out who killed Addison Mason."

Eva had made a notebook, marked all the relevant pages, and tabbed them for easy access. Marco pulled up another document. "I see that the Notary Public registered the sale, but I don't see a registration for the initial sale of the painting," Marco said.

"The first transaction was initiated in the UK," Tuille said.

"Did the seller pay the VAT for transporting the painting and completing the first transaction?" Marco asked.

"I'm not certain what the seller did. At one point during the auction, we discovered that a fake bidder tried to shill bid to run up the price. Fortunately, we monitored the bidding and discovered it was a false account and excluded their bid. We then changed the transaction to a preferred sale," Tuille said, furrowing his brow.

"Did you find out the identity of the fake bidder?" Marco asked.

Tuille shook his head no. "It could have been anyone. That happens sometimes with private auctions. People get wind of a sale in trade papers or somewhere, and they purposely try to undercut the bid. Thankfully, with our new technology, we can spot it right away, and the bidder is forbidden to go further in the transaction."

"I see. So, the fake bidder had no influence on the bidding?" Marco asked.

"Thankfully, No. As I said that person was quickly shut down."

"What about import taxes on the sale to Señora Sanchez?" Marco asked.

Tuille threw his head back. "Imports of collectors' art not intended for sale, which are imported by museums, are exempt from taxation," Tuille said.

"I see," Marco said.

Tuille shifted in his chair. "Señora Sanchez sold the painting to the museum in another private sale, we facilitated."

"Did you know the painting had been stolen from Morocco right before the Spanish Civil War?" Marco asked.

Tuille stared at Marco, his mouth agape. "Stolen? I had no idea. Everything seemed to be in order." Tuille pulled out papers from a folder marked, The *Ruyna Transaction*, and handed them to Marco. As you see, the seller presented proof of ownership of the painting."

Marco took the document from Tuille. It certified the authenticity of the

Ruyna painting. "This document was manufactured. The true owner of the painting lives in Morocco. Your auction house helped to facilitate the sale of a stolen painting that may have been the impetus for the murder of Addison Mason. Under these circumstances, the police will require you to divulge the name of the original seller. They will go through all your sales records," Marco said.

Tuille frowned. He didn't speak for some time. He stood up from his chair. "Excuse me for a minute," he said, walking out of the office.

"I'll need to keep those," Marco said, tucking the forged certificate and the sales ledger into his case.

Tuille left the office for over fifteen minutes. Marco sat leafing through his papers. Tuille returned accompanied by an elderly white-haired gentleman.

"Good afternoon. I am Paul Tuille, owner of this auction house." Paul looked at Marco with a cool gaze. "As I'm sure my brother told you, we make every effort to protect the integrity of our clients. However, since criminal activity has been alleged in this case, it's our duty to cooperate fully with the authorities." He pulled out a document from the portfolio he carried. The original seller was a Jules Moore of the UK. I will have my assistant provide everything we have about the sale on file."

Chapter Thirty-Seven

lores met with his team. He'd been convinced he'd solved Addison's murder, but the prosecutor said he didn't have enough evidence. Junior officers gathered around him as he reviewed the pictures of the two victims on the whiteboard. Arrows in red marker were drawn on the board going in different directions next to pictures of the deceased and names of potential suspects.

"The chief wants these murders solved ASAP. I need you to put your everything into this. We're starting to make some headway. I know these murders are complex, but we can get it done."

Flores's growing anxiety from mounting pressure from upstairs was affecting his health. Media attention continued to focus on the failure of the police to solve two murders. *"Are Our Citizens Truly in Danger?"* the headline said, blasted on the front page of the local newspaper. The Chief's patience had worn thin with that last article. Each day, Flores felt his job to be in peril. So, Flores pushed his team to dig deeper. Overtime had been authorized, and they worked late into the night, reviewing surveillance footage, cross-referencing auction house records, and sifting through financial transactions. Each new discovery brought more questions, as suspects were Xed off the whiteboard.

Mid-afternoon, the sun slanted through the window of his office, casting a reflection on his computer screen. Flores sat at his desk with his hand on his chin, looking at the screen. At last, a ray of hope appeared when one of the uniformed officers walked in.

"Sir, I've found something," she said, pointing to a series of flagged transactions. "Amy sent a large wire transfer from an account registered in the UK, the day of the Runya auction. The purchaser used an alias, but his address matches a known fence for stolen art."

The weary detective sat up in his chair. "We've got something to go on now. Good work. Instruct the team not to let Thompson and Bloom out of your sight," he said.

Flores needed the name of the art fence. The prosecutor would require him to testify. Sometimes, nailing the culprit involved coordination with other countries. He hoped two nations working together would be able to solve the murder. Flores contacted his counterpart in the UK. The person he initially spoke to referred him to the Antiques unit of England's Scotland Yard, a part of Britain's Metropolitan Police. The antiques section, part of the Specialist, Organised & Economic Crime Command, specialized in investigating the theft of antique silver. Flores was put in touch with Detective Inspector Michael Sargeant, who said he had twenty years of experience in antique silver recovery.

"You wouldn't believe the value of some of this stuff," Sargeant said.

Flores filled the officer in on the capers of Nicholas and Amy. He shared all the information he'd gathered, including text messages, fake websites, and email exchanges. He told Sargeant about the large wire transfer Bloom had made the day of the Runya auction.

DI Sargeant agreed to look into the wire transfer. "There's a lot of something here," he said.

Flores told him that he also suspected that the two may have been involved in a murder.

"That's quite a pair. Bonnie and Clyde of the UK," Sargeant said, chuckling. Flores laughed.

Flores checked back in with his own officers once he hung up the call. Things seemed to be rolling fast, like a log pushed off a hill. Amy, they said, had been keeping a low profile while on bail since her arrest. With respect to Thompson, his officers reported odd behavior, including going to meetings at odd hours and whispered phone calls to non-traceable numbers.

"Keep digging. We'll get to the bottom of it," Flores admonished his team.

* * *

DI Sargeant contacted Flores after a week. "I have some interesting news," he said.

Flores sat up in his chair.

"We traced that transaction you asked about to a well-known art fence," Sargeant said. "We were able to bring him in. In interrogation, he told us that he'd been hired by a man with a Scandinavian accent, he didn't know his name. He was asked to pretend to be a bidder on an important painting being auctioned in Spain. The people who hired him promised him a large cut when the painting was sold. He said he didn't know the name of the person who hired him, but they told him the painting was worth a fortune."

"The auction house said there'd been a suspicious bidder," Flores said.

"That's right, fortunately, the auction house identified the bid as being false and cut off the transaction. Our fence wasn't too happy about it either, ha, ha, ha," Sargeant said.

Flores thanked DI Sargeant for his assistance.

"Ta," Sargeant said, in a crisp English accent.

Flores felt a sense of relief. He now had concrete information that could tie Thompson and Bloom to the murder of Addison. The murder of Diego remained outstanding, but one crisis at a time. Flores received more good news a few hours later. His team had followed Thompson to Torremolinos, where before their surveillance, he'd blended in with other English expats and tourists clamoring for a tranquil life on the warm beaches of the Mediterranean. They'd followed him to a well-known meeting place of the right-wing conservative group, Vox.

As Thompson had violated the conditions of his bail by driving to Torremolinos, the police had cause to re-arrest him. This time, he wasn't the arrogant and defiant young man he was before. He entered with his head down, when Detective DeLuca brought him in to the interrogation room.

"Señor Thompson, we've become aware of additional information. Further charges have been brought against you," Flores said.

Flores slid the written report emailed to him by DI Sargeant down the table. The report detailed the transaction and wire transfer between the fence and Amy.

Thompson's lawyer scrutinized the report. No one spoke for a time. The anxious Flores tapped on the table with his pen.

"That says Amy Bloom entered into a conspiracy to sabotage the bid for the painting. My client isn't mentioned in this document."

Flores smiled a half smile, the corners of his lips upturned. "Señor, we have sufficient evidence that Amy and Nicholas are joint conspirators. Amy received money from an unidentified person, which she wired to the auction house to secure a false bid."

"There's no proof Thompson was involved in any of that," his lawyer said.

"When we examine all the evidence, I'm one hundred percent sure your client will be implicated. We'll find proof the two lovers conspired to steal the lost Runya painting for purposes of sale on the underground art market. This establishes a motive for murder. That, and the stolen silver scheme, should put him away for life."

Thompson's lawyer arched his eyebrows. "Even if you find other evidence, I don't believe you can prove a nexus to Mason's murder."

Flores watched the cocky young lawyer. He wondered how'd he react to the next bit of information. "I've got a bit more here." Flores pulled out more papers and sent them down to the end of the table. Thompson's lawyer scooped them up and reviewed the documents.

Flores turned on the video of the surveillance of Thompson attending Vox meetings.

"I need to show you something else. We can also prove that Thompson intended to divert museum donations to the right-wing political organization, Vox, including money from sale of the Ruyna. Text conversations, our forensics team recovered, show that they'd planned to amass funds from various sources in order to permanently leave the country," Flores said.

Thompson gestured for his client to come closer. The two whispered for some time.

"What are you offering?" Thompson's lawyer asked when they finished conferring.

Thompson's business in Gibraltar, as well as his bank accounts, had already been seized and confiscated through international cooperation and the Spanish Asset Recovery Office. (ORGA). The UK was in the process of revoking his legal license. There was nothing left for Thompson, and he knew it. He'd been trapped in a maze of evidence.

Thompson blinked rapidly. He shook his head, as if to indicate he understood his options.

Flores advised that he'd consult with the prosecutor, but most certainly it would involve substantial jail time and deportation. The murder charge was separate.

"We can't resolve the murder case now. That will have to go to trial," Flores said.

"My client didn't murder anyone," his lawyer said.

"We'll let the court decide that."

Thompson made a move as if jumping over the table to attack Flores. DeLuca restrained him and led him back to his cell.

* * *

Once she heard Thompson's fate. Amy confessed. She said someone she didn't know had contacted her and said they wanted to buy the Ruyna painting. They'd solicited her to arrange the shill bid in order to inflate the price. The fake buyer claimed he worked for a Scandinavian art dealer, who financed the operation. They'd intended to sell the painting for a fortune if the bid had been successful. Thompson knew about the operation, but he hadn't been directly involved, according to Amy.

"That still makes him a part of the conspiracy," Flores said.

The two faced years of imprisonment and deportation. The indictments handed down listed numerous charges. A separate charge for conspiracy to commit the murder of Addison Mason was filed. This time, both were denied bail.

* * *

It'd turned dark by the time Flores finished the paperwork. He reached into his desk drawer and extracted the bottle of American whiskey he kept. He poured a healthy amount into the glass he kept next to the whiskey. He took a large gulp and let out a breath. He rubbed his neck trying to reach the crick, but the pain lingered. He took another shot of whiskey. He'd have to limit his celebration, though. Diego Sanchez's murder hadn't been solved. Carmela Sanchez was a wealthy and important member of the community. Pressure continued from the mayor's office and the government to find out who killed Sanchez, and why.

Flores put his hands behind his head and reared back in his chair.

Chapter Thirty-Eight

Marco had something to celebrate. Belen would be returning home from her dance tour. He woke up happy, singing U2's "Beautiful Day." He still smiled as he walked to work through the brick streets of town.

Eva noticed his cheery disposition. "You look happy today, jefe," she said.

"I am. Belen's coming back this evening."

"That's great," Eva said. "Did you clean the house?"

Marco snickered. "I'm going to put everything away, including my dirty socks, before she gets there."

"Good."

Marco switched on the light in his office. He'd only come in for a short time to do some research on the murders. He needed to get everything ready before Belen arrived. Marco didn't believe Thompson and Bloom murdered Addison. They had no motive. There'd been no evidence Addison ever knew of their crimes, nor that Amy was storing silver in the basement of the museum. Marco reviewed his Excel sheet, eliminating suspects. He paused when he got to Sven Bjorgen. Hmmm. They'd never considered him as a possible suspect. Now that he thought about it, Sven had a powerful motive. Professional rivalry. His own museum hadn't been doing well. Bjorgen's was in debt and on the verge of bankruptcy. He'd also publicly expressed his feelings about an Islamic Museum in Vivirrambla, in what Marco thought were racist articles. Perhaps Bjorgen decided to shut down the new museum before it even opened.

Marco also recalled that Sven said something at the museum opening that had given him pause. When Amy Bloom went to search for Addison, Sven made the statement that, "Addison could be lost forever in this big museum." Everyone laughed at the time. Now, Marco thought that there was perhaps something more to that statement. Projection.

Marco phoned Flores to tell him what he'd discovered. He also wanted to talk to him about Jules Moore.

"I think I've nabbed Addison Mason's killers," Flores said before Marco could speak.

"That's what I wanted to talk to you about. I think you should look at the other museum owner, Sven Bjorgen as a suspect," Marco said, explaining the pieces he'd put together.

"What would Sven gain by killing Addison?" Flores asked.

"Addison's museum was competition for him. By all accounts, it was a much better museum; but if Sven could stop the museum from opening and get a hold of the Ruyna, he'd be rich and could save his museum for years to come."

"Hmmm. I don't know. Thompson and Bloom also have a strong motive. Amy Bloom tried to sabotage the acquisition of the painting," Flores said.

Marco let it drop. He knew once Flores had decided something, he'd stick to his conclusion. Marco would have to continue sleuthing on his own.

"Now, about Jules Moore, you're saying the man you went to see in England had possession of the stolen painting for over eighty years? That he was the seller at the auction?" Flores asked.

"That's right. He was Anonymous. The auction house represented him. Carmela bought it from him. Then she sold it to the museum. Something about the tax debt," Marco said.

"Did Moore actually steal the painting?" Flores asked.

"The auctioneer didn't know where Moore acquired it. They make it a policy not to question an anonymous seller. I doubt if Addison knew about Jules Moore. The auction house didn't even know the painting had originally been stolen," Marco said.

"Amy Bloom and Nicholas Thompson may have known Moore stole the painting. Amy worked for him. They could have been blackmailing Moore, threatening to turn him in to police unless he supplied them with silver to sell," Flores said.

"That's a possibility. I think we need to meet with Jules Moore," Marco said.

"This Jules Moore character is in England. You said he didn't travel. How are we supposed to get him over here?" Flores asked.

"I had an idea about that. Oliver Hall, one of the museum Board members, is close to Jules Moore. Oliver introduced me to him when I went over there. Señor Moore invited me to dinner at his house; he's a frail elderly man with cancer. He told me he used to travel to Spain often. He wished he could visit one last time before he dies. Let's make his wish come true. Let's try to get Oliver to induce him to come over. We can tell him Amy Bloom needs his help," Marco said.

"That's not a bad idea," Flores said.

"Okay, I'll call Oliver Hall tomorrow."

Marco hung up the phone. Then he shut down his computer and told Eva he'd be leaving for the day. He'd prepared a special meal for Belen and needed to get home to finish cleaning and cooking. Eva looked at him with a wry smile. "Have a good night and tell Belen hello from me."

Chapter Thirty-Nine

"By November 1, 1939, the Nationalists Occupied All of Spain and the fighting was over."

—*Spain in Hearts*, Adam Hochschild

A knock on the door broke his concentration. Flores checked his watch. It was getting late. He'd been engrossed in documents for longer than he thought. "Come in," he said.

An officer poked his head in the door. "Excuse me, sir. There's an attorney here to see you."

Flores cocked his head. "Did he say what it was about?"

"No, sir. He said he needs to speak to you directly. He says it's urgent."

"Ok, show him in."

The officer returned a few minutes later with a rotund man wearing large red framed glasses. His hair was salt and pepper, as was his goatee. He wore a blue suit with a multi-colored kerchief in his front pocket.

"*Buenas tardes, Señor Abogado,*" Flores said. "Please have a seat. How can I help you?"

"*Buenas tardes. Soy, Eugenio Tomasa,*" the man said, shaking Flores's hand with a crushing grip. "I'm here to talk to you about my client, Nicholas Thompson. I'm afraid you'll have to drop the murder charge against him."

Flores narrowed his eyes. "What happened to his other lawyer?"

"I'm afraid they had some irreconcilable differences. I'm a criminal defense attorney," the lawyer said.

"What do you want to speak to me about?"

Eugenio sat back in his chair. "My client cannot have committed this murder. He has an alibi for the time of the murder, Detective."

Flores put down the papers he'd been holding. "This is the first I've heard about it."

Eugenio smiled. "Well, frankly, Detective, my client was embarrassed about his behavior, and he didn't want his wife to find out. He never thought he'd be blamed for murder."

Flores wanted to laugh. *Embarrassed? Nicholas wanted to steal money, pilfer a famous painting, and start a new life in a new country after leaving his wife.* "What's his alibi?"

"Nicholas and Amy were…should I say, *en flagrante* at the time of the killing," Eugenio said, moving his eyebrows up and down.

Flores knitted his brow. "What do you mean?"

"To be blunt, they were having sex in one of the exhibit rooms in another part of the museum at the time of Addison Mason's death. They did not go back into the exhibit hall until Amy announced she was going to search for Addison. She could not have killed him that short amount of time. A witness, Señora Mercedes Ruiz, has come forward to say she saw them having sex. She'd wandered out of the exhibit hall looking for a bathroom. She accidentally walked into the wrong room. Of course, she backed right out," Eugenio said, smiling again.

Flores furrowed his eyebrows. "Why haven't I heard anything about this up until now? It's very convenient that this witness came forward now."

"As I said, my client didn't want his wife to know. Señora Ruiz was also embarrassed. She'd been reluctant to tell anyone else. You can question her yourself. She only came forward when she heard that my client and Amy Bloom had been charged in the papers. Then she contacted me. She was afraid she'd be in trouble if she went directly to the police."

"I see. We'll have to verify this, of course," Flores said, trying to maintain his cool.

"Of course," Eugenio said, drawing a breath from his huge frame. "Feel free to talk to Señora Ruiz. She understands now that she won't get in trouble with the police. Here's her contact info."

Flores took the information from him.

The lawyer stood up and extended his hand to Flores. "Thank you for your time, Detective. Please don't hesitate to contact me if you need anything more."

Flores watched the attorney leave his office. He felt his heart sink, as if he'd been hit in the chest by a mallet. The late afternoon streamed through his window. He grabbed the whiskey bottle from the bottom desk drawer again. This time, not to celebrate. He needed the courage to go and tell the Chief that neither murder case had been solved.

Chapter Forty

"[W]hat we call our despair is often only the painful eagerness of unfed hope."
—Middle March, George Eliot

Flores braced himself for the expected wrath from the Chief when he told him that the murder cases were both still outstanding. The Chief had backed down when he thought one of the murderers was in custody. He took his time going to his office, giving himself a pep talk along the way. He popped a couple of Altoids in his mouth.

"Sit down," the Chief, dressed in full uniform, said when Flores arrived in his office.

The meeting had gone as expected. Flores left the Chief's office with his job hanging by a thread. His head hanging low, Flores went back to his office to plan his next steps. At lunch time, while he sat at his desk eating his tuna sandwich, the phone rang, causing him to jump and spill coffee all over his computer keyboard. Another keyboard he'd have to get replaced. Property scolded him the last time about not being careful with his equipment.

Oliver Hall identified himself when Flores rang him. Hall said Marco had asked him about getting Jules Moore to come over. Hall said he would try, but he suggested Flores also contact Moore.

"I think he'd listen to the police," Hall said.

After mopping up his desk, Flores phoned Jules Moore on the number Oliver had given him in England. He and Moore had a lengthy conversation. Moore turned out to be an interesting old man, who'd had a fascinating life. Moore said that after he heard about Amy's arrest. He'd taken inventory of his shop. He discovered several pieces of expensive silver missing. Some silver from his own collection was also missing. He admitted he'd become something of a hoarder in his advanced years.

"No family, nothing to do but acquire stuff," Moore said.

He'd had no idea Amy had been pilfering his silver.

"Will you come to Spain then?" Flores asked.

Moore said that his health was failing, but he thought he could make the two-hour flight to Malaga. He wanted to see Amy in person to ask her why she'd steal from him when he treated her like a daughter.

"I want to see Vivirrambla again, one last time, too," Moore said.

When he hung up, Flores pinged Marco and told him of his conversation with Jules. He asked Marco to accompany Oliver Hall to pick Jules up at the airport when he arrived.

Chapter Forty-One

"Miguel was dressed as a vizier of the Arabian Nights."
—*Leaving Tangier,* Tahar Ben Jelloun

Marco and Oliver met a frail-looking, white-haired old man in baggage claims at Malaga airport a couple of days later. Marco was struck by how fast Moore had deteriorated since he'd first met him in London just a few months ago. He seemed much older in that short time. Moore hugged Oliver and shook hands with Marco, as he picked up his bag.

"It's good to see you again, young man. I hadn't expected to see you so soon, and in Vivirrambla," Jules said to Marco, his old eyes twinkling.

The old man still had an air of flamboyance. He wore a bright orange tracksuit and glasses with black and orange Betsey Johnson frames, which stood out against his mass of white hair. On his age-spotted fingers, he wore several diamond rings which appeared to be antique. He smelled as if he'd been drowned in cologne. He trotted through the airport with his jewel-encrusted antique cane out to Oliver's Mercedes.

Jules spoke in a weak voice. "I forgot how nice the weather was here, perhaps if I'd moved here, my health would be better," he said, laughing, as he climbed into the front seat of the car. Oliver took Jules's bag and threw it into the trunk. Oliver had agreed to let him stay in his home during his visit.

Marco said that they needed to go straight to the police station as Detective Flores was expecting them. They drove one-half hour to the Malaga police station. Jules seemed animated as he looked out the window. IIe commented

193

on the scenery and reminisced about the last time he'd been in Spain. An officer ushered them into Flores's office when they arrived at the precinct. Flores had tried to tidy up his office, much to Marco's surprise. His desk wasn't filled with the usual Styrofoam coffee cups and paper wrappers.

Flores invited everyone to sit. "Señor Moore, thank you for flying over here to help us with this matter. I hope it hasn't been too much of a hardship for you."

"How is Amy?" he asked. "I thought she was ill."

"Ahh, she's fine. You'rehere on police business, Sir."

Flores explained the nature of the charges against Amy. We were hoping you could help with our investigation.

Jules pursed his lips tightly and shook his old head. "You brought me here under false pretenses."

"Yes sir," said Flores. It was the only way we could get you to come to Spain."

Moore made a hissing sound with his mouth. "I still can't believe Amy would steal from me. That isn't like her. This boyfriend of hers, Nicholas Thompson, must have talked her into it. You knew Nicholas Thompson at school, didn't you, Oliver?" Jules asked.

"Yes, he went to school with Addison and me. You met him a couple of times when he visited me. He became a successful lawyer. I was shocked too. It just doesn't make sense that Nicholas would be involved in theft and possibly murder."

"We dropped the murder charges. From my experience of years as a detective, people can sometimes surprise you, unfortunately," Flores said.

Marco and Flores had made the strategic decision to ask Moore about the Runya painting before letting him speak to Amy, in order to get as much information from him as possible before he could be influenced. Flores turned to Moore.

"There's another matter I need to ask you about, Señor Moore," Flores said.

Jules sat back in his chair. The creases on his old face appeared prominently in the light of the sun beaming through Flores's window. He knitted his brow. "Oh, really? I thought you just said you dropped the murder charges."

"Si, Señor, we did. This is about the painting that Addison Mason intended to unveil the night he was killed, the lost Runya. I'm sure you heard about it," Flores said.

Moore took a wrinkled hand and brushed back a strand of white hair that had fallen into his face. "Painting? I heard something about a lost painting."

Marco got out the information he'd amassed from Tuille auction house and showed it to Moore. "Señor Moore, we know that you were the person who sold the painting to Carmela Sanchez through Tuille auction house."

Jules sat silent, unmoving. Then he coughed a deep cough. Oliver Hall went to find him some water. When Hall returned, Jules still had not spoken.

"What's all this about?" Oliver Hall asked. "I thought you wanted Jules here to talk to Amy. Are you ok, Jules?"

Jules shook his head, yes. "I'm okay," he said in a barely audible voice.

Marco continued. "I've spoken to Emir Mohamed, a gentleman in Morocco, whose family is the rightful owner of the Runya painting. A servant stole it from them in the nineteen thirties. I've seen all the documents of authenticity. The painting had been with Emir's family since the time of Boadil. Emir's father had been devastated when the painting he'd been entrusted to guard was stolen."

Jules Moore coughed again and took a large gulp of water.

"You set up that auction, didn't you, Señor?" Flores asked.

Oliver Hall stared at Jules, his eyes wide. It was apparent Hall knew nothing about the painting being stolen. He stuttered. "I...it was me who arranged the sale. We set up a private auction. Jules told me he wanted to get rid of the painting before he died. He was delighted it was going back to Spain."

Marco looked at Oliver Hall. "So, he never told you how he got the painting?"

Oliver shook his head. "No, I just assumed he acquired it like he acquired all his paintings. Jules is an art expert. He knows a lot of important buyers. I knew the painting was special to him. It hung in his dining room over the buffet for several years."

"As an art historian, you never found any information about the painting being stolen?" Flores asked.

Hall shook his head. "I'm afraid not. I never studied Islamic art. As odd as it sounds, unless it was something like a Rembrandt, if it weren't in my discipline, I'd have no way of knowing about the Runya, due to the lack of information available to me."

"I see. So did you authenticate this particular painting?" Marco asked.

Oliver raised his eyebrows. "I told him it seemed to be an authentic fifteen century painting. Little tracking is done of these paintings unless a question is raised."

Jules took a sip of water. "So, is that why you really brought me here?"

Flores and Marco remained silent.

"You can't arrest me. You brought me here under duress," Jules said.

Oliver Hall looked over at him, his face contorted in confusion.

"You're right, but I can contact my colleagues in England and Interpol. I have my officers standing by, ready to make that call. I have a contact in the UK who's an expert in stolen antiques. Your next trip won't be a nice, pleasant business class flight to Spain," Flores said.

Jules scrunched his creased forehead. He folded his hands. He looked almost prayerful. "I tried to do the right thing in the end."

"Tell us about it, Señor Moore. A man may have been killed because of what you did," Marco said.

Again, there was silence except for periodic coughing from Jules.

"It's a long story," Jules said.

"We've got all day," Flores said, sticking an Altoid mint in his mouth and offering them to the room.

"You don't have to tell them anything, Jules, I'll get you a lawyer, and we can find out what this is all about," Oliver said.

Moore wagged his index finger back and forth. "No, no. I've flown all the way out here now," (cough). "My doctor said I only have a year or so left if I'm lucky. I'm glad the truth is coming out. I needed to get it off my chest."

Jules turned to Flores and Marco. "I'll tell you what happened all those years ago. I was more of the middleman. I ended up with the painting, as there was nothing else I could do with it once we had it. There was no buyer's market."

"Jules, you don't have to say anything," Oliver urged.

Jules put his finger to his mouth. "Shhhh, don't worry, Oliver, it's my time to talk and time is something I don't have much of left."

"How did you get the painting?" Flores asked, his voice sounding harsh.

Marco wished Flores weren't so abrupt at times. He lacked the ability to discern when a circumstance called for more tact.

Jules narrowed his eyes. "The thirties, as you know, were a turbulent time in Spain. The country was on the brink of civil war. Franco was poised to take power. I visited Spain frequently in those days. Let me just say my lifestyle wasn't as accepted in London as it was here; besides, I had the sun and more lovers than I could count."

Flores wiggled in his seat.

Jules pretended not to notice. "In those days, I attended those legendary parties given by Salvador Dali. Dali, as you know, supported Franco and the Nationalists. I met a lot of Franco supporters at those parties. I personally didn't care one way or the other. England had its own troubles during that time."

Marco and Flores looked at one another. "Salvador Dali, the artist?" Flores asked.

Jules looked up at them. "Yes. He had great parties. I loved good-looking Spanish and Moroccan men and they gravitated to Dali's house. Some of the Moroccans had been involved in the military uprising in Melilla in nineteen thirty-six. They loved to share their stories."

Marco had learned of the uprising as a student. The Army of Africa, as it was called. Arabs who supported Franco, along with other units in the Spanish Army, joined together and rose up against the Second Spanish Republic. They fought on the side of the Nacionales. Their support helped the succession in July 1936 of Generalissimo Francisco Franco.

"What does all of this have to do with the stolen painting?" Flores asked.

Jules glared at him. Small creases formed when he narrowed his eyes. "It has everything to do with it. We developed a circle of friendships at those Dali parties. The Moroccans, in favor of him, needed funding to support

Generalissimo Franco. I'd been dating one of them, Abdul. We were in love." Jules's eyes lit up as he spoke about his old lover. "One night as we sat around sharing a hookah, Abdul told us that he worked for a family that had a valuable painting. He knew how to get his hands on it. If we could sell it, we could raise a lot of money."

Jules coughed again for a long time, a deep cough that made his chest cave in. Oliver Hall looked over at him. Once he caught his breath, Jules spoke again.

"As I said, I wasn't on one side or the other, but I would have done anything for Abdul. True to his words, after a month or so of planning, Abdul stole the Runya painting from the house he worked in in Morocco. He brought it back to Spain, but we had to figure out how to sell it. We couldn't very well go to Sotheby's and say, "Hey, we've got this stolen Runya if you want it." Miguel Sanchez agreed to hide the painting in his family's restaurant until we decided what to do with it."

"Carmela Sanchez's father was a part of your group?" Marco asked.

Jules shook his head. "Yes, the restaurant became the hub for our activities."

Now Marco knew what Carmela meant about her father being a fascist. Why he'd meet with strange men in the back of the restaurant.

"Miguel Sanchez used his restaurant as a front for Francoists?" Marco asked.

Jules nodded. "Yes, he was a good friend of ours and the movement. I was the same age as his son, Diego. We all grew close. Miguel Sanchez approached me and asked me if I could afford to buy the painting. I told him I could. I had plenty of money. I'd inherited it from my parents, who died before the Great War. I agreed to purchase the painting and take it back to London, where it remained until I recently sold it to Carmela."

Oliver sat up in his chair. "How did you smuggle the painting back to England?"

"It was easy to go back and forth then as an Englishman. No one really paid attention if you had money. Later, I discovered Diego had stolen the money I paid for the painting. He never given it on to the group. My lover, Abdul, thought I'd stolen the money from them and kept the painting. He never forgave me. I never returned to Spain. Abdul threatened to kill me if I returned." Jules sank back in his chair. "My heart's never healed. I've had many men, but I've never gotten over Abdul."

"You never returned to Spain after that?" Marco asked.

Jules shook his head. "Until you brought me here today, under false pretenses…"

"They aren't false pretenses. Amy has been arrested."

"Anyway. No, I just couldn't bring myself to come back here knowing I'd be so close to Abdul's grave even though died many years ago. I found that out from some other members of our group."

The room was quiet for a time. Marco broke the silence.

"Señor Moore, I think you were here one other time," Marco said.

Jules's head jerked back. "What do you mean, young man?" he asked, coughing.

Marco placed printouts and a ticket on the table in front of Jules. Marco had checked with the airport in Malaga to see if they had any record of Jules entering the country at any time. He'd combed through airport records and manifests. He'd interviewed airport employees, including ticket agents and porters who may have helped an old man with his luggage and remembered him.

He learned the most information from a ticket agent at JetBlue airline, which made frequent flights between Malaga and London. The agent verified that an elderly man fitting Jules's description, smelling of cologne, had taken a recent flight to Spain.

"These are statements I got from the employees at the Malaga airport, plus a copy of your ticket. Jetblue flight JBI1023, round-trip ticket from London to Malaga for the day before Diego was killed. Marco pointed to a grainy photograph, depicting a man walking to a gate with a cane. You're captured here on camera," Marco said.

Jules squirmed in his chair but didn't respond.

Just then, the air in the room filled with the smell of Jules's cologne, the scent of Hugo Boss, combined with the sweat of an old man.

"The ticket agent remembered a well-dressed, white-haired old man who smelled of cologne. She said it stuck out in her mind that someone so elderly took the time to smell good," Marco said.

Flores wrinkled his nose at the overpowering smell. "What do you have to say to that?" he asked.

Jules didn't respond.

Then Marco added. "A while ago, someone accosted my girlfriend and me and warned me about Diego Sanchez. Do you know anything about that?"

Jules nodded. "Yes, I sent someone to warn you. You were getting too close to learning the truth."

"What?" said Oliver.

Marco continued on. "The manager at Sanchez's remembered a white-haired old gentleman coming into the restaurant a little before Diego was killed. The man smelled of cologne. He said the gentleman slipped out before completing the reservation. Then everything turned chaotic. Everyone became distracted when the murder occurred. That white-haired man was you, wasn't it, Señor Moore?" Marco asked. "Your cologne is your calling card. We've all been smelling it since you arrived. I smelled the same scent in London."

Jules shrugged his shoulders and hung his head.

"You slipped into the restaurant's kitchen. When all the wait staff went to the other room for a meeting, you confronted Diego and stabbed him with one of the kitchen knives," Marco said.

Jules stared at Marco, then turned away. "Can you believe Diego wanted to talk after all these years?"

"How did you get into the kitchen without anyone seeing you?" Flores asked.

"I'm an old man. No one pays me any attention. I slipped through the door when they went to their meeting. They were busy. Thankfully, they left the knives out. I might be on my last leg, but I'm still nimble. It only takes a minute to kill if you know what you're doing. Abdul was a rebel fighter; he taught me how to kill in an instant," Jules said.

Oliver Hall recoiled. "Jules, I don't believe what I'm hearing. You killed Carmela's brother in cold blood?"

Jules arched his thick, white eyebrows. "I hated that bastard for making me lose Abdul. Diego had the gall to call me when he found out I had arranged to have the Runya painting brought back to Spain. He said that if I came over, we could have dinner at the restaurant and talk. I agreed."

Tears began to fall from his tired old face.

"Emir and his family were devastated to lose that painting," Marco said.

"I had no idea where Abdul got the painting. It's true he was a servant in that house. I never knew how I could return the painting to the police without incriminating myself. I saw this as the perfect opportunity for me to purge myself of this crime before I leave this earth."

"You killed Diego, out of revenge. How does that make you atone for what you've done? How does that cleanse you?" Marco asked.

Jules gave Marco with an icy stare of resignation. "It took me seventy years to exact my revenge. At least I got that."

Oliver stood up and walked over to Jules and rubbed his shoulders. "Don't you see he's exhausted now?"

Chapter Forty-Two

*"The enormous gulf between rich and poor was a major tension underlying the
Spanish Civil War."*
        —*Spain in Our Hearts*, Adam Hochschild

A crowd of a dozen or so assembled around a large gold plaque on the wall next to the painting. Marco stood amongst them. The plaque had a picture of Emir and his family. The written narrative told the story of Sumya Runya, painter to the ruler Boabdil, the last Caliphate of Spain. Marco and Belen had been invited to the small celebration before the Musea de Galeria de Arte officially reopened.

A resolution had been worked out after some haggling between Emir's family, Farah, and the Board. At last, everyone seemed happy with the agreement. Marco had briefed Emir Mohamed on Jules Moore and how the Francoist stole his painting to finance Franco's rise to power. He also told him about the murder of Carmela's brother. Emir had expressed shock at the news; however, he felt relieved to finally know the truth. Carmela, ashamed of what her family had done, agreed to pay four million Euros plus one million dollars in restitution for the Runya. She agreed to donate the painting to the museum as a part of its permanent collection. After a vote, minus Marc Thompson, the Board chose Oliver Hall as its interim director.

Emir said that he'd prayed about it with his family, and that they'd decided the painting should go to the gallery, where no individual would be responsible for its safekeeping. The theft had caused his family eighty years of guilt and shame. That would never happen to another generation. They agreed to license the painting for the planned interactive exhibit Farah's husband had been working on.

***

Now, Marco and Belen were attending a posthumous ceremony celebrating the life of its founder, Addison Mason. Oliver's new assistant, a young American, invited guests to step out to the garden where a memorial sculpture had been erected to be placed at the spot where Addison had been found dead. Marco and Belen joined the group in the garden. The sun was hot, beating on the stone. Women fanned themselves with decorative Spanish fans while men dug for something to wipe the sweat off their brows. Marco hoped it wouldn't be a long ceremony as they stood under the beaming sun, listening to tributes to Addison.

Farah Zine, standing on the other side of the garden, looked over at Marco and winked. Marco smiled back at her.

Belen nudged him in the rib. "I see Señora Zine is here. Is her husband with her? I don't see him?"

As he was about to respond, a gray cat with vivid green eyes crossed in front of Marco prancing over the stone tile and through the grass. Marco looked down at it, happy for the diversion from Belen's scrutiny. The agile cat frolicked and started playing with a bright orange small wooden figure near one of the statues, patting it back and forth with its paws. The figure gleamed in the sunlight.

Marco nudged Belen. "Look over there," he said, whispering and pointing to the object.

"What is it?" she asked.

Marco grabbed her hand. "Let's move over there."

They sidled past guests, towards the wooden figure. The cat scurried away. Marco bent down to look at the figurine. It was in the shape of a horse. Its saddle, composed of a light blue floral design, had been hand-crafted. Marco saw where the figure had been buried. The cat must have dug it up.

"Does this look like the figurine you saw at Sven's Museum shop?" Marco asked.

Belen looked down at the object. "Yeah, that's it. I remember it was the only thing in that place that didn't look creepy. Sven told us it was called a Dala horse, remember?"

Marco nodded. "He said something about it being the national symbol of Sweden. Sweetie, I think you just solved a murder," Marco said, kissing her on the cheek.

Belen's eyes grew wide. "Why? What have I done?"

"I'll tell you when this is all over. I'm going to have to go to Malaga right after this. I'll drop you off at home first," Marco said.

Marco headed straight to Flores's office to tell him about the small curio in the garden. He found Flores sitting at his desk amongst a pile of papers. His ubiquitous teetering coffee cup rested dangerously close to his computer keyboard.

"You'd better move that cup before you have an accident," Marco said while taking a seat.

Flores fumbled and shifted the coffee cup to the other side of the desk. "What are you doing here?"

"Good news, Alberto. I think I've identified our killer," Marco said.

Flores sat up. "Really? Now that would indeed be good news. I'm really in danger of a demotion. The Chief called me upstairs again this morning."

"I think you'll be able to get the Chief off your back, soon," Marco said.

Marco relayed the tale of the Swedish Dala horse and Sven's museum. He told him how they'd spotted the figure in the sculpture garden near where Addison had been murdered.

"If you think about it, it all fits. Sven Bjorgen is very tall. Javier Bortello said the perpetrator likely had to be tall to get something around Addison's neck before he could fight back. He's also left-handed. I noticed it when we visited his museum. He wrote me a note with his personal information on it."

"Hmmm. We didn't look at him, you're right," Flores said.

"Javier seemed pretty certain about it from the position of the body, concluding the killer had to be tall," Marco said.

Flores sat up in his chair. "Now this is getting interesting. Did you bring the figurine?"

Marco shook his head no. "I left it in the garden. So, you could get prints."

"Ok, good. I'll send someone right away. If Sven's prints *were* on it, he must've buried that Dala horse in the garden as sort of a calling card. Murderers, especially those with a personal motive, sometimes leave their signature behind after they do the deed. It's sort of a "catch me if you can" move. They're proud of their caper. Obviously, Sven didn't think we'd find the figurine," Flores said.

"You sound like a forensic psychologist. Have you been taking classes?" Marco asked, laughing.

Flores chuckled. "I've learned one or two things attending those seminars, over the years. Let's hope Sven Bjorgen doesn't find out we're on to him and flee to Sweden. I'll talk to the prosecutor right away."

"Great, thanks, Alberto," Marco said.

"Thanks for bringing me good news. I may get a reprieve once the Chief knows we've identified a new suspect."

Chapter Forty-Three

Farah asked Marco to meet him in Puerto Bella for a celebratory dinner. She wanted to thank him for all he did for the museum.

"No funny business. I promise," she said when she called him. Marco laughed, "Sure, why not?"

Belen was in Madrid for the weekend, visiting her family. So, Marco was free. He walked home, showered, and changed into a fresh pair of dark linen pants and a light blue Lacoste shirt. He splashed on a dash of Aftershave. When he arrived in Puerto Bella, he found Farah waiting for him in front of the door of the restaurant in the same building complex as Sven's Museum. She wore an apricot-colored maxi dress with slim spaghetti straps. Her long, dark hair hung to her shoulders. Large dangling gold earrings highlighted her bronze complexion. She wore her large dark shades, as the sun remained high in the sky, reflecting on the large windows of the modern buildings. Marco kissed her on the cheek. "You smell good," she said.

Farah had chosen *Breath*, a trendy restaurant with a Michelin-starred chef. They climbed the white stone steps to the entrance. The hostess seated them outside on the terrace, at a table decorated with orange and white flowers and illuminated by small, dimly lit candles. They sank into beige upholstered chairs with wide backs. A slim waiter dressed in black and white handed them a menu.

Farah ordered an orange cocktail with white cream and chocolate on top. Marco thought it looked like dessert, but Farah said it tasted great. Marco ordered a beer. They shared sushi as appetizers. For dinner, Marco had salmon with truffle fries, "Hmm," he said, to one of the best meals he could remember. Farah ordered lamb with well-cooked vegetables. She, too, expressed her delight with her meal. As Farah stuck her fingers into one of Marco's fries, she looked at him through the flickering light of the candle.

"It's too bad we didn't have better timing," she said.

"Yeah, too bad. I haven't heard any more about your stalker. Has he gone away?" Marco asked.

Farah swirled her swivel stick in her second cocktail and took a sip, "I hope so. The Malaga police may have scared him off."

For dessert, they shared chocolate, sugar-coated pastry surrounded by strawberry pieces. When they finished dessert. Marco rubbed his stomach in a circular motion. "I don't think I can move."

Farah sipped her cocktail, which was down to the last slurp. "I know I said no funny business tonight, just one question. Are you going to marry Belen?"

Why do women always jump to marriage? Marco thought. "I want to marry her one day. I'm just not ready right now."

Farah threw her head back and laughed. "Typical man. Don't want to be told what to do. Not ready to be a father and a husband. You men think if you don't commit to anything, time will stand still, and you'll always be young, like the Picture of Dorian Gray."

They both laughed.

"I saw that movie. Didn't he turn ugly when the painting was destroyed? Time is definitely not standing still. The cliché about time flying seems more and more true the older I get," Marco said.

"You're right," Farah said, smiling.

As they finished the last of the dessert, Farah handed her credit card to an ogling waiter.

"Thank you for a wonderful meal," Marco said.

"Thank you for all your help. You've done a lot for me and for the museum. Do you have time to go back to the museum? There's something I want to show you," Farah said.

"Sure," Marco said. "I've got all night."

They drove separate cars back to Vivirrambla. Once they reached the door, Farah took out a key and opened the museum door. Marco followed her inside.

The room was pitch black. The sun had set since they'd begun dinner. It looked like one of those old mansions you see in movies. Marco expected a man in a steel suit of armor to fall out in front of them. "It's spooky in here at night," he said.

Farah laughed as she switched on the lights. "Yeah, it's like one of those horror movies. Come over here, I want to show you a new exhibit we're putting up. I wanted you to be the first to see it."

"I'm intrigued," Marco said, going where Farah directed him.

Farah switched on the light in another room. An illuminated glass case dominated the wall in front of them. Inside the case, a pillar of white marble decorated in Bas-relief hung against a solid black background.

"Emir donated this to us. It's also from the fifteenth-century, from the palace of Boabdil," Farah said.

Marco walked closer and looked at the featured piece. "Wow. It's incredible. Jaddah would love this. I'll have to make sure she sees it."

"I thought you'd like it. Emir's become a real friend of the museum," Farah said.

As Farah finished speaking, something loomed up behind them, a figure in the shadows.

"Certainly not the quality of a Donatello," the intruder said.

Farah gasped.

Marco turned to face the speaker. "What are you doing here?"

"I followed you and the beautiful Señora Zine here," Sven Bjorgen said.

"How did you get into the museum?" Farah asked.

Sven sneered. "Why, beautiful Farah, I have a key. Addison was kind enough to let me have it when he...let's say went to that great museum in the sky, ha, ha, ha. Why are you two always together?"

Farah shivered. She wrapped the gold shawl hanging from her arms around her shoulders and put her arms closer to her chest. "Sven, have you been drinking?"

Sven glared at her. "Of course I've been drinking, ha, ha, ha."

Marco inched closer to Farah. "I found the Dala horse you buried in the sculpture garden. Addison had orange paint on his shirt when they found him. The paint came from the newly painted figurine. Clever of you to put it right near the sculpture where you killed Addison. A cat dug it up, though," Marco said.

Sven's face contorted. He pulled a gun from inside his pants and stuck it in Farah's side. "Don't try to move or make a noise."

"Sven, what's this all about? You killed, Addison?" Farah asked. "You didn't tell me that, Marco."

"The investigation's still open. I couldn't tell you anything about it," Marco said.

Sven laughed. "Ha, so, beautiful, Farah, your lover doesn't tell you everything after all. Addison Mason was a joke. His museum was a joke. A whole museum featuring ancient Islamic art. Who wants to see that? Still, I wanted that painting, you know. A lost painting tied to royalty no matter who it is, is worth a fortune. I begged Addison to sell it to me. I told him I'd give him one-hundred thousand over the price he paid for it."

"Why would he have agreed to anything like that?" Marco said.

"He stood to make a profit for his new museum. When I couldn't persuade him to sell, I wrote articles about the museum, hoping to shut it down before it even opened," Sven said.

"I read some of your articles, very scathing against Islamic art," Marco said.

"Sven, what *do* you want from us?" Farah asked, her voice shaking.

Sven poked the gun into Farah's back, causing her to squirm. "You know what I want, Farah."

Sven's eyes momentarily softened. Then he glared at Marco. "What does this Gypsy have that I don't?"

Farah tried to steady her voice. "Sven, I have no idea what you're talking about? You smell like liquor. I think you've had too much to drink. You should go home before you do something you regret."

Marco reached for his phone. He felt his heart pound.

Sven shoved the gun harder into her back. Farah recoiled. "Give me that phone, or she dies."

Marco handed him his phone. "Was money all you were after? You had no respect for the art did you?"

"You've driven me to this, Farah. You've ruined my life."

"Farah has done nothing to you. You've been following her, haven't you? You scared her, and now you're pointing a gun at her," Marco said.

Sven looked surprised. "My museum's closing, did you know that, Gypsy? People prefer this Islamic trash to my beautiful European art. The whole world's becoming too 'woke.' I needed to get that painting. It was the last hope to save my museum. I had a buyer lined up in England."

"The art fence who tried to bid on the painting at the auction. You arranged that, didn't you? Where did you get the money?" Marco asked.

"You certainly know a lot about what's going on, Gypsy. I've been using my wife's money to keep everything going. She told me that if the museum doesn't start making a profit, she was going to close it. I took money from her account to purchase the painting. I had a buyer lined up. My wife would never have known. I would have sold it and given her back her money. I'd have enough money that I never needed to depend on her anymore," Sven said.

"I met your wife at a party I had at my house. She said she couldn't find you for a time during the museum opening. That's because you were in Addison's office, forcing him out onto the patio to kill him, right?" Marco said.

Sven ignored the question. He tugged Farah with the gun, "I loved you, Farah. You brushed me off like an annoying pest."

"Sven, I had no idea," Farah said. "We're both married."

Sven had tears in his eyes. "Why couldn't you represent my museum like you did for this one? Why couldn't you become my spokesperson? We could have been a great team."

"I don't love you, Sven. You can't intimidate me into loving you."

Sven looked down at the ground. Marco sensed an opportunity. He took a step forward and reached for the gun.

Sven snapped back and pointed his gun at Marco. "Don't move, Gypsy. I followed you on that ferry to Morocco. I knew you two lovebirds would be meeting up there."

Farah recoiled.

"That's right. I saw you on the ferry. You said you were going to visit friends. How did you know I was going to see Farah there?" Marco asked.

Sven snarled. "I know everything Farah does. I've been tracking her for months. I figured out that you two were having an affair from the beginning. You planned a little tryst to Morocco."

"There was no tryst. We went there on business. Nothing is going on between Marco and me. So, you're the one that's been following me?" Farah asked.

Sven grabbed her hair. Farah jerked her head away. "You're so beautiful, Farah. I've loved you ever since I saw you for the first time in *Vivirrambla Today*. I'm the one who truly loves you, but you chose this Gypsy trash over me."

"Marco's my friend. I'm married." Farah said.

Sven laughed a deep belly laugh. "That so called 'husband' of yours is a nobody. Useless. He could have been useful if he'd developed a 3D immersive show for my museum, like he's doing for Addison. I called him about it, before Addison died, but he said it wasn't possible in my museum. Then I found out Addison's filed for a patent for that 3D exhibit of Runya. With a patent, he'd own the rights to the software. I'd have to pay him to use the software."

"Addison's my husband's client, Sven," Farah said.

Sven ignored her. "I'd lost the Runya painting, but I found one last chance to save my museum and my life. That night in the garden, I begged Addison to sign the patent he'd filed over to me. I'd thought of having an immersive art exhibit first, I told him. He'd stolen my idea. I'd sue him, I said."

Marco sneered. "Why on earth would he have signed a valuable patent over to you?"

Sven glared at Marco. "What do you know about it, Gypsy? I discovered one of the museum's board members is high up in the right-wing group, Vox. I told Addison and threatened to expose him. How would it look, a museum that featured Islamic art, one of its own, a member of an ultra-right-wing group?" Sven laughed. "Addison didn't believe me. He said Marc Thompson was one of his oldest friends. I told him I'd send it to all the papers. Addison practically laughed in my face. He said he couldn't be bullied. He said he'd find out for himself if it were true. If it was, he'd deal with it."

"Good for him. What do you plan to do with us?" Marco asked.

Sven walked over and punched Marco in the stomach. Marco doubled over gasping.

"Shut up, Gypsy. I need to think."

Sven was silent for a time. He looked over as if he'd heard something. "What was that?"

* * *

Marco worked to catch his breath back. "It's probably just the building settling. It's an old house."

"I'll take you too to the basement, where no one will find you for some time," Sven said as if Marco hadn't spoken.

"You already tried to kill me once, after I got off the ferry," Marco said.

Sven grinned a sinister grin. "Yeah, too bad I missed. I won't make that mistake again." He nudged Farah forward. You and Farah are going to come with me. My beautiful Farah, you're going to be found with the gun in your hand, having committed suicide, distraught over your affair with the Gypsy." He rubbed the gun against her face. "I hate to mess up this glorious face, but it's clear to me now that you don't want me."

"You won't get away with it. The police will find you," Marco said.

"Ha, ha, ha, I'll be back in Sweden before they even find your bodies."

Sven waved the gun towards the exit. He shouted at Marco and Farah. "Move it."

* * *

Just then, a man, barely visible, dressed in a police uniform crept up behind

CHAPTER FORTY-THREE

Sven and held a gun to his head. "Don't move one inch," he said.

Sven stood frozen in place, trying to weigh his options. A loud bang commenced. The main museum doors flew open, and a swarm of police stormed in, yelling, "Malaga Police, put the gun down." Sven looked around, wild-eyed.

"Put the gun down now!" the officer shouted again. He pointed his own gun directly at Sven's temple. Several officers stood behind and around him.

Sven looked around as if calculating his options. "I could just kill her now," he said.

"We'll kill you before you make the shot," the police officer said.

They stood at a standoff for what seemed like an eternity. After a time, Sven threw his gun down and shot his arms up in the air, thereby releasing Farah, who nearly fell to the ground.

The officer, who'd saved them, caught Farah before she could fall. "Buenas tardes. I'm Officer Gil. Detective Flores assigned me to protect you, Señora Zine. I've been watching you this whole time. I saw the man follow you all into the museum; I slipped in behind you in the dark, but I had to wait for backup to arrive. I didn't want to risk any of your lives," he said.

Farah smiled. "Oh, thank goodness, I'm eternally grateful," she said, running to Marco.

Marco held the shaking, sobbing woman in his arms. "Thank you," he said to the officer.

Police handcuffed Sven. He looked at Farah as he was led away. A single tear dropped from his eye. "All I wanted was for my museum to do well so you'd want me, Farah," he said.

Farah turned her head away from him.

Chapter Forty-Four

Flores spent the next several days researching the life of Sven Bjorgen. A raid of Sven's home yielded hundreds of photos and magazine pictures of Farah Zine hidden behind a bedroom closet in a secret wall space Sven had erected. His wife hadn't been aware of his obsession, nor of his secret room.

Flores discovered that Bjorgen faced financial troubles. He had large gambling debts. Flores found footage of an old story where Sven had been filmed when his museum opened. Sven touted it as being a new kind of museum, on the edge, avant-garde, with bold new pieces highlighting lesser-known artists. A few years later, he'd lost most of his investors. The museum averaged two visitors a day. One critic described it as: *Just Plain Weird* with *Weird Paintings and other Weird Pieces Run by a Weird Owner.* Another critic described Sven's gallery as *"Creepy Art in a Creepy Museum.* The writer said he didn't find one piece that was interesting, except the hand-painted Dala horses in the gift shop.

* * *

Flores had Sven brought into the interrogation room. Marco sat across from him. Detective Luca stood behind. Sven now wore prison garb. His blond hair was uncombed and wirily. Sven twisted in his seat and turned his head to the wall. Like most criminals, he seemed unnerved by Marco's eyes, which looked as if they could see right through him to pierce his dark soul.

"I see your museum's about to shut down," Flores said.

"I can't help it if so-called art critics don't recognize great art."

"You had only a few visitors last year. You were about to lose everything," Flores said.

Sven shrugged his shoulders.

"You couldn't compete with Addison Mason," Flores said.

"What do you know about art?" Sven asked.

"He knows enough to know that no one's interested in your so-called art," Marco said.

Sven lunged at Marco. Detective DeLuca grabbed his shoulders in a tight grip and restrained him.

Flores commanded him. "Sit down, sir."

The interrogation lasted several hours. In the end, Sven, worn down and beaten, finally admitted to the murder of Addison.

"Take him away," Flores said when Sven finished his confession.

Detective DeLuca snatched the Swedish man up from the table and led him away.

As DeLuca led him away, Sven stared at Marco, his irises pools of darkness like a black hole. Marco felt a cold chill running down his spine.

Chapter Forty-Five

Marco sat on Alvarez's stool, drinking a café con leche and reading *El País*. All the newspapers carried the news about the sinister Swedish museum owner who'd committed the murder of a rival. A grinning Flores told the press that Sven Bjorgen had confessed to killing Addison Mason. The police, he said, had solved all pending cases and recovered a very valuable lost painting. The Chief stood behind Flores, dressed in uniform, peacocking, and wearing a broad toothy smile.

* * *

Belen and Marco took some time off from work to do nothing but be with one another. They strolled along the beach, swam, ate, and made love. It felt perfect. On the gallery's official reopening date, Marco and Belen glammed up in black cocktail attire and mingled with guests at the museum, renamed: The Addison Mason Galeria d'Arte, which was painted in green and gold on a sign above the wooden door. Addison's wife accepted a plaque in his honor bearing the new name.

"Mason would be so honored to receive this," she said, tears dropping down her cheeks.

They unveiled *The Gates of Justice* painting at last. The press called it a beautiful site. Emir Mohamed and his wife ventured from Morocco to attend. Emir spoke a few words about the importance of Runya in Islamic history. His wife stood beside him, holding his hand. Emir and Carmela Sanchez hugged one another as flashbulbs from every paper in Spain and

Europe lit up the room.

Oliver Hall, wearing a black suit, white shirt, and purple bow tie, and cummerbund, breezed through the gallery, cheerfully welcoming guests. His new assistant handed out souvenirs, original prints of *The Gates of Justice,* which included a write-up explaining the painting's history and the story of how it was used to help finance the Francoist in *La guerra civil.*

The Runya painting, displayed in an antique gold frame, hung proudly in its permanent place in the room. In another part of the museum, a live interactive immersive 3D exhibit displayed the life of Runya, the artist, in the courtyard of Boabdil, surrounded by Arabian Knights dancing before the king in red and green pantaloons. Runya, himself appeared portrayed painting on an easel.

"That exhibit's remarkable. It really feels like you've gone back to the fifteenth century and walked through the *Gates of Justice,*" Belen said.

Marco put his arm around her waist. "Yes, Farah's husband, Bernard, did a wonderful job." Marco pulled her in closer to him. "Some things haven't changed since Ruyna first painted his masterpiece though. Countless pilgrim passengers still leave their homelands seeking a better life, seeking fairness, seeking entry through the **gates leading to justice.**"

Belen grabbed his hand and intertwined her fingers in his. Marco felt the warmth of her skin. "I love you," she said.

About the Author

Paula is a trademark attorney. She also has a Master's degree in Public Health (MPH), and previously worked for a healthcare insurer. Paula writes mysteries featuring a colorful private investigator. The stories are set in sunny Southern Spain on the Mediterranean Coast, with a focus on scenery, food, and the diversity of the characters. Paula has published articles in the *Huffington Post* and trademark-related journals. Paula lives in Arlington, Virginia. She is the immediate past President of the Chesapeake Chapter of Sisters in Crime (SINC).

AUTHOR WEBSITE:
  paulabmays.wixsite.com

Also by Paula B. Mays

Murder in the Parador

Murder in La Plaza De Toros

Short Story: "The Muffin Lady"